Mascarada Pass

Please return this book on or before the due date below

nt
ht

Also by William Colt MacDonald and available from Center Point Large Print:

Cartridge Carnival
Gunsight Range
Ghost-Town Gold
Peaceful Jenkins

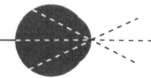

Mascarada Pass

A GREGORY QUIST STORY

William Colt MacDonald

CENTER POINT LARGE PRINT
THORNDIKE, MAINE

This Center Point Large Print edition
is published in the year 2021 by arrangement with
Golden West Literary Agency.

Originally published in the US by Doubleday.
Originally published in the UK by Hodder and Stoughton.

The text of this Large Print edition is unabridged.
In other aspects, this book may vary
from the original edition.

Set in 16-point Times New Roman type.

ISBN: 978-1-64358-848-3 (hardcover)
ISBN: 978-1-64358-852-0 (paperback)

The Library of Congress has cataloged this record under
Library of Congress Control Number: 2020950547

Printed and bound in Great Britain
by TJ Books Ltd, Padstow, Cornwall

Contents

Mascarada Pass

ONE: Powdersmoke

Can it be true, as many of the old-time Westerners swear, that a buzzard—a *zopilote*, as the Mexicans have it—can scent human blood well in advance of the time it is doomed to be spilled and manage to arrive at the scene of an impending tragedy even before it has eventuated? Is it possible that these foul-smelling scavengers with their repulsive heads, raw red necks, and wide-soaring wing sweep possess some psychic knowledge of death to come? To place credence in such a supposition would appear to a realist an extreme absurdity, and yet occasionally something occurs for which your most erudite realist can offer no explanation. For instance . . .

Since early dawn three buzzards had been hovering high in the atmosphere above the town of Rosario Wells. Town? Actually, it was just a small settlement about ninety miles south of the border between the United States and Mexico, undeserving of the name "town." A handful of blocky, thick-walled adobe huts, clustered in no particular fashion, as though they had been flung down helter-skelter from the hand of some careless god. In addition to the dwellings, but differing little in appearance, except in size, were a *cantina* and a sort of general store which served the people and the nearby ranches and small *haciendas*. A narrow road meandered between the buildings but eventually disappeared in the surrounding terrain of sand, alkali, mesquite, and cactus. So that was Rosario Wells, broiling hot during the day, and chilly—sometimes downright cold—before the sun started heat waves quivering above the plant life of the semi-desert which enveloped the settlement.

The sun hadn't yet climbed above the peaks of a distant mountain range when a Mexican, clad in shapeless white garments and barefooted, emerged, stretching and yawning, from one of the adobes near the center of the settlement. He stood before his house, rubbing his eyes a minute before gazing in both directions along the wheel-rutted, hoof-chopped road, deserted at present except for a scattering of early chickens scratching futilely in the dust. Gradually his eyes took in other surrounding points, eventually raising to glance at the sky. Then he stiffened. Almost directly overhead three buzzards wheeled and soared and dipped on motionless wings, tracing small meaningless patterns against the void, never moving far from the center of their orbit. They seemed to be waiting, just waiting—but for what?

The Mexican shuddered, superstitiously crossed

himself, and looked hopefully at the surrounding country, thinking, perhaps, a dead cow or even rabbit might have called the buzzards to this locality. Then he shrugged despairingly; it couldn't be denied the birds were hovering straight overhead. Something, someone in Rosario Wells was doomed before the sun set on this day. Muttering the one word "*Malo!*"— bad—he hurriedly procured an armful of split mesquite roots from the side of his house and scurried within. After a time blue-gray smoke curled from his chimney, but he didn't again appear.

The sun rose higher, heat poured down, but activity in Rosario Wells was almost at a standstill. Word of the *zopilotes* had spread through the settlement. A few women, *rebozos* clutched tightly about their heads despite the warmth of the morning, moved fearfully among the houses. Small naked children were kept close; anxiety showed plainly in their parents' calls. Even chickens and goats, used to wandering at will, were penned. Seraped men met now and then and passed troubled comments, their straw sombreros pulled low on foreheads. The deep shadows between buildings blackened.

And always the *zopilotes* soared directly overhead, as though scenting death in the cloudless, heated atmosphere. . . .

Shortly after midday a rider approached from

the west, slowed to a walk as he approached the settlement's houses and guided his pony to the *cantina*, where he drew to a halt, tethered his mount to one of the uprights supporting the porch roof of the *cantina*, and entered the building. An hour later he emerged, somewhat unsteady from the effects of too much tequila, and lurched toward a chair on the *cantina* porch. Here he settled down in the shade and glowered angrily at the almost empty street. He was a huskily built man. Some might have considered him handsome; others would have decided his eyes were placed too closely together, his lips too slack. A holstered .45 was slung at his right hip, and his yellow silken shirt was almost too flashy for a working cowhand. His name was Jeff Shattuck, and an older brother, Pitt, operated a cattle ranch ten miles west of Rosario Wells.

A teen-aged Mexican girl, full-figured and barefooted, padded past the *cantina*, her toes kicking up small puffs of hot dust. The angry look left Jeff Shattuck's face. A predatory grin twisted his mouth. "I'll be damned," he told himself. "Ain't never saw that one before. Wonder if that cactus wren is local—?" He broke off to whistle in the girl's direction. The girl paid him no attention but continued looking straight ahead until she turned through the doorway of the nearest adobe shack. Shattuck scowled. "These damn Mexes is getting right uppity. 'Bout time somebody told 'em where to get off."

He started to rise from his chair, then sank back again as he heard the creaking of saddle leather approaching the *cantina*. The rider—a puncher named Ed Jorgens—dismounted and ascended to the porch. Shattuck glared at him. "Don't bother telling me," he forestalled the other's words. "Pitt is mad and wants me to come straight back. He don't want me hanging around Rosario Wells. The Mexes is down on me now due to my foolin' around their women. Also, tequila is no good for me—"

"The way you drink it, it ain't," Jorgens said mildly, sinking into a chair at Shattuck's side. He removed his sombrero and fanned himself. "Gesis! It's hot—"

"—and I'll do something I'll be sorry for," Shattuck continued as though there'd been no interruption. "And if I'd just settle down and work like my kid brother, Todd, we'd make a going outfit of the spread. My Gawd, I'm so sick of raisin' beef! But ain't that what Pitt said, Ed?"

Jorgens sighed. "You saved me a lot of *habla*, Jeff. Why'n't you and Pitt stop your squabblin'? It don't get you no-place. He's boss."

"Like I said," Shattuck growled, "I'm sick of cows and being stuck down here in this Gawdforsaken hole with nothing to do but work.

I'm aiming to leave here *pronto*. After quitting Pitt once, I was a fool to come back."

"You'd best reconsider, Jeff. When you come back, Pitt says Cookie needs a sack of flour and you're to get it. Also, Todd wants you should buy him some .45 ca'tridges—"

"Dammit to hell!" Shattuck exploded. "Am I a messenger boy for Pitt—and that kid brother of mine?"

"That's for you to decide," Jorgens said quietly.

"I got to admit that Pitt makes sense." Shattuck swore a bitter oath. Neither man spoke for a few moments. Jorgens commented, "This sinkhole looks deader'n ever today. Must be the heat keepin' people inside—"

"Naw"—disgustedly—"it's some fool belief these oilers have got, about death headed this way. I was talking to Tony"—jerking his head in the direction of the bar inside the *cantina*—"and he says it's due to some buzzards flying over the town since sunup or before. Bad omen, Tony tells me. The damn fool believed it too. You know these Mexes, superstitious as hell. Spook up like the devil at the first sign of somethin' like that. Personally, I figger 'em as just plain lazy and lookin' for an excuse not to work—"

"I'll be damned!" Jorgens exclaimed, and at the questioning look from his companion gestured toward the road. "Reed Haldane!"

Some of the color left Shattuck's face. He

14

started to rise, then sank back, his gaze glued on the big, solidly built man who was passing on the back of a chestnut gelding. Haldane had been gazing straight ahead, the lines of his stern jaw taut and grim. A dust-beaten sombrero was pulled low on his forehead; his open vest hung limply from woolen clad shoulders. A holstered Colt's gun lay along his corduroyed right thigh. Now some movement from the *cantina* porch caught his attention. His head swung around, then he slowed and reined the horse toward the porch.

Jorgens said, and there was a certain tremor in his voice, "H'are you, Reed? Long time no see."

Reed Haldane's cold gaze shifted momentarily to Jorgens, then back to Shattuck, slumped down in his chair. He spoke to Jorgens, but his eyes were steady on Shattuck, saying, "Hope you're well, Ed." The words were short and sounded as though he didn't give a tinker's damn whether Jorgens was well or not. He dismounted but didn't move from his horse's side, then continued, "I want to see you, Shattuck."

Shattuck stiffened his frame. "You see me, Haldane. Take a damn good look."

Haldane's cold eyes blazed, but he held his temper. "You know what I mean. Come down off that porch."

Shattuck started to rise but changed his mind. Defiantly he said, "I got good ears. Speak your piece, Haldane."

Haldane said steadily, "You want I should come up there and tear you loose from that chair?"

"Look here, Reed," Jorgens commenced, "we don't want no trouble with you—"

"*You,*" Haldane said without removing his eyes from Shattuck, "aren't going to have any trouble with me, Ed. What Shattuck wants is up to him. I didn't come here to start a ruckus. I just want some information. You coming down here, Shattuck?"

Reluctantly Shattuck left the seat and descended the two steps to the roadway. He stopped about six feet from Haldane, belligerent lights shining in his eyes. "All right, mister, what do you want to know? Make it fast. I've got to get back to the ranch."

A cold smile curved Haldane's lips. "You always were one to take out fast if you thought trouble was coming," he said contemptuously.

"Make it fast, I said." Shattuck's tones quivered.

Haldane nodded shortly. "Where is she?"

Shattuck hesitated. His tongue licked at dry lips. He said after a moment, "I don't know."

"Don't lie to me, Shattuck."

"Prove me a liar!"

Haldane's mouth had angry bulges of white at the corners, though his voice was steady when he said, "I'm asking you just once more. Where is she?"

16

Shattuck's reply came through a rush of sudden rage. "I don't know." He added venomously, "And for your information, I don't give a damn! If you're not man enough to hold your woman, don't come begging to me—"

The words remained uncompleted as Haldane's clenched fist collided against Shattuck's jaw. Shattuck's legs wilted and he sank to his knees. Before he could roll over, Haldane jerked him upright by the collar, holding him there while his other hand slapped smartly across Shattuck's face. Shattuck shook his head groggily. After a minute his brain cleared.

"Now," Haldane said grimly, "I want an answer to my question." He added, "And look me straight in the eye when you talk. Now speak up!" He released his hold on Shattuck's collar.

Reluctantly Shattuck's gaze came up to meet Haldane's burning eyes. The words, when they came, trembled with mingled fear and anger. "I've told you I don't know, Haldane. I—I ain't seen her since—since that night you came. She—she went away—someplace." Haldane just looked steadily at the man. Shattuck half sobbed, "It's the truth, dammit! I tell you I don't know, I don't know. You've got to believe me. I don't want no trouble with you. I regret what happened—"

"By the Almighty!" Haldane exclaimed. "I believe you are speaking the truth. For once!"

17

Disgustedly he started to turn away, back toward his horse. Then, with some further question in mind, perhaps, he spun back toward Shattuck. It may have been he had some inner warning, a premonition of impending danger.

For in that moment rage had overcome fear, and Shattuck had jerked his six-shooter from holster. Haldane swore and leaped to one side, drawing his own gun as he moved.

The two explosions came almost together. Shattuck's slug flew wide of its mark. For a brief interval Haldane thought he, too, had missed aim. Shattuck had stepped back a pace and was lowering his weapon. Then he spun slowly toward the center of the road, took three stumbling steps, and crashed face down in the dust.

Haldane whirled to cover Jorgens, on his feet now, face the color of dirty ashes. Haldane said, "You want any part of this, Ed?"

Jorgens replied shakily, "Not any part, Reed. You was within your rights. He drew first." He repeated, "Nope, not any part."

Haldane nodded shortly and sheathed his weapon. "Go see how bad I hit him." Powder-smoke drifted along the hot, quiet street.

Jorgens moved out to the center of the road and stooped down. Frightened faces of Mexicans peered from windows and slightly opened doors, but there was a sort of deathly silence all along the street. The buzzards overhead had soared lower. . . .

"Well?" Haldane asked impatiently as Jorgens rose to his feet.

"It ain't well at all," Jorgens returned in a not-too-steady voice. "You finished him."

Haldane drew a deep sigh. "I never wanted to kill him," he observed to no one in particular; then, "Ed, there's no law here yet, I suppose." Jorgens replied in the negative. Haldane asked, "Pitt at the ranch?" Jorgens nodded and added the information that Jeff's brother Todd was there too. Haldane went on, "Get on your horse and go tell 'em what happened. I'll wait here until you bring 'em back."

"Do you think that's wise?" Jorgens asked. "Pitt will be mighty upset about this. You could avoid trouble by riding—"

Haldane said again, "I'll wait here until you bring 'em back."

Jorgens nodded and went to his horse. When he had pounded out of Rosario Wells, Haldane turned into the *cantina*. At the bar Tony, the proprietor, set out a bottle. He didn't ask any questions. There was no one else in the low-ceilinged room. Haldane had a second drink. Tony muttered something in Spanish that had to do with the *zopilotes* and their smell for blood. Testily Haldane uttered one word, "Bosh!" then after a second thought strode toward the doorway.

A low curse was torn from his lips as he looked toward the silent figure huddled in the dust.

The three buzzards had landed in the road by this time and were hopping eagerly toward the dead man, repulsive heads and red necks stretched in anticipation. Haldane swore again and reached for an empty beer bottle on a table nearby with the intention of hurling it at the birds. At that moment a Mexican came hurrying from the nearest adobe with a blanket to fling over Shattuck's still figure. The buzzards hopped clumsily, protestingly, a few yards away from the body, their wings rustling dryly, though they refused to take flight. Hadn't they, they seemed to be inveighing, more right than anyone to be here at this moment? They had known—they must have known—this was to happen, was the angry thought that coursed through Haldane's mind as he remembered old-timers stating earnestly that a buzzard could predict death by its very actions.

"Damnable stink birds," Haldane growled. The Mexican who had brought the blanket had returned to his shack by this time, and the buzzards were once more closing in. Haldane drew his six-shooter and strode out to the roadway. "Sure as hell those birds'll pluck that blanket off," he fumed. His gun spoke once, and a buzzard was slammed savagely against the earth, where it lay quiet after a few rustlings of wings. The other pair of birds rose heavily in the air and took up a position above, beyond the reach of gunfire, where they once more resumed their soaring and dipping, like black newspapers blown hither and yon by vagrant winds. Haldane reloaded his gun and sat down to wait a few feet from the body.

He was still seated there a little after sundown, the birds still floating far above, when a rattling of harness and the pounding of hoofs announced the arrival of Shattuck's two brothers, Pitt and Todd. A third man tooled the mules drawing the wagon. Haldane climbed to his feet and stood waiting until the horses and wagons had halted and the men dismounted. Pitt Shattuck glanced at the blanket-covered body, then at the birds above. The grim lines of his face softened somewhat as he realized what Haldane had been doing.

Haldane said, "I'm sorry, Pitt. How do you want to play it?"

Pitt Shattuck said gruffly, "We don't want any trouble, Reed. What's done is done." Haldane started explanations. Shattuck interrupted wearily, "I know. Ed Jorgens told me what happened. There wa'n't anything else you could do under the circumstances. Ed's not a liar; I can believe him. I know Jeff too. I should have warned you two years back when he went to work for you that there'd be trouble. Him and me had quarreled then. I figured I should keep my mouth shut. Now I wish I'd talked to you, warned you."

21

"Mebbe it wouldn't have done any good—two years back," Haldane said quietly.

"Pro'bly not," Pitt Shattuck agreed. "It was a techy subject. I'll tell you one thing though, Reed, you never had any reasons for suspicions 'bout your missus. Oh, I know, Jeff always was a blinger with the ladies, but he never got no-place with her. He, hisself, told me that, and Jeff wa'n't one to speak of his defeats. He liked to boast of his triumphs—"

"Thanks for telling me, Pitt," Haldane said soberly. "Like I say, I'm sorry. If there was anything I could do—"

"Take yourself away from here fast," Pitt Shattuck said bitterly. "Jeff was at fault, but he was my brother. I can't forget that. And I can't make myself like you for what's been done. But I keep thinkin' that it was forced on you, so there won't be no trouble—"

"T'hell there won't!" Todd Shattuck burst in furiously. "I'm sick of this palaver." His young voice shook with rage. He wasn't yet twenty—nearer seventeen. "This talk of forgiving and forgetting makes me sick to my stomach. Haldane, I'm going to get you if it's the last thing I ever do—"

"Hush it, Todd," Pitt Shattuck cut in sharply. "We don't want no more trouble—"

"Maybe you don't," the younger Shattuck flared. "I do! Haldane, jerk your iron!"

22

Pitt Shattuck swung swiftly on his younger brother, jerked the six-shooter from Todd's fist, and slammed the long barrel of the weapon with savage impatience against Todd's head. Todd stumbled and went crashing to the earth, where he lay half stunned. Pitt whirled back on Haldane. Haldane's gun was half out of holster. Now he let it slip back. He said soberly, "Much obliged, Pitt."

"*Por nada*," Pitt Shattuck growled. "For nothing. I don't want any thanks from you, Haldane. You killed Jeff. On your account I just struck my own brother. For me and mine you spell bad medicine, Haldane. You saw how Todd felt. You'd better ride. Come tomorrow, I might feel a heap different about you too. And Jeff has friends on the outfit." He said again, "You'd better ride."

Haldane nodded and went to his horse, climbed into the saddle. By this time Todd Shattuck had lifted himself groggily to his feet and stood swaying on uncertain legs. Furiously he watched Haldane turn the horse away from the *cantina* and head it north. He raised one clenched, trembling fist and shouted thickly, "I'll get you for this someday, Haldane!"

Haldane didn't reply but quickened the horse's pace.

Pitt said harshly, "Todd, you shut your mouth and help me lift Jeff's body into the wagon. And

23

I don't want no back talk. Remember, you ain't the only one what'd like to see this business squared. But now ain't the time, and threats never got anybody no-place."

Sullenly Todd moved to obey. Within a short time riders and the wagon with its grisly burden had disappeared from Rosario Wells. When morning came the frustrated *zopilotes* had likewise vanished except for a few scattered bones and some ruffled feathers in the roadway. Coyotes had been busy in the street during the night. And at this point your realist might point out that one buzzard of the trio hadn't foreseen its own death, or it would have stayed far away from Rosario Wells.

TWO: Suicide?

And now, approximately twenty years later, Fred Haldane lay dead at the undertaker's in Masquerade City, "a victim of his own hand," as Dr. Yost Woodward had put it. Sheriff Matt Tillman concurred, though reluctantly, in what the doctor announced, as he could think of no reason, he said, "for Reed to kill himself. It just wasn't like Reed to do such a thing." It was difficult for other people to believe too. There were those who hinted darkly that the coroner's inquest might produce evidence to change the doctor's verdict, though no word was forthcoming that could be used as a basis for such surmises. True, the name of Shattuck was mentioned once or twice, but there'd been no trouble with the Shattucks since they'd come to this country several years back. Exactly what had caused the original trouble between the Shattucks and Haldane no one was certain—there was something about Haldane having killed a Shattuck at some time—but details were missing.

Just to complicate matters at the time, there'd been a train wreck about four miles west of Masquerade City the night before Haldane's body had been discovered. A large portion of the townspeople had taken to horses and buggies and wagons and traveled out to view the wreckage. Those not so curious had gone to bed early. Consequently no one in Masquerade City could be found who had heard the shot that ended Haldane's life.

A Texas Northern & Arizona Southern freight train had left the rails on the steep downgrade where the tail end of the Masquerade Mountains dropped off to level sand-mesquite-and-alkali desert country. The engineer and fireman and the crew in the caboose had all met death in the disaster. When it was discovered that the wreck had been man-impelled, the T. N. & A. S. Railroad had at once dispatched its top investigator, Gregory Quist, to look into the matter. A gang of freight thieves had been preying on various railroads in recent years; it was assumed that this same gang was responsible for the T. N. & A. S. wreck.

Quist had made good time in reaching Masquerade City from his headquarters in El Paso, though it had meant losing sleep and covering one stretch on horseback in order to make better train connections between certain points. The last stage of the journey had been accomplished on a handcar sent out from the nearest junction, the T. N. & A. S. line being temporarily closed until the wreckage farther along could

26

be cleared away. An employee of the railroad had met Quist at the depot when he arrived and furnished certain pertinent facts. When the man had concluded, Quist nodded shortly, promised to be at the scene of the wreck later, and departed to get a room at the local hotel where he could clean up after his dusty, gritty ride. The train wreck had occurred at ten o'clock in the evening, and only twenty hours had elapsed when Quist stepped into his hotel room.

"Not bad time at all," Quist mused as he placed his satchel on the bed and started taking out his shaving equipment. He stripped off his woolen shirt, then paused momentarily to glance from a corner window of his second-floor room. The sun was dropping fast but hadn't yet touched the lower saw-toothed peaks of the Masquerade Range, which lay twenty miles or more to the west. He turned back from the window, a broad-shouldered man with thick tawny hair, and poured water into a basin on the dresser. Quist's features were rather bony, the nose aquiline, the skin well-tanned except for the lighter streak across his broad forehead where a hat brim had afforded protection from burning sun. His face held a quizzical expression, slightly sardonic. His movements were lithe and easy, seemingly half catlike, half lazy. In a country where most men wore mustaches and many full beards, Quist was clean-shaven—or would be when he had concluded the razor job he'd set himself before the mirror. The keen steel made ringing sounds as he sliced through the lather.

Quist had finished washing up and was donning a fresh woolen shirt from his satchel when a knock sounded on his door. He tensed and finished buttoning his shirt. The knock came again, this time louder, impatient. Quist reached for a blue bandanna and knotted it about his throat before he called, "Who is it? What do you want?" The tones were deep, almost musical, as they welled up from his thick chest.

As though the words were a signal to enter, the door started to open. There came from outside in the hall a brief scuffle. Abruptly the door was flung violently open and two men started through the doorway at once, each trying to precede the other. Quist gazed in some amazement as the two struggled in the opening a minute before they somehow succeeded in entering side by side, though it was a tight squeeze.

Quist laughed softly. "You could have saved a heap of trouble by tossing a coin," he commented.

Neither heard him. Once through the entrance, they both plunged across the room, as though each was anxious to make himself heard first.

"Meestair Quist?"

"I've come to ask a favor, Mr. Quist—"

"Pay heem no attention. Eet was my idea—"

"You lie in your teeth, Ramon—"

28

Immediately the two, as though they'd forgotten the object of their visit, turned furiously on each other. A stream of vituperation, angry accusations, insults, mixed with some Spanish profanity, filled the air. Quist curiously eyed the pair a minute, a smile twitching the corners of his lips. Unnoticed by either of the two angry men, he reached to the dresser for the pitcher of water and calmly tossed its contents in their general direction. There'd not been much water remaining after Quist's ablutions, but the effect was instantaneous. Both men fell silent, drops of water trickling down their features.

"There, that's better," Quist observed quietly. "Now what in the name of Jehovah is this all about? Have you two gone insane?"

At once the pair again burst into speech, each trying to outdo the other.

Abruptly Quist thundered, "Shut up! Both of you. If you came here to see me, state your business. I'm not interested in listening to your personal opinions of each other. Talk sense—or get out—now!"

That did it. The pair fell silent while they drew bandannas and started mopping their faces. They were young. The eldest of the two wasn't more than twenty-two, a slim-hipped, wide-shouldered fellow with good features and brick-red hair. The other appeared around twenty, was as tall as his companion, but there the resemblance ended.

29

A rather handsome fellow, Quist mused, with a sort of devil-may-care air at the moment, blue-black hair and keen dark eyes. Lots of Spanish or Mexican blood too. Both were in denims, weathered sombreros, and high-heeled boots; six-shooters were slung at their sides.

The Mexican—or Spanish—fellow forced a rueful smile. His red-haired companion glowered at him, then his gaze came back to Quist, and some of the resentful color faded from his face.

"You theenk we are a pair of fools, Señor Quist—"

"Don't pay no attention to him—" Redhead flared.

". . . your water cure ees what we deserve—"

"It's like this, Mr. Quist—"

Quist swore an awe-inspiring oath in Spanish and followed it with one in English. "Now, get out *pronto*!" he concluded. His hands shot out, seized each man by a shoulder and spun him around. Then he shoved—hard—and the pair went spinning toward the open doorway. Redhead crashed against the jamb and bounced back. The other came up short against one wall. Both turned, jaws dropping, toward Quist and stared unbelievingly at him.

Redhead was the first to find his voice. "J-jeepers!" he said shakily with reluctant admiration. "You play rough, Mr. Quist."

And from his companion: "You have the strength of the *toro*—"

"I said to get out and stay out," Quist said harshly. Then he sighed wearily as curiosity overcame him. "No, wait! Come back—but remember to just speak when I ask for it—and one at a time."

The two returned to the center of the room and stood waiting. "You"—Quist spoke to the Mexican—or Spaniard—"what's your name?"

"Ramon Serrano, Señor Quist."

"And you?" Quist shot a glance at the red-head.

"Chris Baxter, sir."

"Thanks, Chris," Quist said shortly. "Now keep your lip buttoned until I ask Serrano a few things." He turned to Serrano. "Now what did you want to see me about?"

"The Señor Reed Haldane is dead."

"I suppose I should express sympathy," Quist said shortly. "All right, consider it done, but I don't know him, never heard of him."

"He was my boss. Also, Señor Quist, he owned the Rafter-RH Rancho and the Saddlehorn Saloon. I—"

Quist lifted one hand to silence Serrano and turned to Baxter. "What's your relation to Haldane?"

"I worked for him, and he was the best man who ever lived."

Quist scowled. "Commendable sentiment. Now what have I got to do with all this?"

"You being the head detective of the T. N. & A. S., I figured to ask you to find his murderer—"

"Eet was *my* idea—" Serrano cut in indignantly.

"You're a liar by the clock!" Baxter flared.

Serrano swore in Spanish. Baxter drew back his clenched fist. Quist stepped in quickly, blocked the blow intended for Serrano's face, then seized both men by shirt collars and urged them forcibly toward the doorway, refusing to listen to their contrite apologies. Once they were outside in the hall, he slammed shut his door. He could hear them still arguing furiously as they departed. Quist drew a long breath. "Of all the damn young wildcats I ever saw—" He paused, scowling. "Something was said about a murder. Maybe I was a bit hasty. Oh well, I'll get details eventually. I didn't come here to run down murderers—or did I?"

His scowl increased. He glanced down and deciding his corduroys were pretty soiled by his travels, reached into his satchel for a clean pair. He had donned these and was seated on the bed, fastening on a pair of spurs, when again a knock came at the door. Without lifting his head Quist called, "Come in—but keep your talk to a minimum," thinking, Maybe those youngsters have learned their lesson this time.

He heard the door open and close again. Then

silence. Quist finished buckling a strap and said impatiently, "Well?"

A rather timorous voice said, "Mr. Quist?" It was a feminine voice with a sort of throaty quality.

Quist whirled up and around from the bed like a shot and surveyed his visitor. "Well"—this time softly—and again, "Well, this is a surprise. I might add, a very pleasant one. I expected some-one else—"

"I know." The girl nodded. "Ramon and Chris said you gave them the—the bum's rush. Those were Chris's words."

"And did they tell you why?"

"They said you refused to listen—"

"So help me, Miss—Miss—?"

"Haldane. I'm Francisca Haldane."

Quist bowed. "Miss Haldane. So help me, I tried to listen, but they were too busy arguing for me to learn what they wanted—something about finding a murderer—"

"I know. It was my father who was killed." The girl's large dark eyes filled with tears. She had unbelievably long lashes.

"I'm sorry," Quist said, hurrying to place a chair for her. "Now take it easy a moment." The girl seated herself. She was rather tall and slimly built, with creamy skin, an almost perfect nose, and full lips. A flat-topped fawn-colored sombrero topped her head of heavy black hair,

33

drawn to a thick knob at her nape. She wore a mannish shirt, divided riding skirt, and high-heeled boots. Quist decided she was one of the prettiest girls he'd ever seen. No, pretty wasn't quite the word for it. And she couldn't be termed actually beautiful. There was too much determination, character, in the girl's chin and mouth for that.

It was growing darker in the room by this time. Quist struck a match and lighted the kerosene lamp on his dresser. Then he turned to face Francisca Haldane again. She was just replacing her handkerchief and forced a wan smile as her dark eyes met Quist's gaze. She said, "I'm sorry. I'd sort of braced myself for something different, and—and—well, you've been so kind. You're not the sort of man I expected to find here—"

"So?" Quist asked softly. To put the girl more at ease he seated himself on the bed. "And what have you heard about me?"

"That you're cynical, hard, ruthless. A cold-blooded killer. A bloodhound on a trail—" She checked herself suddenly. "Oh, I shouldn't say such things."

Quist smiled thinly. "I've heard them all before. It doesn't bother me. Yes, I've killed when I had to—but I never liked it. I am what my work has made me, I suppose. I'm surprised, Miss Haldane," he added mockingly, "that you'd step into such an ogre's den."

"I've also heard"—she lowered her eyes—"that you're a mighty smart detective and that you—you have a way with women."

"Bosh!" Quist said harshly. "There's no time in the sort of life I lead for women—" He broke off. "You're trying awfully hard, Miss Haldane. Exactly what is it you want from me? Maybe we can save time by getting down to business."

She looked steadily at Quist a moment, wondering if his eyes really were amber-colored or yellow. No, topaz was the word. "It's about my father, Reed Haldane, Mr. Quist. He was found dead this morning—"

"So recently? You shouldn't be here—"

The girl slightly lifted one impatient hand. "I'm all right. When we heard that you'd arrived in town to investigate the railroad wreck—somebody at the depot recognized you when you arrived—we got the idea you might help us—"

"Who is 'we'?"

"Chris and Ramon—and myself. We feel sure Dad was murdered. You see, he—he was found early this morning, and they called it suicide—"

"Who called it suicide?"

"Dr. Woodward and Sheriff Tillman. We just know Dad wouldn't—wouldn't do anything like that. There wasn't any reason for him—" The girl paused and reached for her handkerchief.

Quist said quickly, "Just where do Baxter and Serrano fit into this business?"

"Dad practically adopted them when they were young. They acted as a sort of bodyguard." Quist interrupted to say something about one of them having failed in his job, apparently. The girl raised a protesting hand. "No, neither of them are to blame." The handkerchief had disappeared by this time. "Neither was supposed to be with Dad when—when it happened."

"They did little except call each other names when they were here."

The girl sighed. "I can well imagine. I know how they are. Always fighting. You see, they both worshiped Dad and were jealous of each other. Each has always tried to outdo the other, and it's resulted in a strong dislike between them."

"I'd say that was putting it mildly," Quist observed dryly. He added shrewdly, "And how do they feel about you?"

The girl flushed. "I—well, they like me, I guess."

"You've said enough." Quist smiled. "I can begin to appreciate the attitude of that pair now. So you refuse to believe your father would end his own life. Any basis for that? Do you suspect anyone?"

The girl hesitated. "I'd rather not accuse anyone without proof."

"But you do feel there's someone had reason

36

to kill him. He must have felt that way himself, else he'd not have had a bodyguard. Look, Miss Haldane, why don't you leave this to the regular constituted authorities? I'm here on a job to investigate that wreck. I'll have my hands full. If the sheriff and doctor state that—"

"You don't believe he was murdered?" The girl's voice rose.

"I didn't say that. That's for the local authorities to determine," Quist said quietly. The girl renewed her plea for aid. Quist shook his head. "I'd like to help you, Miss Haldane, but my regular job comes first. This wreck was caused by freight thieves and—"

"Suppose I said that there's a connection between my father's death and your freight thieves," Francisca Haldane said slowly.

Quist looked sharply at her, studied her a long moment, then slowly shook his head. "That was a good try, too, but it doesn't go down. You don't really believe that yourself now, do you?"

The girl's cheeks went crimson, but she met Quist's penetrating gaze steadily. "No, I don't," she confessed. "I was just trying to persuade you to—Oh, what an awful thing for me to do." She looked helplessly at Quist now and started to rise.

Quist laughed softly. "Forget it. I can always admire a good try and resourcefulness." He paused suddenly, brow furrowed with tiny thought wrinkles. "Wait!" The girl sank back in

37

her chair. Quist was on his feet now, pacing the floor, speaking half to himself. "The wreck and your father's death coming within a few hours. It could be coincidence. Probably is. But I—don't—know. Maybe it's an idea to be followed through—"

"You will help us then?" the girl said eagerly.

Quist shrugged broad shoulders. "I'll make no promises beyond looking into this a little more. Maybe it will come to nothing, so don't get your hopes up."

The girl was also on her feet now, words of thanks pouring from her lips. Quist brushed aside the outpouring. And at that moment there came a third knock on his door.

THREE: A Suspect

Quist called, "Come on in," and the door was flung wide. On the threshold stood Chris Baxter and Ramon Serrano. Both looked instantly at the girl, then cautiously toward Quist. Neither took a step to enter the room. Quist laughed softly, and the sound was sheer organ music from his deep chest. "I said to come in. It's safe. I've got the dog tied up."

Somewhat subdued, the two entered. Serrano spoke first. "We just came to see if Fran was all right." Now that he'd cooled down there was only the slightest trace of Spanish accent. Quist judged that he reverted to an earlier form of speech only in moments of stress. That Baxter hadn't resented that word "we" and burst into violent speech surprised Quist. Perhaps the girl had a quieting influence on the pair, or maybe they had come to some sort of temporary agreement. Quist asked amusedly, "Why shouldn't Miss Haldane be all right? I never put anyone out of my room unless he gets obstreperous. Miss Haldane and I have had a very interesting conversation—"

"Oh, Chris—Ramon! Mr. Quist has promised to help us," Francisca Haldane exclaimed.

"Not promised," Quist objected. "I only said I'd cast around for a few details. Maybe I can help. Frankly, I don't know."

"Is very good." Ramon nodded. "Is appreciated, Mr. Quist."

Baxter laughed self-consciously. "For once I'll agree with Ramon, Mr. Quist. And I can't say I blame you for running us out. We acted like a pair of fools—"

"Speak for yourself, Chris," Serrano bridled. "But I also played like the fool."

"Look here, you two," Quist said sternly, "if I'm going to have a hand in—in what's happened here, I'll need your co-operation likely. Now scrap all you like when you're out of my sight, but I don't want to be annoyed by any childish squabbles. Is that understood?"

Baxter and Serrano nodded, their faces red.

"And you'll take orders from me when I want help?" Quist continued. "I don't intend to boss you around, understand, but if there's a decision to be made, I'm the one to make it. Clear?"

Again the two nodded. Quist smiled. "Maybe we're making headway. Scrapping won't get you anyplace when there's intelligent work to be done. If you two had showed sense when you first came here, it wouldn't have been necessary for Miss Haldane to see me. You've made things rough for her at a time when she should be in bed, or at least resting."

Baxter didn't reply, but his color heightened. Serrano said, "I'm already admit I'm the fool, señor. If you have an order, I should like to redeem myself."

"I've an order." Quist turned to the girl and asked a question. She replied she was staying at the hotel overnight. Quist turned back to Serrano. "Accompany Miss Haldane to her room, then go to your best livery and hire a horse saddled for me. And I don't want any crow baits. I'll leave it to your good judgment. I've got to get out to that wreck and look things over as soon as possible. Meet me in front of this hotel in ten minutes. In addition to the horse, get me a bottle of beer and a sandwich someplace. I've had no supper yet and I won't have time to go to any dining room. Now get going. Miss Haldane, I hope to see you again in a day or so."

Baxter looked somewhat jealously after Serrano as he followed the girl through the doorway, but he didn't say anything. He looked at Quist when the door had closed. "Now what do you want of me?"

"Information," Quist replied, "and make it fast. Never mind details. I understand that Reed Haldane owned the Rafter-RH spread and the Saddlehorn Saloon. He was found dead. The local peace officer and doctor claim it was suicide. You and Serrano and Miss Haldane think he was murdered. Who do you suspect?"

41

"Todd Shattuck. He's one of the owners of the Triangle-S outfit."

"Why suspect Shattuck? Got any sort of proof?"

Baxter shook his head. "But there was bad blood between them. I don't know the details, but I understand Mr. Haldane killed one of the Shattucks a long time back."

"How many Shattucks are there?"

"I can't say. Two, here. Todd and Pitt. They run the ranch."

"Why not suspect Pitt Shattuck too?"

"He's always tried to get along with Mr. Haldane." Quist asked a question. Baxter said, "It was the barkeep found him dead in his bed, with his own gun in his hand and a bullet through his heart. The body was found in the combination bedroom and office Mr. Haldane kept at the rear of the Saddlehorn."

"Why didn't Haldane sleep at his ranch? You're one of his bodyguard, I understand. You should know something about it."

Baxter's face flushed hotly. "Don't get the idea I wasn't on my job when necessary," he snapped. "I was off duty. Mr. Haldane had Ramon and me guard him during his waking hours. He claimed he could look after himself when he was in his bedroom. Yes, he slept at the ranch sometimes, but mostly he stayed in town. Is that clear to you?"

"Clear," Quist said tersely. "But don't get belligerent with me. I never knew anybody could fly off the handle as easy as you. And Serrano. I suppose the body has been removed to the undertaker's." Baxter nodded. Quist continued, "We'll go take a look."

He donned his tan, flat-topped sombrero after whipping dust from it against his leg, then reached in his satchel for a leather harness equipped with an underarm holster holding a short-barreled .44 six-shooter. This outfit he quickly fitted to his thick chest. Baxter eyed it curiously, saying, "That's quite some rig-up."

"It's convenient," Quist said. "Been using it for a number of years now. You see, with this holster, when you draw, you just pull the gun straight out through its open side instead of up and out as you would with a belt holster. That dispenses with one movement, and sometimes a fraction of a second spells the difference between life and death. A flat steel spring sewed within the leather holds the gun in place until it's needed. This rig is a heap more comfortable to wear than a hip gun and, as I said, faster to the draw." Picking up his coat, he shrugged his muscular arms into the sleeves.

Baxter glanced at the plain wide-buckled belt that supported the corduroys. "Don't you wear a ca'tridge belt, Mr. Quist?"

"Too heavy." Quist again dipped into his satchel, opened a box of .44 cartridges, and thrust a handful into one coat pocket. "Any man that can't finish whatever job he undertakes with what's in the gun and an extra handful just hasn't any business toting a gun."

"Cripes! I'm beginning to think you said something there."

Quist chuckled. "I hope I did. But don't lay any bets on it. I can make mistakes as bad as any other man. C'mon, let's go look at that body. If I don't get out of Masquerade City before much more time passes, I'll have to do a heap of explaining to the T. N. & A. S."

Quist turned his lamp low, and together the two men left the room. At the edge of the sidewalk before the hotel they found Serrano awaiting them with a buckskin gelding, saddled, an opened bottle of beer in one hand and a thick beef sandwich in the other. Quist said, "Much obliged," and accepted the provender. He stood looking at the horse a few moments, then nodded. "You know horseflesh, Ramon."

Serrano flushed with pleasure. "*Gracias*! Of the stirrup length I am not too sure, though. You are so broad a man misjudge' your stretch of leg." Though both Serrano and Baxter were about six feet in height, Quist seemed to tower over them.

"They look about right to me, Ramon." Quist climbed to the saddle, eased himself gently down. He studied the horse a moment. "Nice pony. Didn't know but what he might buck a mite."

Ramon handed up the sandwich and bottle. Quist took a bite and a swallow of beer. "All right, lead the way. If it's not too near I'll be through by the time we get there."

"About a block and a half from here," Baxter said. They started off, Baxter and Serrano walking on either side of the horse's head.

Most of Masquerade City's business establishments were closed by this time, but here and there rectangles of yellow light shone from windows of saloons and other buildings. The three men passed a general store, a pair of restaurants, a couple more saloons, a feed store and bank, and various other establishments of commercial enterprise.

"Hmm, quite a sizable and going burg," Quist told himself, noting the people passing on the plank sidewalks. He'd been so interested in sizing up the town that he'd not realized at once that Serrano and Baxter were again involved in one of their seemingly endless quarrels. Bitter words were passing beneath Quist's nose from either side of his mount. Quist scowled, tossed the empty beer bottle to the edge of the dirt roadway, and choked down his last bit of sandwich. Abruptly he plunged in his spurs. Indignantly the buckskin reared, shocked by the sudden pain, then its hoofs came down and it commenced to buck. Baxter and Serrano hurriedly stepped out of reach of the flying hoofs.

A proper use of the reins quieted the horse almost instantly. Quist said sternly to the two men, "I told you once I didn't want to put up with your damn wrangling. Did you think I was talking to exercise my jaw? Now keep away from me—both of you. I'll find the undertaker without your help."

"But, Meestair Queest—"

"I'm sorry, Mr. Quist. I reckon we forgot ourselves—"

"Forget me too, will you?" Quist said harshly. "If I never see you hombres again, it'll be too soon." He again guided the horse into motion, leaving Baxter and Serrano standing open-mouthed behind him in the middle of the street. Half a block farther on, on the left side of the street, Quist saw a sign above a lighted building which read: E. X. Hume, UNDERTAKING AND FURNITURE. And in smaller letters: "Fine Funerals & Home Furnishings."

Quist chuckled. "E. X. Hume. What a misnomer. He should advertise resurrections too." He wheeled the buckskin toward the hitch rack and dismounted. The building was a two-story frame affair with a wide cheap glass window spreading across most of the lower floor, with a two-doored entrance at one side. Through the window Quist saw a display of parlor furniture. The entrance doors were closed. Two men stood talking before them. One was a big paunchy man with jowls, a four-day beard, and wide straggly mustaches. His battered sombrero was shoved back to reveal thinning blond hair strongly streaked with gray. On his skimpy vest was pinned a sheriff's star of office. His companion, in cowpuncher togs, was short and thin. In the light from the display window Quist had a brief glance at his features and didn't like what he saw. The fellow, despite his lack of stature, looked mean, vicious. There was something queer about his eyes. His lips were a thin slit, colorless.

"Where do you think you're going, mister?" asked the man with the badge as Quist side-stepped the pair and reached for the doorknob of the undertaking establishment.

Quist paused. "I understand Reed Haldane's body has been brought here."

The sheriff eyed Quist a moment, chewed meditatively on his cud of tobacco, spat a long brown stream, and then said, "You understand correct. What's your interest in Reed?"

"I'm a friend of Miss Haldane's."

The sheriff frowned, shoved his sombrero to one side, and scratched his ear. Finally he arrived at a decision. "Sorry, friend, you'll have to wait a spell before the body can be viewed. There's too many folks want to come crowdin' in here. Ed Hume asked that I keep 'em out. This gent here"—gesturing with one thumb toward the undersized cowpuncher—"was just trying to get in. I had to stop him too. Come around tomorrow when the inquest's over."

"I may not be in town tomorrow. I've other business."

The sheriff spat again. "That's just too damn bad," he said unfeelingly. "So why don't you go on about your other business now?"

Quist commenced a protest, but the undersized cowhand cut in contemptuously, "Look, pal, why don't you take Matt's advice? Go peddle your fish."

Quist turned his head to survey the man. He said pleasantly, "I don't remember asking any word from you—pal."

"You're getting it, see, pal? Come on, show us you're smart by sloping out of here." The man appeared spoiling for a fight. His jaw outthrust menacingly, he took a step nearer Quist.

"Now, Mustang," the sheriff said reprovingly, "don't you start any fuss. This gent don't want any trouble."

Quist said quietly, "It's no trouble for me, Sheriff." He didn't remove his gaze from the cowhand. The fellow's six-shooter holster was tied down by a buckskin thong about his thigh as an aid to quick drawing. Quist thought: Ah, a would-be gunman. Raising his right hand, palm outspread, Quist placed it against the cowhand's face and put all the weight of one shoulder behind a single violent thrust.

FOUR: Garroted

So swiftly had Quist acted, the cowhand had no time for evasive tactics. His feet seemed to be torn violently from the sidewalk. His body hurtled through the air as though projected from a cannon. There came a sudden shattering of splintered glass as the man's head and shoulders plowed through the glass window and into E. X. Hume's showy display of parlor furniture. A table toppled over. A fancy lace spread from its top enveloped the cowhand's head. A chair crashed to its side. A lighted oil lamp on a marble-topped stand teetered drunkenly before deciding to remain upright to shed its soft glow over the wrecked furniture display. Broken glass littered the floor of the display window. The cowhand sprawled, half stunned, and while one arm moved feebly he made no move to arise.

The sheriff eyed the wreckage, then his gaze came back to Quist. "Now you've done it, mister," he commented reproachfully. "Mustang ain't going to like this a-tall." There was a certain cautious look in the sheriff's eyes now.

Quist laughed softly. "I didn't like the way *he* was acting either."

"You should understand that Mustang Neale is a bad hombre to fool with."

"I wasn't fooling, Sheriff."

The sheriff scowled. "I could put you under arrest—"

"You could *try*," Quist corrected. "Then you'd learn I'd not be fooling with you, either. You might get your sit-spot in a sling."

The sheriff hesitated. A crowd was gathering, drawn by the sound of the shattering glass window. At the sheriff's rear, the two entrance doors banged open and a cadaverous-looking individual with a long nose and no hair at all on his head plunged out, demanding, "What in hell's happened out here?" He paused. "My God! Look at my display. What's Mustang Neale doing in there?" Neale, by this time, was pawing his way shakily up from the floor. "Arrest him, Sheriff! Neale's already made too much trouble around here—"

" 'Twa'n't Mustang's fault, Ed," the sheriff said. "This hombre shoved him through your window. They had some words."

Ed Hume whirled on Quist, features working angrily, but before he could speak, Quist cut him short: "Look here, your window will be paid for. Present your bill to the T. N. & A. S. Railroad. I'll okay it for payment. I came here—"

At this point the sheriff broke in, "Sa-a-ay, you aren't Gregory Quist, are you?" Quist admitted his identity. "Jeez," the sheriff asked, "why'n't

you say so? I heard you was around town, but—"
He interrupted himself to speak to Hume. "It's
all right, Ed. This is Greg Quist, the railroad
detective. Friend of Fran Haldane's. He come to
see the body. Best let him go right in."

There was further talk. Mustang Neale had
raised himself to his knees by this time and
was gazing blearily through broken glass at the
grinning crowd on the sidewalk. A new respect
had entered the sheriff's attitude as he and Hume
led the way into the undertaking establishment.

Quist followed the pair along a corridor to the
rear of the building, through what Hume called
his viewing parlor, a small room with trestles on
which a coffin could be placed, some artificial
potted palms, and a group of religious pictures
on the wall, and thence into a large room lighted
with oil lamps. At one side of this room a number
of caskets were stacked on wooden horses; at the
other a man stood working over the dead body
of Reed Haldane, which reposed on a long table
covered with white oilcloth. Above the table,
on a long shelf, rested gallon bottles of alcohol,
embalming fluid, and several boxes containing
other equipment necessary to the undertaker's
trade.

Ed Hume said, "Doc was just probing out the
bullet that finished Reed. Doc, this is Greg Quist,
the big railroad detective. Mr. Quist, this is Doc
Woodward."

The doctor turned, his hands occupied, and nodded pleasantly to Quist. He was a thin graying man with tired eyes. A basin of dark pinkish-stained water stood near his open black physician's bag. A few instruments lay nearby. The doctor was in his shirt sleeves; beads of perspiration stood on his forehead. "It was a tough one to get out," Woodward said, "but I managed to get a grip on it just before you came in." He raised his forceps to display a small dark metallic object gripped in the jaws.

Quist stepped nearer. "Looks like a .45 to me."

Dr. Yost Woodward nodded. "That's how I figure it. Sort of battered, but if there's any doubt, we can weigh it. And Reed always carried a .45."

"It came out of his gun," the sheriff put in. His name was Tillman.

The doctor asked, "Did you know Reed Haldane, Mr. Quist?"

Quist shook his head. "His daughter asked me if I'd sort of take a look around. I'm not sure there's anything I can do, of course."

"Nothing to do," the sheriff said promptly. "Darn'd if I can figure out any reason for it, but Reed killed himself. That's plain as the nose on your face."

Quist said quietly, "If you can't figure a reason for it, it's not quite that plain." He looked questioningly at Woodward.

The doctor sighed. "Poor Francisca. She feels

52

so certain her father wouldn't commit suicide, and yet there's no other answer. I looked things over before we brought the body here. No, I haven't the least idea why Reed would do a thing like this."

Quist asked, "Mind if I look over the body?"

"Certainly not," Woodward replied. Quist went to the table. He heard the doctor ask about the breaking glass that had been heard at the front of the building, then he settled into an inspection of the corpse which lay stretched, almost naked, before him. There wasn't, at first, much out of the ordinary to Quist's eyes. Haldane had been a well-built man with iron-gray hair. A small purplish-red hole showed just below the breastbone where the .45 slug had found a gateway to the heart. The dead man's eyes were only partially open; his jaw had dropped. The flesh felt cold and clammy to Quist's touch. Finally he turned away from the table.

Woodward said, "I hear you had a little fuss with Mustang Neale, Mr. Quist. You'd better watch sharp. Neale has a bad reputation around here." Quist replied with something to the effect that he wasn't worried about Neale. The doctor nodded and asked, "Finish your examination?"

"It didn't take long," Quist replied. "Offhand I'd say Haldane died around three or four this morning. Right?"

A sudden respect for Quist showed in the

doctor's eyes. "That's how I placed it," he replied. "How did you know?"

"Condition of the body. It seemed to me *rigor mortis* has started to pass off. It would take about that time."

The doctor started to agree, but Sheriff Tillman interrupted: "In case you'd like me to tell you how I found the body, Mr. Quist——"

"No time now, thanks," Quist cut in. "I've got a job awaiting me out to that wreck. I've got to be pushing along."

"Then you agree with us," Woodward said, "that it was suicide? That is, you found no evidence that would lead you to a murder theory?"

Quist frowned. "Did Haldane wear high starched collars?"

The doctor, sheriff, and undertaker all looked puzzled at the question. Woodward replied, "I don't think I ever saw Reed in a starched collar but once or twice since I knew him—and I've known him a long time. He always wore flannel or woolen shirts. That's a queer thing to ask——"

"Look here," Quist interrupted, turning back to the corpse. He turned the dead head to one side and then the other. "I don't see how you could miss this, Doc."

"You mean that thin reddish line? Well, it isn't reddish now. More purple-like now. But it was red when I first noticed it. What about it?"

"Doesn't it mean anything to you?"

The doctor's forehead knotted. "Why, no, not exactly. I just figured that line around his throat had been made by his shirt collar—Look here, Quist, what are you getting at?"

"As I get it," Quist explained, "the man was found dead in his bed. I take it he didn't sleep in his shirt, so a collar mark would have time to wear off. Even if he did, would a flannel or woolen shirt leave a mark like this? An extremely high starched collar might—just might, y'understand—but only for a short time after it was removed." He again turned away from the table. "Examine it closely and you'll see the skin has been broken at spots. Whatever caused those abrasions was mighty tight around the throat."

"By Gawd, Doc," Tillman exclaimed, "I think Quist has something there. It wa'n't no collar made that line around the neck."

The doctor's voice sounded hoarse when he spoke. "Mr. Quist is right, of course. What a fool I was not to think of it. I should have made a closer examination instead of just jumping to conclusions—but—but what do you think caused that mark, Mr. Quist?"

"A piece of wire could have been responsible, though I won't say it was wire—"

"But what's the answer?" Woodward persisted.

"I think Haldane was garroted," Quist said flatly. "Somebody choked off his breath; then, when he was insensible, took his gun and shot him."

Tillman swore in shocked profanity. The doctor and Hume remained silent, staring wide-eyed at Quist. Finally the doctor spoke. "I'm going to want your testimony at my coroner's inquest in the morning. You make this sound like murder."

"I've tried to make that clear," Quist said quietly, "but I won't be at your inquest. I've a job to do out at that wreck."

Woodward said, "I'd like to have you there, Quist. I could have a subpoena served on you, you know."

Quist shook his head. "You could, but you won't. I'd just ignore it. If you wanted to make trouble, I'd turn the whole business over to the T. N. & A. S. Are you big enough to buck the railroad, Doc? You'd just be making trouble for yourself." The doctor started a further protest, but Quist cut him short. "Look here, I'm not needed at your inquest. You can testify as to what I've said and that you agree with me. Later, when I get this wreck business looked into, I'll be back. Now don't go ornery on me. I'll be more help as a friend than an enemy. Just remember that."

And without waiting for any of the others to speak, he nodded and strode out of the building. Emerging from the wide doorway to the sidewalk, he saw Mustang Neale standing a few yards away. On either side of Neale stood Serrano and Chris Baxter. The instant they saw Quist they came hurrying toward him. Quist glanced at

Neale, who turned and strolled off in the opposite direction.

"So now what?" Quist looked at Baxter and Serrano.

"Mustang," Baxter said, "has been making some threats."

"You heard what happened?" Quist asked.

"We saw what happened," Serrano said. "We stayed right behind you, even when you told us to keep out of your sight."

A smile twitched at Quist's lips. "So you two transferred your bodyguard activities to me. All right. And thanks. Even if I didn't need you." He paused. "Maybe I did at that. Thanks again. We'll start over. Maybe we can get along. Meanwhile, get hold of Doc Woodward and have him tell you what I uncovered. I've a hunch you're both right: it's murder, the way I see things."

And to forestall questioning, he hastened around the hitch rack and stepped up to his saddle. An instant later the buckskin gelding's hoofs were raising dust along the street.

FIVE: Warning

The sun was a dull red disk in a brassy sky, the air filled with tiny, sharp-biting flying particles that drove people indoors. A fiendish wind drove savagely in from the desert country, twisting trees and smaller plants and stripping vegetation from the branches. Animals out on the range huddled for shelter in the hollows or sought the protection of cutbanks. For two days the sandstorm had raged, but now it was commencing to slacken.

"An hour ago," Quist mused as he rode wearily toward Masquerade City, "I couldn't even see trace of the sun. It was almost like night." He rode slumped down in the saddle of the buckskin gelding, sombrero pulled low on forehead and a bandanna drawn high across nose and chin. Only his eyes showed between hat and bandanna, and these he kept almost closed, squinting against the drive of cutting sand and grit. "Horse, you've proved you could take it. If you don't deserve a good feed and rubdown when we get in, I'm a liar by the clock."

The wind was dropping rapidly now. Within another hour it had almost died away, except for occasional sand-laden gusts that cut through the atmosphere. The sky cleared and the sun emerged in full force, bringing perspiration to Quist's forehead. He lowered the bandanna from his face and straightened in the saddle, his gaze surveying the terrain that lay ahead. "Jeepers," he exclaimed, "we're nearer town than I'd figured we were. Yep, pony, you sure know the way home."

Less than a mile ahead were the houses on the outskirts of Masquerade City, low adobe shacks, and beyond rose the roofs of larger buildings. A double line of dust-laden cottonwoods flanking the banks of Rio Mascarada showed where the stream cut past the southwestern edge of town. It wasn't much of a stream or river, either one—just a slow-flowing, shallow bed of water that rose in the mountains and eventually, after passing Masquerade City, sank into the alkali flats some miles south of the town.

Quist touched his pony with his spurs and a short time later was clattering across the wooden bridge that was the beginning of Main Street and on into town. Already store- and shopkeepers were working in front of their establishments, sweeping piles of drifted sand from the sidewalks into the road. On all sides Quist could hear comments regarding the severity of the storm, but now people were abroad, laughing and talking again, and those who had been besieged within saloons were emerging to look at the sun once more.

Quist pulled the buckskin to a walk as he entered the town. He crossed Apache Street and a block farther on, at the corner of Main and Yucca streets, he spied Chris Baxter standing on the hotel corner. The redhead grinned broadly as Quist drew to a halt at the hitch rack. "Thought you might be arriving when the air cleared," Baxter said. "Wasn't that storm a lulu? How did you ever find your way back?"

"I didn't," Quist said quietly as he stepped down. "I was lost for a spell. But that buckskin knew the way, once I gave him his head."

"I'll take him over to the livery for you, Mr. Quist, if you want to go right up to your room. You must be fagged out."

"I'll be obliged to you, Chris. Don't know when I've had such service before—" He broke off. "What in time you chuckling about?"

Baxter grinned. "I was just thinking," he admitted a trifle sheepishly, "how Ramon's going to be burned up when he hears it was *me* on the job to help you." Quist stared at him. Baxter explained, "You see, we sort of got off on the wrong foot with you at first. I'd sort of like to make it up to you—"

"Hell's bells on a tomcat!" Quist exploded. "I never saw such a pair for trying to outdo each other. When you aiming to grow up and act like men?"

Baxter reddened. "I reckon it does seem sort of

childish to you—but, cripes, you don't know all that's gone before—"

"And the more I hear of you, the less sure I am I want to know," Quist snapped testily. His voice softened. "Nonetheless, I appreciate your taking care of that horse. See that he gets fed right and rubbed down." Lifting a burlap sack from his saddle, he turned away.

Brushing off Baxter's further words, Quist climbed the steps to the hotel porch and entered the lobby, then mounted the stairs to the second floor. As he approached the door to his room, he stopped short. There, standing in the corridor, Ramon Serrano lounged against the wall. On the floor at his feet was a tray holding a half dozen bottles of beer. From the looks of the bottles, they'd not been long removed from the ice. Quist felt his lower jaw relax. Serrano grinned widely.

Quist exclaimed, "What the hell!"

"There is nothing like *cerveza* to wash the sand of the dust storm from the throat, Señor Quist—"

"Truer words were never spoken." Quist smiled. "How the devil did you know when I'd arrive?"

Serrano explained: "When the storm slackens I ride a short way from town to watch from a high point of land. I did not think you would remain away long in such blowing and flying sand. When I see you are coming, I return and procure the *cerveza*. May it wash all the weariness from your body, señor."

Quist was touched at the young fellow's thoughtfulness. He said, "Come on in and help me with the washing," and added words of thanks.

Serrano refused courteously, stooped, and, picking the tray from the floor, presented it with a bow to Quist. "I go now to make the sarcastic laughter at Baxter. He will be very turbulent when he learns it was I, Ramon Serrano, who has awaited you with refreshment."

For the second time within the space of minutes Quist felt his lower jaw slacken. "I'll be blasted! You two sure do act like a couple of kids!" Then, glancing at the cold beer, he relented. "Thanks, anyway. Sure you won't have one with me?"

"*Gracias*, no. Anyway, someone awaits your coming in your room. I have heard him in there."

Quist stiffened momentarily, then nodded. If Serrano had heard someone in the room, there was no need for caution. Besides, Quist had some idea of his visitor's identity. Carrying the tray, he turned toward the door, saying to Serrano, "And, Ramon, you might ask Chris Baxter what I said to him a few minutes ago. You two seem to be running a dead heat. See if you can't get together in other ways too."

Serrano gasped. "You mean Baxtair, he hav' already see you before me?"

"Yeah. He was on hand to take care of my horse." And without awaiting Serrano's next words, Quist stepped into his room and closed the door behind him. It wasn't simple, burdened as he was by the tray of beer and the burlap sack he carried, but he managed it. Then he glanced at his visitor. "Thought it was probably you, Jay."

"Got back at last, eh, Greg? It's about time."

Quist laughed shortly and pried the stopper from a bottle of beer. Ignoring the glass on the tray, he tilted the bottle to his lips. Finally he set it down with a long sigh of satisfaction, apparently ignorant of the fact that his visitor was glaring angrily at him. "All right, Jay," Quist said, "I think I know what's coming. Get it off your mind while I clean up and get into some clothing that isn't sand-encrusted."

"Where the devil have you been?" Jay Fletcher demanded.

"I'll tell you later, Jay. Go ahead, relieve your mind."

Jay Fletcher, division superintendent of the T. N. & A. S. Railroad, was a thin, gray-haired man in a dark gray suit of wrinkled "town" clothing. Tired eyes gleamed angrily behind rimless glasses. He had a worried, harassed air as he talked, sometimes pleading, sometimes demanding.

". . . and I certainly expected to find you out at

the wreck when I arrived," he was saying testily while Quist shaved. "But no, not a sign of you. Oh yes, you'd been there, but you hadn't stayed. What I want to know, Greg, are you working for the T. N. & A. S. or aren't you?"

Quist wiped lather from his ears and reached for another bottle of beer. "I've a contract that says I am," he replied quietly.

"Then by the Almighty you'd better live up to it, Greg. You're here on railroad business. Have you forgotten? It appears you have."

Quist paused in his toweling. "What gives you that idea, Jay? By the way, I didn't offer you a beer—"

"You know damn well I can't drink that slop. I'll tell you what gives me that idea. I arrived in Masquerade City, and the first thing I heard is that you've undertaken to prove a murder when there's a plain case of suicide—"

"Oh, you've heard about that, eh?" Quist said quietly. He was getting into a clean shirt now.

"Who hasn't heard of it?" Fletcher snapped. "The whole town seems to feel you just came here on Haldane's account." Then, mockingly, "The great Gregory Quist is here to solve a murder mystery. If you're not careful, you're going to find yourself the subject of a book." Fletcher swore. "Do I hear anything pertaining to your railroad duties? Not a word!" Quist asked a question. Fletcher said, "Oh yes, I attended the Haldane inquest. Had to do something to fill time while I awaited you. In trying to learn where you'd gone, I made the acquaintance of Miss Haldane and a pair named Baxter and Serrano who had worked for her father. All they could talk about was Haldane's death. Where you were—"

"What did the coroner's inquest bring out?" Quist asked.

Fletcher said reluctantly. "A verdict of murder. And all due to the fact you found a red mark around Haldane's throat. Nonsense!"

"Then it doesn't look too much like suicide, Jay."

"That's neither here nor there," Fletcher flared. "You're here on company business. You'll have no time for running down murderers."

"Suppose that murder was connected with the wreck?"

Fletcher stiffened. "Have you proof of that?"

"I haven't said so—yet."

"What have you to go on in that direction?"

Quist said tersely, "Hunch. Sure you won't join me in a beer?"

"Damn it, no!" Fletcher sounded exasperated. "Now, listen here, Greg, why not just forget this murder? You'll have no time—"

"I don't know where my mind can be," Quist interrupted mildly. Going to the burlap sack he had brought, he delved into it and came up with a bottle of James E. Pepper whisky, then found a corkscrew on the dresser. "If I'm not wrong, Jay, Pepper bourbon is a favorite of yours." He poured some liquor into a glass.

Fletcher sourly accepted the drink. "What else have you got in that sack?" he asked, lifting the liquor to his lips.

Quist shrugged. "A few odds and ends I picked up at the wreck," he replied evasively. "A man can always use whisky."

"That's not all whisky in that sack?"

"I haven't claimed it was," Quist said mildly. "There're a few samples of the freight I picked up at the wreck. Things the thieves didn't take, or already had enough of, or overlooked. Don't forget, I've been away a few days. I had to eat. There were foodstuffs on that train."

"You're certain it was freight thieves caused the wreck then?"

"No doubt of it. Rails had been pried apart. Wagon tracks showed where stolen freight had been carried off—"

"That reminds me," Fletcher interrupted. "I've a copy of the waybill with me, so you can see what was being carried, if you need it." A momentary gleam entered his eyes. "We fooled the thieves this time, though."

Quist frowned. "Just how do you mean, Jay?"

"It's like this," Fletcher explained. "The company had a load of gold bullion to deliver, consigned to the San Francisco mint. We feared the freight-thieves gang that has been operating in the Southwest the past couple of years, so we set loose a rumor that the gold bullion was to be carried on that freight train that was wrecked. The news was pretty widely spread. Actually, the gold was forwarded two days before that wrecked freight train pulled out." Fletcher smiled smugly. "Truth is, all that train carried was a lot of machinery, mining and otherwise, consigned to northern California, clothing, packaged and canned food, wagons, lumber, liquor, some guns for Fort Tress, furniture—you know, the usual stuff. Our scheme saved the expense of a heavy guard—"

Quist swore a sudden oath and slammed down his beer bottle. Fletcher looked startled and asked what was wrong.

"I'll tell you what's wrong," Quist said angrily. "You and that whole company crowd think you're almightly smart. Actually, I've never heard of anything so cruel and imbecilic—Oh lord, anyone who'd be a party to pulling a stunt like that wouldn't understand what I mean. Jay, this is the damnedest thing I ever heard of. I don't see how you men could conceive such a—" He broke off, speechless, glowering.

Fletcher said timorously. "I still don't see what's wrong."

Quist lashed out savagely, *"You* wouldn't.

Maybe if I explain it simply, you'll get it through your thick head—"

"I don't like your tone, Greg," Fletcher bridled.

"Now I'm really bothered," Quist said caustically. "And what are you going to do about it?"

"When your next contract comes up—" Fletcher commenced hotly.

Quist laughed harshly. "Don't even try to offer me another contract. I'm sick of working for a set of dim-witted, stupid—Hell! Jay, you can have my resignation right this minute. I'm through!" He scowled at Fletcher. "I'll stay on until you send another operative—"

"Now, now, Greg"—Fletcher commenced to cool down—"don't talk foolishly. You and I have had our differences before, but we've always managed to iron them out for the good of the road. There's no use of us flying off the handle. Let's both keep cool until we get straightened around. Now what were you explaining?"

"It's this way"—Quist was holding his anger with an effort—"the T. N. & A. S. hasn't had too much trouble with freight thieves the past few years, though all the other lines in this section of the country have—"

"If the T. N. & A. S. has been free of thieves," Fletcher said placatingly, "it's due to your good work, Greg."

"Buffalo chips!" Quist said savagely, then got a better grip on his emotions. "Here's the situation as I see it. I went out to the wreck long before you got there. It was pretty much of a mess. What boxcars weren't in splinters—like matchwood—were burned or still burning. The wrecking boss, Carstairs, figured he might as well burn up everything that wasn't savable—quickest way to clear the tracks. But the fire had been started before that—by the thieves. I found several empty kerosene cans that had been thrown in the brush. Carstairs had his derrick working, lifting stuff clear. The whole wrecking crew was working like beavers, as they always do for Carstairs. He told me our trains were being rerouted over the Rock Buttes Southern and—"

"The tracks are clear by this time. We're running on schedule again."

"I'm so pleased to hear it," Quist said caustically.

Fletcher bit his lip. "I'm still wondering why you object so to that story we circulated."

Quist swore testily. "Can't you see, you just invited those freight thieves to wreck that train? Consider the damage to cars and locomotive, the time wasted in rerouting, the extra expense of a wrecking crew and—"

"But the gold went through. Can't you see that—?"

"At the expense of the lives of the whole train crew," Quist snarled. "Did you know the whole crew had been killed, Jay, or don't you consider those lives mean anything? Have you thought of the sorrow brought to their families? Oh no! You and those other brass hats and ditchwater minds never take into consideration the lives of men working for the road. All you think of is dividends for stockholders and trying to outsmart your competition to make more money so you can freight more gold and kill more men—Hell, you don't understand and you never will understand. I'm sick of this whole business. If I have to make a god of the T. N. & A. S., I'm getting out. You can have my resignation right this minute—"

"I'm not empowered to accept it," Fletcher said weakly. "The office—"

"T'hell with the office," Quist said bitterly. "I've had enough of your meddling. I'm through!"

"Now, Greg, now, Greg, that's no talk for the best investigator in the railroad business—"

"Investigator," Quist sneered. "Railroad dick. There's no other name for it. And even in that you can't keep out of my hair. Just because I'm not at the wreck or here in my room when you arrive, you immediately try to jump me and tell me my business—"

"But it's the company that pays your salary for company work," Fletcher persisted, "and not for investigating some local death that likely has nothing to do with freight thieves, despite your hunch."

Quist sighed wearily, opened another bottle of

71

beer, and poured more whisky into Fletcher's glass. "You want to know where I've been?" he asked. "I've been following the tracks of those wagons I found near the scene of the wreck—freight thieves' wagons carrying off stolen goods—"

"Good, Greg, good! Where did they go?"

"How in hell do I know where they went?" Quist snapped. "They were headed north—and traveling fast. From the sign, I'd say they had six horses to a wagon, and there were at least ten wagons—maybe twelve. The trail was so cut up—"

"Headed north?" Fletcher had brightened considerably. "They must have been going to Rawnston—that's a fair-sized town on the Rock Buttes road. They could dispose of the stolen goods there—maybe reship—" He paused; then, "Did you go to Rawnston?" Quist shook his head and swallowed some beer. Fletcher said sharply, "Why not, Greg?"

"In the first place"—Quist's tone was cutting—"I wasn't actually sure they were headed to that Rawnston town. And in the second, have you forgotten, Mister Fletcher, that we've had a sandstorm for the last couple of days?"

"Yes, naturally I knew of the sandstorm. I've remained indoors most of the time, here in my room, at this hotel. But what has a sandstorm to do with it?"

Quist groaned. "Everything. Now don't be any more stupid than you can possibly help. But everything. That sandstorm simply blew away or covered all the tracks, so it was impossible to follow the trail of those wagons. Whether they continued north, or turned off somewhere, I've not the least idea. And just to set your mind at rest, Jay, I've spent no time on the murder business here in town, with the exception of maybe an hour the first night I was here. You see, I was too interested in certain murders—and I feel the T. N. & A. S. was responsible—out at that wreck."

"You can't hold the road responsible for the deaths of the train crew, Greg. That's in line of duty."

Quist said wearily, "No, I can't, but I wish to hell I could."

There was silence for a few minutes. Finally Fletcher said soberly, "I'm sorry as the devil, Greg. I never looked at it your way before. You're right, of course. I'll see that the families of those men are taken care of. We owe them that much. I own enough stock in the company so my word will carry weight with the directors. I'll make them see—"

"All right, all right"—Quist raised one protesting hand—"I know you'll do all possible, Jay. More words won't solve anything. Maybe I've said more than I should. We're both on hair-trigger. How long you staying here?"

"I'm leaving on the seven twenty-three in the morning. Now that I know you're on the job, I'll rest easier. I suppose you'll head for Rawnston the earliest possible?"

"I will if something takes me there, Jay. I've a hunch those freight thieves are centered here-abouts. Consider the other roads that have been raided the past few years—and no apprehensions made, either. The various spots where trains were wrecked due to somebody spreading rails, or taking them up altogether, are all within less than a hundred miles of Masquerade City. I may be wrong, but until I'm proved wrong, I'm aiming to work around here and see what can be picked up. Maybe Haldane's death is connected someway with the thieves, maybe it isn't. I have no way of knowing—yet—but you can count on one thing, Jay: the road won't suffer by letting me have my own way."

"I know, Greg. I should never have intimated I thought otherwise. Actually, I didn't—"

"What's that?" Quist interrupted suddenly. Striding to the bed, he snatched up a folded paper from the cover. On it was written simply, *Gregury Quest.*

"Oh, that—I'd forgotten. Shortly after the clerk let me into your room, someone shoved that paper under the door. I heard the footsteps leave immediately. I suppose it's some sort of message from the hotel desk. I didn't read it. Probably a note from one of your many clients"—this, caustically. "I was too riled up at the moment to be interested in your correspondence. I noticed your oil lamp had burned out, though the wick had been turned low. Figured you'd dashed off on the Haldane matter without giving thought to railroad business, and I jumped to conclusions that made me mad—"

"Think twice before you jump hereafter," Quist advised tartly. "I often leave my light burning, turned low. It's not always wise, on my job, to enter a darkened room—" He broke off and studied the paper and handwriting in ink. "*Quest,* eh?" he commented. "Now I wonder if that's sarcasm, a mistake, or written purposely to deceive me." Unfolding the paper, he studied the note it contained. His lips tightened a trifle, and he said softly, "Well, this looks rather interestin'. Now, who do you suppose—?"

Fletcher asked a question. Quist passed over the sheet of paper, saying, "You'll note some sort of letterhead has likely been torn off that paper." Fletcher read:

Quest, why don't you go someplace else to do your detecting? There's healthier places than this town for a man of your talents, pal. Better take warning.

75

The note was unsigned. Fletcher looked troubled when he'd finished reading it. He exclaimed indignantly, "This is a definite threat, Greg."

Quist nodded, his lips twitching. "Do you think you're breaking news to me, Jay?"

"No—but—but your life may be in danger, Greg."

"That's possible," Quist said lazily.

"You don't seem concerned." Fletcher looked worried.

"I've seen too many notes of that sort to get worked up."

"Any idea who wrote it?"

Quist hesitated, then said, "No."

"What are you going to do about it?"

Quist shrugged his broad shoulders. "Nothing. I'll let whoever wrote it do the following up. In that way he may come into the open."

Fletcher said indignantly, "But you can't just sit around and wait for someone to make an attempt on your life, Greg."

"All right, I'll stand some of the time, if that pleases you—"

"Greg, be sensible—"

"I try to be, Jay. Right now that note pleases me a heap. It shows somebody is worried at my being here. When he gets worried enough, he may try something that will tip his hand."

"But who is it?"

"You tell me and I'll tell you. One thing is

certain. Either he's responsible for Haldane's death, or he's connected with the freight thieves. I've a hunch I'm going to find out before too long a time passes."

SIX: An Old Grudge

Quist emerged from the hotel—Jay Fletcher had left an hour earlier—and into the bright morning sunshine that cut across one corner of the hotel porch. Men were moving along the sidewalks on either side; a few women were in sight, carrying market baskets and parasols as a protection against the heat. Horses and wagons were strung spottily along the almost unbroken line of hitch racks. There wasn't a cloud in the sky of unblemished turquoise. Standing at the corner of the porch, Quist glanced toward the distant range of Masquerade Mountains, their serrated peaks and ponderous buttes etched sharply in the bright light. Two thirds of the way to the topmost peaks, a pair of bluffs, shaped to a large degree like human heads, stood out in bold relief against their granite-gray background, the "heads" being of a more reddish-brown color, each having a wide section of stratified bluish-black rock across it, giving the heads the appearance of being masked.

Quist remembered now that someone had told him the original name of those mountains had been *Cordillera Mascarada*—Masquerade Range. The reason was plain to him as he looked

79

at the masked "heads." "That's the difference between the Spanish and the people who own this country now," Quist mused. "Whatever Spaniard named that range was immediately reminded of a masquerade ball, with dancing and music. An Anglo would be more likely to think of a masked bandit." And then Quist thought of something else; one definition of masquerade connoted acting or living under false pretenses. He frowned. "Maybe it all fits in," he concluded.

Quist's gaze roved over the street. Directly across Main Street, at the corner of Yucca, Chris Baxter stood before the Lone Star Livery. Quist cast his eyes diagonally to the other corner and saw Ramon Serrano waiting near Johnson's Feed & Hay Store. Both men were looking toward Quist, as though hoping to catch his attention. As Quist started to descend the steps of the hotel porch, both Serrano and Baxter started across to meet him. As they moved, each quickened step until they were fairly racing to greet him.

"Another dead heat," Quist chuckled as they practically skidded to a stop on the sidewalk before him.

"Morning, Mr. Quist. Could I get your horse for you?"

"Is fine day, Señor Quist. Permit me to be at your service."

"I'm not in need of any service, thanks, Serrano."

Baxter grinned triumphantly. "Mr. Quist isn't interested in what a spick could do for him—"

"Nor do I want a horse now, Baxter. Much obliged—"

"Who are you calling the spick, you Bowery gutter rat?" Serrano's olive skin flushed darkly.

Baxter bristled to the roots of his red hair. "You call me a Bowery gutter rat and I'll knock all your teeth down your throat—"

"Cut it out," Quist snapped. The two young fellows were closing menacingly on each other. He pushed one muscular arm between them. "I've just thought of something you can do for me."

Instantly personal differences were forgotten as the two gave Quist their attention. Quist went on, "Now get this straight. I don't want any servants and I don't want a bodyguard. I'm much obliged to both of you for keeping an eye on Mustang Neale a few nights ago, but if Neale makes trouble, I figure I can handle it myself. Just get out of my life and stay out—that's what you can do for me."

Without giving them an opportunity to reply, he strode off down the street. "Damned if I ever saw such a pair," he growled.

A block farther on, where Austin Street crossed Main, he spied the jail and sheriff's office, a low blocky affair constructed of rock and adobe, situated next to a two-story frame building across the front of which was painted in sun-faded, sand-blasted letters the words "Courthouse." Quist's steps raised small clouds of dust from the roadway as he stepped diagonally across the street. A narrow porch fronted the sheriff's office. Above it jutted a wooden awning, its outer edges resting on uprights at the edge of the plank sidewalk. To one of the uprights was nailed a sign which proclaimed: "Office of the Sheriff, Mascarada County." There was a window in the front wall of the office, and next to it stood an open doorway.

Quist crossed the narrow porch and stepped into the office. A pleasant-faced man with bristly, sandy hair—his sombrero was shoved almost to the back of his head and seemed to remain in place as though glued there—and wearing a woolen shirt and denim pants glanced up from the desk where he'd been sitting. "Anything I can do for you, mister?"

"I don't know yet. I was looking for the sheriff. I'm Gregory Quist."

Instantly the man was on his feet, shoving a chair in Quist's direction. "I'm glad to meet you, Mr. Quist"—shoving out his hand. "I'm Clem Vincent, deputy sheriff. I heard you were in town." The deputy had a drawly manner of speaking, and Quist liked the handshake he gave him. Clem Vincent continued, "The sheriff hasn't come in yet."

Quist dropped into a straight-backed chair

and started to shake Durham out of a sack into a brown cigarette paper. He didn't wet the edge of the paper, just gave it a firm twist that seemed to keep the paper in place. Vincent struck a light. Quist inhaled deeply and glanced about the office. To the right of the doorway was the desk. In the rear wall was a closed door that presumably led the way to the jail cells at the rear. A couple of packing-house and gunmakers' calendars adorned the adobe walls. At one side was tacked a topographical map of Mascarada County, with below it a cot with neatly folded blankets.

"If there's anything I can do for you—" the deputy commenced.

"What time will the sheriff be in?"

Clem Vincent grinned. "When he gets up. If it's anything important I can direct you to his boardinghouse."

Quist chuckled. "If he's the sort of man who isn't up yet, I wouldn't want it to be important. When does he usually get here?"

"Round noon would be a good guess," Vincent drawled. "Matt Tillman likes to eat heavy—"

"I noted his chest seemed to have sagged toward his middle."

"—and then sleep it off like some men do liquor. In short, Matt don't like to move around much, especially in hot weather. Day like this, I'm surprised you're wearing a coat."

"Yeah, that's one of the disadvantages," Quist

replied. He didn't add that the coat covered his underarm gun, and at the deputy's puzzled expression Quist said, "I like heat."

"Oh, I see," Vincent said blankly.

Quist went on quickly, "I ran into Tillman a few nights ago. Struck me as being rather pompous and overbearing."

Vincent shrugged uncomfortably. "Could be," he admitted. Quist could see that Vincent disliked criticizing his boss. Vincent went on, "Aw, Matt's all right. He's been a right good man in his time, I understand. Maybe he's slowed up some now, but there really isn't much to keep him busy. The town's right orderly, and mostly anything that comes up I can handle without bothering Matt. If he wants to feel important, it's no skin off my bronc."

"I reckon not," Quist agreed. "There comes a time when we all hate to move more than necessary."

"Oh, the sheriff can stir himself all right if anything serious comes up. For instance, the other night when that wreck happened, it was Matt who saddled up and rode out there. I'd been expecting it would be my job."

"Now why would Tillman bother his head over that wreck?"

"It happened in Mascarada County. Keeping law here is our job. There's a rumor freight thieves were responsible for that wreck."

Quist shrugged his shoulders. "Could be," he conceded, "but how could Tillman know about it that soon?"

"He couldn't, of course, but if there'd been anything to learn, he might have picked something up."

"That's true. Did the sheriff learn anything?"

"I reckon not. Told me the next morning that everything was in a state of confusion and there was nothing he could do. He stayed around a spell and then rode back to town."

Quist drew on his cigarette, exhaled. "I was hoping to get some line from the sheriff regarding Reed Haldane's enemies. You any idea who might have killed Haldane?"

"Not the slightest," Vincent said promptly. "Matt—and everybody else he knew—couldn't understand it when they thought it was suicide. If Haldane had enemies, I wouldn't know much about it. I was only appointed to this job about six months back. I come from Sage Wells, twenty-five miles north of here. Course a feller hears rumors on occasion."

"Any particular occasion?" Quist asked.

Vincent shook his head. "I've just heard it said now and then that Haldane had had trouble with the Shattucks at one time. I guess he killed one of 'em—though I don't know what it was about. I haven't talked to anyone else who knows, either. Then a few years back—" The deputy paused.

"You understand this is all hearsay with me? I haven't any proof." Quist said he understood, and Vincent continued, " 'Bout six or seven years back there was a bad drought hit this country. Cows were dropping like flies. Haldane's herds came through in pretty good shape, for the reason that the Rio Mascarada runs through his holdings. While there wa'n't too much water in the river, still and all, he managed to hold on and not lose many cows."

"And I suppose the other outfits resented that."

"Mostly Shattuck's Triangle-S. The other outfits were too far off to take advantage of the river, even if Haldane had offered it. The Triangle-S, being adjoining to Haldane's Rafter-RH, felt Haldane should share his water. All the Shattuck water holes had gone dry. Haldane's point was that if he shared his water there wouldn't be enough for either outfit. I understand he and the Shattucks had words about that too, and hard feelings were roused. Matter of fact, I've heard that Haldane did allow Shattuck to throw small bunches of steers along the river about once a week, and that probably helped some. Anyway, like I say, there was a lot of bad feeling over the matter, but I reckon it died out as the years passed."

"Or maybe it didn't," Quist said slowly. "Some men carry grudges a long time, and Haldane was found dead in his bed."

86

The deputy nodded. "Anyway, there you are."

"You ever see any evidence of bad feeling between Haldane and the Shattucks?"

"None to speak of. Pitt Shattuck and Haldane used to nod to each other when they met. Todd Shattuck was always saying how he would even the score someday, but he said that so often that nobody paid him any attention. For that matter, the whole Triangle-S crew were always running down Haldane, but there were never any open breaks. The Triangle-S crew is pretty loudmouthed anyway—and rough, when the hands think they can get away with it. Especially Mustang Neale."

"Where was Todd Shattuck the night—or rather it was early morning—that Haldane was killed?"

"Out at the Triangle-S."

"You know that for sure?"

"Pretty positive. The minute the coroner's jury brought in its findings of murder, Sheriff Tillman sent me *pronto* to bring in Todd Shattuck for questioning. Todd had an alibi. Pitt Shattuck swears he was at the ranch."

Quist whistled softly and dropped his cigarette butt in a nearby cuspidor. "And so they alibi each other."

"That's about the size of it." Clem Vincent nodded.

"And nobody else was questioned?"

Vincent shook his head. "Neither Matt or I

had any idea who else might have killed him."

"So you've given up looking."

Vincent flushed. "That's not so," he stated indignantly. "I'm doing my best, and so is Matt. We ask questions here and there. Matt's posted a reward of five hundred dollars for information. But we're just up against a stone wall, Mr. Quist. Where would you start?"

Quist said heavily, "I've already started," but didn't offer further explanation.

Before the deputy could ask questions, further discussion was interrupted by the sounds of angry yelling from across the street. Some sort of scuffle was taking place. Both Quist and Vincent were in the doorway now, gazing across the roadway. Vincent stepped out across the porch, followed closely by Quist.

Three men were struggling in a narrow passageway that ran between the post office, which stood on the corner of Main and Austin streets, and the next-door building, occupied by the Red Ball Saloon. Quist had no trouble recognizing Chris Baxter's red hair and Serrano's lithe form. After a moment he saw Mustang Neale struggling between them. The deputy and Quist were across the road now. A crowd had quickly gathered.

"Break it up," the deputy ordered sharply, stepping in and separating the struggling men. It seemed everyone was talking at once. Eventually a modicum of quiet was restored. Serrano stepped back, holding a six-shooter in his hand. Baxter released his hold on Neale, whose flat, obsidian-like eyes slid angrily toward Quist. The man's mouth was just a thin slit in his face. He remained silent when Vincent demanded, "What's the trouble here?"

"Serrano and I," Baxter explained, "saw Neale following Mr. Quist, so we thought we'd see what he was up to. Serrano went down the alleyway back of these buildings—"

"Neale was standeeng in theese passage-way, watching across the street at your office, Clem—"

"He had his gun out, like he was waiting a chance to bushwhack Mr. Quist," Baxter put in. "The shadow's deep here between buildings, and—"

"While Baxter keep the eye on Neale from across the street," Serrano interrupted, "I'm come up in the rear of heem and take away hees six-shootair—" Serrano laughed ruefully. "Neale is moch stronger than I'm think, and he makes me moch trouble. Then Baxter arrive' to help—"

"Aw, that's a damn lie," Neale growled. "I stepped into this shade here to get outten the sun while I waited to speak to Quist. Didn't know how he might take it, so I was just looking over my gun to see if it was in good working order. I didn't have no intention of shooting. Then these two punks jumped me—"

"I think, Neale," the deputy said coldly, "I'd better place you under arrest—"

"No, wait," Quist interrupted. He turned to Neale. "What did you want to see me about?"

Mustang's gaze dropped to Quist's thigh and, seeing no gun, he again raised his face toward Quist. It couldn't be said he raised his eyes. Something queer about those eyes—like a snake's. Flat, almost motionless, opaque. There was no way of telling from the eyes what was passing in the man's mind. For all his small size, he looked vicious, ominous. Again like a snake. A sidewinder.

"What did I want to see you about, pal?" He spoke from his thin slit of mouth. "I was going to warn you to get a gun or get out of town. Ain't no hombre going to push Mustang Neale through a window 'thout he gets what's coming to him. Is that clear, pal?"

"Couldn't be clearer," Quist said quietly. "Is this your second warning—pal?"

Something akin to a look of perplexity came into Neale's features. "What—what do you mean?" he asked uncertainly. "This is the first warning I've give you."

"I suppose you're right," Quist said pleasantly. "Generally a rattler strikes after his first warning."

Deputy Vincent said again, "Neale, I think I'd better place you under arrest and have the j.p. bind you over to keep the peace."

"Cripes!" Neale protested. "I ain't done nothing—yet. Go ahead. Arrest me. Todd'll get me out on bond so fast it'll make your head swim. Then where'll you be? If you want to avoid trouble in this town, pal, persuade Mister Quist to slope outten here—fast!"

"Start walking toward the jail, Neale," Vincent said coldly. "And I don't want any more of your lip—"

"Look here, Clem," Quist put in, "maybe Neale's right in what he claims. I happen to know that Baxter and Serrano are sort of impulsive. Maybe they made a mistake."

Vincent's mouth twitched. "Is impulsive the word for it?" He smiled at Quist. "Putting it sort of mild, aren't you?"

"That could be." Quist nodded. "But how about letting Neale go?"

"If you say so," Vincent said reluctantly. "All right, Mustang, get on about your business. And I don't want to hear any more of your threats."

"I'll try to make 'em when you're not around," Neale sneered. He turned to Serrano. "Give me my gun."

Serrano glanced at Vincent. Vincent nodded. Serrano returned the gun, which Neale shoved into his holster.

Quist asked quietly, "Are you still gunning for trouble, Neale? If so, I'm ready."

"Now look here—" Vincent commenced.

Neale ignored him. "I'm still gunning for trouble, Quist, but I don't draw on an unarmed man."

"That I find hard to believe," Quist stated. "But don't worry about me. I'll take care of myself."

Neale stiffened a trifle, then relaxed. His hand was nowhere near his gun. He'd noticed that Quist's arms hung easily at sides. Something in Quist's apparently careless assurance unsettled Neale momentarily. The flat, obsidian eyes slid sidewise, then returned to study Quist. After a moment he nodded as though some conclusion had been reached in his mind. "Hide-out gun, eh?"

Quist smiled thinly. "If you want to call it that, Neale. Maybe you'd like a look at it. It's up to you."

"Now, look here—" Vincent renewed his protests.

Neale cut in, backing away a step, "Not now, Quist. You got too many pals with you. I already been jumped once today while I was minding my own business—and I'm aiming to settle a score with a coupla punks when I've done with you too. My time will come, Quist. When it does you'll see, by Gawd, that—"

"And is that your third warning?" Quist interrupted.

Neale looked puzzled. "I don't know what you're drivin' at with all this second- and thirdwarnin' talk—and I don't care neither." He backed uneasily another step, then turned and pushed through the crowd, headed in the direction of the Red Ball Saloon. Just before he entered the bar, he paused and said angrily, "Just remember I warned you, Quist. And you'd best take heed."

"I'll remember—pal," Quist called after him.

Neale cursed and flung himself through the swinging doors of the Red Ball.

SEVEN: The Doctor's Story

Deputy Vincent spoke to the crowd, which started to disperse. Within a few moments only Quist, Baxter, Serrano, and Vincent were left standing on the sidewalk. Pedestrians flowed past as before.

Vincent scowled. "I think you're wrong, Mr. Quist. I should have put Neale behind bars. You'll yet have trouble with him. I don't like it. I know the sheriff would agree with me."

Quist shook his head. "He'd just get out on bail. We couldn't actually prove he was set to ambush me. It'd be his word against what Serrano and Baxter claim."

"But I'm sure I'm right," Baxter insisted earnestly. "I saw him draw his gun. He'd been watching the sheriff's office ever since you went in—"

"He was following you for no good purpose, I think," Serrano said soberly.

Quist considered. "I doubt he'd have shot without first warning me. He's a typical killer, but the code of his kind is to warn first."

"But how much time would he have given you between the warning and his shot?" Baxter pointed out.

Serrano put in shrewdly, "And even with the warning, hidden as he was in the deep shadow there, it would require time to adjust your eye to the change of light, Mr. Quist."

Quist laughed softly. "You two certainly are about the most persistent cusses I've seen."

At that moment Deputy Vincent saw somebody entering his office. "Well, I've got to get back on my job. See you later, gents." He stepped from the sidewalk, rounded a hitch rail, and headed across the street.

Quist studied Serrano and Baxter. "Yep, just plain persistent," he repeated. "What in the devil am I going to do with you two? You place me under obligation to you, whether I like it or not. I'll admit there's a chance you're right about Mustang Neale too. But I still don't want you bird-dogging me all the time. What am I going to do with a pair of hombres like you?"

"Put us to work," Baxter said promptly.

"We want to help," from Serrano.

"And I could use help too," Quist said, "but I couldn't count on you two. If I gave you a job, you'd forget my needs and start squabbling the minute my back was turned. I've got to have men I can trust to do what I want done."

"Just try us once more?" Baxter pleaded.

"Give us the chance?" Serrano asked.

Quist drew a deep sigh. "On my account you've both earned the enmity of Mustang Neale.

96

You may be kept busy looking out for your own skins. But I feel I owe you something. We want to learn who killed Reed Haldane. You two know this town better than I. Likely you could be a lot of help. Let's look at it this way. We're trying to do something for Reed Haldane and his daughter. If he were alive, do you think he'd like the idea of you two fighting all the time and ignoring his interests? Your way is just setting up a brick wall in front of things I want to learn."

"Is right. We are the idiots," Serrano said. Baxter nodded agreement.

"I've heard you say that before too," Quist reminded, "but it didn't seem to do any good. But I'm going to give you another chance if you two will promise me that you'll declare a truce until we've learned who killed Reed Haldane. Once that's done, you can tear each other limb from limb, for all I care." He smiled, adding, "And I hope you'll let me know when it happens. It should make a nice brawl."

"We'll do anything for you, Mr. Quist—" Baxter commenced.

"You're not doing it for me," Quist snapped. "You'll be doing it for Reed Haldane. I'm not asking you to shake hands. Spend all your spare time scrapping if you like, but when there's business afoot, just remember you mustn't do anything to endanger Haldane's interest."

"We'll do it, Mr. Quist," Baxter said.

"And forget the 'mister' from now on," Quist growled. "And if you don't behave as I say and cut out your nonsense, I'll go to Miss Haldane and tell her to give you the sack. Remember, she's the boss now."

Baxter and Serrano exchanged quick glances. Neither spoke, but it was plain that Quist's words had sunk in. Quist went on, "Now I don't want either of you tailing me. I can protect myself. Go about your business, talk to people, see if you can uncover any clues. That's all for present. Where does Dr. Woodward live?"

"Over on the next street," Baxter said. "I'll take you there."

"*I* will take you to the doctair's—" Serrano commenced, then checked the words reluctantly. "No, is good for Chris to show the way."

Quist smothered a smile. "That's a good start, Ramon. Is Woodward married?"

Baxter said, "No. His wife died six or seven years back. Doc was pretty broke up at the time, but he continued to keep their house."

Quist nodded. "Anyway, I don't need either of you to show me the way to his place. Just give me directions."

Five minutes later the three men had separated, Quist cutting over Austin Street to what was known as the residential section of Masquerade City. Dr. Woodward's home and office were located in a one-story frame house, painted white, near the corner of Austin. A white picket fence surrounded the property and there were some huge old live-oak trees in the yard. Woodward hailed Quist from a seat on the porch as Quist was stepping through the gateway. "Come up and sit a spell. It's cool here."

Quist agreed as he reached the porch and dropped into a rocker at the doctor's side. A fresh breeze was rustling the leaves of the big oak trees. Quist said, "I didn't know but that you might be busy with patients."

The doctor shook his head. "Had a few patients a short while ago. Later I've got a few visits to make—kids with measles or mumps or whooping cough. A couple of broken limbs. This is pretty healthy country. Gun wounds now and then. I get most of my visits after supper, when men are through work. Mostly men patients. I sometimes wonder why that is, too."

Quist smiled. "You know the old saying that women's work is never done. Maybe the women keep too busy to think of their ailments. It takes a man to really squawk when he gets a bellyache."

"How true that is," Woodward agreed. "In the long run I think a woman can stand pain far better than a man." He broke off. "You didn't come on a professional visit, I hope."

Quist shook his head. "I'm after information. Expected to talk to Sheriff Tillman, but he hadn't got to his office when I was there."

"As to be expected." Woodward snorted impatiently. "That fat windbag! Ever see anybody act so important as he does? And he leaves ninety-five per cent of the work to Clem Vincent. Luckily Clem's a good man. He should be sheriff. But what information can I give you?"

"I'm trying to learn who might hate Reed Haldane enough to kill him. I know there was some trouble with the Shattucks years ago, and of more recent years when there was a drought. Do you think either of the Shattucks might have done it?"

"They alibi each other," Woodward said shortly. "I can't overlook that."

"Suppose they're lying?"

"It's possible. Still, I've seen a lot of Pitt Shattuck, and he doesn't strike me as the sort to wait this long before settling any grudge he might be holding."

"What about the other brother—Todd?"

"Todd is the more likely candidate in my mind, but, again, why should he wait this long? He's been making threats for years, but it seemed just talk."

"Would either of them hire somebody to do the job?"

Woodward considered the question. "It's possible, but both Shattucks strike me as the sort that would like to settle their own scores. Actually, I've always felt that Pitt Shattuck, at least, was

100

anxious to avoid trouble with Reed. When they met on the street, they nodded. Don't misunderstand; they weren't friendly by any means."

"I understand it's rumored that Haldane killed a Shattuck one time. What led to that, do you know?"

"As Reed's oldest friend, I ought to know. And I do. But I'm not sure I should tell you. Reed always wanted the matter kept quiet. I'd like to respect his wishes." Quist asked a question. Woodward replied, "Yes, Francisca knows the story. Reed told her when she was old enough to—to understand things."

Quist asked quietly, "Are you going to force me to go to Francisca, Doctor? Or the Shattucks? One way or another, I'm going to get at the truth in this business. You can either help me or prove to be an obstacle. Which is it to be?"

Woodward's tired eyes surveyed Quist from behind the rimless spectacles. Finally he sighed. "No, I'd rather you didn't go to Francisca. The girl's been through enough, with the funeral and all. She's out at the ranch now, trying to get herself back on an even keel after holding on like a thoroughbred until after Reed was buried. There's no use stirring her emotions with talk of an old trouble. I don't know, Quist, maybe I owe you something. Only for you, Reed would have been buried as a suicide. Yes, you might as well have the story."

"I'm waiting," Quist said.

"It was more than twenty years ago," Woodward commenced, "when Reed was younger, more hot-tempered than he was in later years, that he was down in Mexico City and met a Spanish girl named Magdalena Ruiz. Good blood and education. An orphan. And beautiful, Reed told me. I guess it was one of those love-at-first-sight affairs, and Reed married her. Land and cattle were cheap in Mexico those days, and Reed was well heeled. He got a ranch nearer the border and he and his bride went to housekeeping. A nearby ranch was owned by the three Shattuck brothers, though one of the brothers, named Jeff, quarreled with the elder, Pitt, and left the ranch. At that point Reed Haldane made a serious mistake; he hired Jeff as his foreman. Jeff at that time had a reputation as a ladies' man, but Reed paid no attention to that. Help was scarce. He needed a foreman. Reed hired a man he could get."

"I'm commencing to see what's coming," Quist put in.

"Maybe so. Reed's ranch prospered, and he and his Magdalena were mighty happy for a couple of years. A baby girl had been born—Francisca—and Reed built an addition to his home. He was working right hard those days. Maybe his wife got bored, being alone so much; maybe she didn't. Reed was never sure. But one night when he came into the house he found Jeff Shattuck kissing his wife. She was trying to fight Shattuck off at the time, but Reed was too hot-tempered to notice that. It didn't occur to him until later—when it was too late."

"A temper never steadied any man's aim," Quist observed.

"How right you are. Anyway, Reed immediately jumped to the wrong conclusions. He refused to listen to any explanations and ordered his wife and Jeff Shattuck to get out of the house. The wife was proud. She refused to say a word in her own defense. She just stood looking at Reed as though hypnotized, Reed told me. Maybe Reed didn't give her a chance to say anything. He grabbed up his baby daughter where she was playing on the floor, left the house, got his horse, and rode back across the border. He left Francisca with the mission fathers at Tucson."

"And never went back to his ranch again?"

Woodward shook his head. "He put every-thing in the hands of an agent and sold to the first buyer. Reed told me he never wanted to see the house again. I guess he was like a crazy man for a good many months, before he got control of himself. Then he commenced to have doubts as to the way he'd acted. He set detectives to find his wife, but they never had any luck. All he learned was that his wife had packed up and left—not with Jeff Shattuck—no one knew where. A year had passed by this time. Reed decided to return, himself, and see if Jeff Shattuck could give him any information. He found Shattuck all right, on the street of Rosario Wells, a small Mexican hamlet. Shattuck denied knowing anything about the wife. What else was said I don't know for certain. Anyway, it ended in gunplay, and Reed killed Jeff Shattuck. It was a fair fight—even Pitt Shattuck admitted that at the time, Reed told me, though I guess Todd Shattuck swore an oath that someday he'd get even."

"And they came to this country to carry out that threat?"

Woodward smiled ironically. "No, that was just a trick that Fate played on Reed and the Shattucks. You see, Reed still had detectives trying to find his wife. Finally he concluded she must be dead and that he'd better start living for his daughter. He bought the Rafter-RH here and started to build up his bank account for Francisca. Not many years passed before a relative of the Shattucks died and willed the Triangle-S to Pitt Shattuck. Meantime the Shattucks had sold their Mexican property and moved up here, never dreaming they'd encounter Reed in the Masquerade country. Later, when Francisca finished her schooling, Reed brought her here. I truly think that Pitt Shattuck has tried to avoid trouble, though I wouldn't put it past him to wish Reed harm at any time since they met again."

"That's quite a story," Quist said. "And nothing ever was learned of Haldane's wife?"

"Not one blessed thing. I suppose she's dead, or she'd have tried to get in touch with Francisca, anyway. That was Reed's idea too."

"How come, Doctor, that Haldane owned the Saddlehorn Saloon? Didn't the Rafter-RH pay well enough to keep him going?"

"You bet it did. Reed was a wealthy man. He never said for certain, but from things he dropped now and then, I think he was too much alone with his thoughts at the ranch. Undoubtedly he brooded a lot over what had happened. Maybe he wanted more people near him to talk to, though he was a rather quiet individual. And there are always people in a bar. When the Saddlehorn came up for sale, he bought it and installed Skimpy Degnan as barkeep. Now and then Reed served behind the bar, but not often. Skimpy didn't mind long hours, and Reed just hung around and talked to everybody, or rather listened to them talk. The bar prospered, though he didn't care about that. Finally he took to sleeping in the back room. Why not? He saw Francisca regularly, and he had a good foreman, Brose Tucker, to manage the ranch." Woodward drew a long breath. "Talking so much makes my throat dry. Do you care to walk over to Main Street for a drink?"

"Now you're talking my language." Quist

smiled. "But first, where do Baxter and Serrano fit into the Haldane picture?"

Woodward chuckled and gazed toward the oak trees. "I'd say they'd find it difficult to fit anywhere—together. Always scrapping. Have since they met. Ramon arrived here first, a scrawny brat with no English beyond a few words that kids shouldn't use. I guess he was starving when he came to Masquerade City. Anyway, he stole a loaf of bread and some beef from a restaurant. Wasn't more than ten at the time. Got caught, of course. Reed came to his rescue. Something about the kid's fighting spirit appealed to Reed, and he practically adopted Ramon. Sent him to school. Taught him ranch work. Where he'd been before he came here Ramon couldn't say with certainty. His folks had abused him and he'd run away. Been roaming around Mexico. Didn't even realize at first he'd wandered across the border."

"And Baxter?"

"An orphan from New York. He wasn't more than a couple of years older than Ramon when he got kicked off a freight that stopped here. And what a nasty little hoodlum he was, straight from the New York slum district. Tough as they come. Thin and starved, too. How he ever managed to beat the rails this far is more than I could ever figure out. And carrying a gun, believe it or not. A little snub-nosed cheaply made ·firearm, but no loads for it. Ramon was at the station when

Chris was kicked off the freight and laughed at him. Chris pulled his toy gun, but when he didn't shoot, Ramon knew it was all bluff. Ramon picked up a rock and knocked the gun from Chris's hand. They were fighting like wildcats when Reed happened to pass by. He separated them and took Chris in hand, got him straightened out."

"Another case of practical adoption, I take it."

"Right, but they've never given up fighting. Reed took care of both their schooling, ranch work, horses and guns, and so on. Both boys worshiped him and were jealous as the devil of each other. Each one has always tried to outdo the other. Ramon is better with horses, but Chris knows cows. With guns they're about even. Ramon has the quicker mind, but I think Chris thinks straighter sometimes." Woodward smiled reminiscently. "The fights those two have had. Ramon learned to use his fists as well as Chris. The last few years I don't think they ever fought anything but a draw. Reed never could quite get them to stop, though he got a solemn promise out of each that so long as he—Reed—lived there'd never be any gunplay. Now I don't know what's going to happen. I've never known such a rivalry. And there's so much good in both of those fellows too."

"Suppose," Quist speculated, "they both fell in love with the same girl."

Woodward swore softly. "Do you suppose I haven't thought of that?"

"Francisca?"

"That's how it looks to me." Woodward sighed. "Last couple of years I've been looking for an explosion to take place most any time, though I don't think anything much has ever been said to Francisca by either of those two."

"How do you think Francisca feels about 'em?"

"Blessed if I know. I don't know her mind any better than I do any woman's. Offhand I'd say she was impartial. She's accompanied both to dances and such. There are other fellows around who'd like to court her too, but she's always seemed to like Ramon and Chris best."

"With her being half Spanish and Ramon's Spanish blood, I'd figure he might have the inside track."

"It seems that might be true, but I couldn't say."

"Did Haldane have any inkling of the situation?"

"I believe he did. I think that's one reason he brought Chris and Ramon away from the ranch and had 'em live in town as his bodyguards— probably that more than any actual fear of the Shattucks. In town Reed could keep an eye on Ramon and Chris. Reed split their bodyguarding into shifts, and that kept them apart. He got them rooms at a boardinghouse here, so they didn't get out to the ranch more than once a week as a rule.

When Reed went to bed, whoever was guarding him went off duty. Reed claimed he never needed a bodyguard after he'd locked himself in his room, as he'd never allow anyone but a friend to enter—"

"That's an interesting point," Quist broke in.

"I suppose." Woodward nodded, though he didn't appear to get Quist's meaning. "I'll say this for Reed: he did a fine job of bringing up those two boys. I figure he always felt his job there sort of evened up, to a small extent at least, for the results of his hasty temper years ago. And I know he'd had no objection to either Chris or Ramon as a son-in-law if he'd been certain Francisca knew what she wanted. He was a pretty fine man, Reed Haldane was. Quist, I'm talking too much. Let's get that drink."

EIGHT: Evidence

The two men strolled leisurely along Austin Street, Woodward carrying his black medical bag. Quist said, "As coroner here, maybe you can help me out, so long as I can't see the sheriff for a time."

"Glad to do anything possible, Quist."

"I want a look at that room where Haldane's body was found. I don't suppose things have been disturbed yet. I want to talk to that bartender who found the body too."

"Skimpy Degnan. That can be taken care of. I locked the room after my coroner's jury had had a look at it. The jury had to know just how the body was laying, and so on, and sort of take a look around. Luckily I've got the key to the room in my pocket. Tillman asked me for it yesterday, but I couldn't locate it at the moment. I'd placed it in my other suit after the inquest and forgotten it."

"What did the sheriff want the key for?"

"He figures it's part of the evidence, and if we ever catch the murderer, the key might be needed."

"There's more than one key, isn't there?"

"Skimpy Degnan has one, but he needs it to let himself into the saloon in the morning and lock up at night, so long as Reed's no longer there to take care of closing up and opening."

The two men had reached Main Street by this time. They continued on across to the Saddlehorn Saloon, which stood on the southwest corner, opposite the jail and sheriff's office on the same side of the street. Entering the bar, they found only a few customers at the long counter which stretched the length of the right-hand wall. The rest of the room was given over to scattered chairs and round-topped wooden tables. There were three windows in the left-hand wall and a broader window at the front, next the swinging doors. At the rear was a partition with closed door.

Dr. Woodward nodded to the men at the bar—a cowhand from the Rocking-H and three men in "town" clothing—and led the way to the farther end. A few moments later Skimpy Degnan approached for their orders. Woodward introduced him to Quist. Degnan was an extremely thin man, rawboned, with a thick shock of iron-gray hair and Irish-blue eyes. There was a smile to go with the eyes. He placed a bottle and two glasses on the bar. When drinks had been consumed, Degnan said:

"I owe you my thanks, Mr. Quist."

"*Por qué*? How do you figure I got thanks coming, Skimpy?"

"For making certain people see that Reed Haldane hadn't committed suicide."

Woodward flushed. "No use rubbing in my mistakes, Skimpy."

"No rubbin' in intended, Doc. But I just couldn't bear a thought of Reed doing a thing like that. He was all wool and a yard wide. Wasn't a better man ever lived."

"You worked for him quite a while, eh?" Quist asked.

"I was tendin' bar here even before he bought the place," Degnan replied. "I stayed on. We got on fine. I never worked for an easier boss to get on with."

"Tell me about finding him that morning," Quist suggested.

Degnan sobered. "It's a thing I don't like to think of." He drew a deep sigh. "I'd left my boardinghouse and got here around a quarter to nine. The front door was locked. A good deal of the time Reed had opened up before I got here, but that morning he hadn't. No, sir. Well, I let myself in and sort of started to tidy up from the mess of the night before. You know, dirty glasses and so forth, refilling bottles from kegs—things like that. Still Reed don't show up. I think he's overslept, so I goes over and gives a knock at that door there"—indicating a door at one end of the partition built across the back wall. "Reed had had that room built in when he decided to do

113

most of his sleeping here. When he didn't answer the knock, I tried the knob."

"Was the door locked?" Quist asked.

Degnan nodded. "On the inside. Reed had new locks—snap locks—put on when he bought the Saddlehorn. On the front door, the door to that room there, and the back door. You have to go through his room to get out the back door."

"And what's out the back door?" Quist asked.

"Mostly open country," Degnan said. "Plus the T. N. & A. S. tracks, seventy-five feet away, and piles of rubbish behind each back door all along the way."

"You mentioned three doors," Quist said. "Is there a different key for each door?"

"Same key fits all three."

"Who had keys besides you and Haldane?"

"Nobody. We each had one."

"There were never any more?"

"Not that I know of, and I was here when the new locks were put in."

"Go on. When you found the door locked, what did you do?"

"I knocked again, and then when there was no answer I unlocked the door. Never dreamed he was dead. Figgered him sick, maybe. But not cold dead. There he was, stretched out on the bed in his nightshirt, the gun in his hand layin' at his side. The blankets only partly covered him, and I could see the nightshirt was all blood. It

114

fair made me sick to the stummick for a minute. 'Bout that time I heard a couple of customers come into the bar. I sent one for Doc Woodward and t'other over to the sheriff's office. Course Matt hadn't showed up yet, but Clem Vincent was there and he come over instanter. And that's all I know. Just like the testimony I give at your inquest, ain't it, Doc?"

Woodward nodded agreement. "Right, Skimpy."

The barkeep said, "The sheriff wanted my key yesterday to get into that room, but I remembered what you said, Doc, not to let anybody in that room. He said he wanted to look around again, to see if the killer left any clues that had been overlooked."

"I meant to keep that door locked until the inquest was over anyway, Skimpy," Woodward said. "I never intended you should keep Matt out."

"Orders is orders," Degnan stated firmly.

Woodward smiled. "I can imagine that the sheriff was sort of riled when you wouldn't let him have the key."

"I told him to get permission from you. Oh, sure, he shot off his mouth some, but that big blow-hard doesn't scare me any. Yeah, he was sorta mad when he left. Said he'd talk to you about such defiance of the law."

Woodward sighed. "That's Tillman for you. He's supposed to be the top law authority in the county, and yet practically anybody can talk back to him. Imagine going to appeal to me. Actually, he didn't even mention you, Skimpy."

"Likely didn't want it known Skimpy had turned him down." Quist laughed. "I'm afraid your sheriff doesn't claim a very high place in my estimation. Well, thanks, Skimpy. Doc, how about taking a look at that room now?"

The two men walked to the closed door in the partition. Woodward produced a key, unlocked, and the pair stepped inside, Quist closing the door behind him. The snap lock immediately took effect. Quist glanced quickly around. In the back wall was the door that led outside, and next to it was a window, the sill halfway from floor to ceiling.

Quist said quickly, "Do you know if this back door was locked at the time the body was found?"

"It was locked when I got here—and I came fast—because I remember taking off the snap and opening it to let in some air. There was a lot of coagulated blood and flies buzzing around—" The doctor broke off. "The catch was on that window too. That's what made me think it was suicide, along with the other evidence. Window and both doors locked, Reed dead in his bed, gun in hand. What else could I think?"

"Don't let your mistake get you down, Doc," Quist advised. "We all make 'em. It was natural." He continued his survey of the room.

Two doors—one giving access to the bar, the other to the outside at the rear of the building—stood almost opposite each other near the west end of the partitioned-off room. Next to the outside door was the window in the back wall, and beyond that stood a washstand and a small oblong oak table littered with magazines, old papers, a six-shooter, a partially empty box of cigars, and an oil lamp equipped with a shade of milky-colored glass. Against the north wall of the room was a single iron bed, its head to the east wall. Near the head of the bed was a dresser with closed drawers. There were two straight-backed chairs and a couple of small Navajo rugs on the pine flooring.

Woodward said, "Do you see anything unusual?"

"Not yet," Quist replied. "Sure nothing in the room's been touched?"

"No more than necessary in removing the body. I remember straightening out those two little rugs when I arrived. You know, how a person will straighten out a rug unconsciously. I don't know now why I remembered that. I was so concerned over Reed."

"Rumpled rugs might indicate a struggle," Quist commented.

"Jeepers! I never thought of that."

"I was hoping"—Quist frowned—"there'd be some sort of desk in here. Sometimes you can pick up clues by going through a man's papers."

"Reed left the running of the Saddlehorn largely to Skimpy. Such accounts as Skimpy keeps are kept in a small safe behind the bar. I suppose Reed's other papers were kept out to the ranch. I know he has a safe out there too."

Quist studied the lamp. The wick was turned low and showed no evidence of having been left to burn dry. Quist tapped the round base of opaque glass with one fingernail. The resulting sound showed him there was still oil in the lamp. He picked up the six-shooter on the table and looked it over. It was new, nickel-plated, and manufactured to resemble a Colt's gun. He replaced the gun and asked a question.

"No, that's not the gun," Woodward said. "I don't know where that came from. Never remember seeing Reed with it. It's not loaded, as you probably noticed. It didn't seem to fit into the evidence, so it was just left here. It looks brand-new."

"Never been fired," Quist said. "I know the gun. It's a new issue, manufactured by Samuels & Tempfield. It's a cheap imitation of a Colt's six-shooter, and priced accordingly. I've heard that the company is already facing a suit for patent infringement. As a gun it's not worth a damn."

"I wonder how Reed happened to buy it," Woodward frowned.

Quist glanced again at the table. He saw a few matches near the lamp. One had fallen to the floor—though the other matches weren't near the edge of the table. Quist picked one match from the table and moved out to the center of the floor. His eyes ranged swiftly over the pine flooring and rugs. Finally he knelt down, scratched a match, and peered beneath the bed. A grunt escaped his lips as the match went out and he crawled part way under the bed. A moment later he arose, holding in one hand a strip of rawhide nearly two feet in length. He studied it, meanwhile brushing dust from one sleeve.

"What you got there?" Woodward asked. "Oh, a piece of rawhide lacing. Does that mean anything?"

"I'm right sure it does," Quist stated.

"Pshaw! That rawhide might have been under that bed for weeks."

"I doubt it. One end looks like a pretty fresh cut."

Woodward glanced at the belt and empty holster hanging on the back of one chair. "I still don't see where it fits in. Reed never tied down the end of his holster. By the way, if you want to see his gun, I've got it at my house. Incidentally, now my inquest is over, I suppose I should turn it over to Tillman."

"You were certain it was Haldane's gun, eh?"

"No doubt of it. It was identified by Baxter,

119

Serrano, and Skimpy. Two empty shells, one fresh-fired. The hammer had been resting on the other one, I suppose. Anyway, there was just the one wound in Reed's body. But I don't get the idea of that rawhide—Wait"—as a thought occurred suddenly—"you mentioned a garrote. You think that is it?"

"I feel pretty sure of it. Here's the way it shapes up to me. Reed Haldane had extinguished his lamp and gone to bed. Sometime during the night there was a knock at this rear door. Whoever it was, Haldane recognized the voice and let the man in. The man got behind Haldane, who probably wasn't wide awake yet, and strangled him with this rawhide. Likely Haldane had started toward the table to light the lamp. That match on the floor could have been dropped by him when the rawhide choked off his breath. Once unconscious, the killer placed Haldane on the bed, shot him with his own gun, placed the weapon in Haldane's hand, and departed, closing the door behind him. The snap-lock immediately locked the door, of course—"

"And the murderer dropped that rawhide in his haste?"

"Perhaps," Quist conceded. "Look here, where was the gun when you found it?"

"In Haldane's hand, as was testified. It was right at the edge of the bed there. I'm surprised it didn't fall off the bed."

Quist studied the bed. "His head was on the pillow?"

"Yes, and he was covered by blankets to the waist."

"As you explain it, Doc, Haldane must have held the gun in his left hand then. Was he left-handed?"

"No, by jeepers! Now how did I happen to overlook that? No one else apparently thought of it either."

"Including the killer. Of course, all this proves nothing, actually. We knew before Haldane had been murdered. This is just additional evidence. I've seen the bodies of dead suicides and dead men who had gone out in a gun fight. The gun fighter often retains a grip on his gun. I've never known a suicide to do so. In a suicide the fingers seem to relax more quickly—an actual suicide, that is. Of course, where a dead man's fingers are wrapped around a gun butt, there's more than a likelihood that they'll stiffen that way. Another point: considering the wound, death must have come instantly to Haldane. I doubt he'd have the strength or consciousness to lift the gun and place it at his side. More likely, when the shot was fired, his arm and gun would have dropped on his body—if he was a suicide."

"You see things mighty clearly, Quist."

"That's my business. Don't blame yourself for overlooking such things. I just wanted to give you a little additional evidence, in case there's a lingering suspicion of suicide in your mind."

"There just couldn't be now," Woodward said emphatically.

Quist said, "I'm glad you see things my way. I'll appreciate it if you'll keep this"—holding out the length of rawhide—"under your hat for the present. I'd just as soon it isn't known I found it, until I can run down whoever used it."

"Sure, sure. I won't let out a peep."

Quist folded the rawhide and thrust it within his shirt, then buttoned the shirt again. At that moment there was a knock on the door, and Sheriff Tillman's voice demanded, "What you hombres doing in there?"

Woodward slipped the latch from the lock and opened the door. "Come on in, Matt. Quist was just taking a look around."

"Howdy, Quist—Doc. Don't reckon you found anything I missed last time I was here. I gave this room a purty good going over. If they's any clues here I didn't find, it'd be dang funny." The sheriffs little pig eyes roamed around the room. He was a rather sloppy-looking specimen. He hadn't shaved for three or four days. His collarless white shirt was stained and spotted. Egg had been spilt on his vest at some time or other. He turned to Quist. "Probably just been wasting your time here, I suspect."

Quist yawned widely. He said something that

sounded like "Probably," though the sheriff wasn't sure.

"Nope, Matt Tillman don't miss much," the sheriff went on. "I owe it to my constituents in this county to give 'em all my abilities. When they put Matt Tillman in office, they know they got a man that don't wear no man's collar. Strict law enforcement is my motter, and nobody can say I don't live up to it. Gawd knows I got my faults—some folks don't like me—but even my worst enemy never said I didn't run a good administration. That's the truth, b'Gawd!"

"There's nothing like a man having confidence in himself, Sheriff," Quist said dryly.

"That's Gawd's own truth." Tillman nodded his head emphatically. "Quist, you looked all over this room, eh?" Quist said he had. "And didn't find any clues you could turn over to me? I'd like to catch the murdering skunk that done for Reed Haldane."

"I haven't got a clue to give you," Quist said.

"Proving," Tillman rumbled, "just how thorough I am. Quist, did you notice that six-shooter yonder on the table?"

Quist nodded. "It's that new Samuels & Tempfield model. Not worth a damn in my opinion." He turned to Dr. Woodward. "You never heard of Haldane making any other enemies when he was down in Mexico, did you? Somebody who might have held a grudge?"

Woodward shook his head. "I think Reed would have told me if there'd been anything like that—"

"This here gun now," Tillman interrupted, again speaking to Quist and picking the weapon from the table, "sort of bothers me. Me, I knew Reed Haldane as well as any man could. He was square and, what's important right now, he knew guns. Now what would a man like Reed be doing with a shiny doodad like this if, like you say, it's no good? I'd already come to that conclusion before you mentioned it, of course. But what would Reed be doing with it? Where did he get it? I never saw any for sale in this town. You ever seen one before, Quist?"

Quist nodded. "Except for the serial number, I've got the identical gun in my room at this minute. Fact is, there's only a difference of seventeen figures between the serial number of my gun and this one here. Might be the cylinder of that gun is a trifle looser than the one in my room, but they all wobble like a duck with a broken leg. Dangerous to shoot, in my estimation."

"I'm surprised you getting suckered into buying such a gun." Tillman laughed fatly.

"I didn't buy it," Quist said quietly. "This particular series of six-shooters is one of a consignment some smart salesman sold in Washington to be delivered to Fort Tress. Lord only knows what a real cavalryman would want with a nickel-plated, glittery chunk of junk like this, but Washington decided for him, I guess."

"How do you know that?" Woodward asked.

"That the guns were consigned to Fort Tress? I've got a copy of the waybill showing what was carried on that freight that was wrecked a few nights ago. The gun I have in my possession I picked up near the scene of the wreck. Apparently the thieves had overlooked it or dropped it in their getaway."

"T'hell, you say!" Tillman exploded. "But how did Reed get this gun?"

"I haven't the least idea," Quist replied.

"But—but look here," Woodward stammered, "this gun in Reed's possession makes it look as though he might have had some connection with the freight thieves. Good lord, Quist—!"

"I didn't say that either," Quist replied quietly. "You're the one making that statement, Doc."

NINE: Mystery Gun

There was a moment's silence while the doctor and Sheriff Tillman arranged their thinking processes to this fresh development. Tillman spoke first. "B'Gawd, I think Doc's right—"

"Oh no." It was almost a groan from Woodward.

"I don't know's a man can view it in any other light," Tillman said. "Hell! I don't want to think nothin' of the kind of Reed any more'n Doc, but we got to face facts. You said yourself, Quist, these guns were on that freight that was wrecked. How would Reed get one of 'em unless he'd been out there, or one of the thieves gave him one?"

"Don't say things like that, Matt," Woodward protested. "Good lord, I've known Reed Haldane for years and—"

"You got to face facts, Doc," Tillman said again.

"Yes, I suppose," Woodward said hesitatingly. He seemed to have aged in the past few minutes. "Maybe I wasn't mistaken after all. It could have been suicide, I suppose—in spite—in spite of things Quist has pointed out—"

"Why should it be?" Quist asked tersely.

"That I don't know," Woodward said. "At

127

bottom Reed was honest as they come, but he might have got mixed into something he couldn't help. Perhaps suicide was the only way out, as he saw it. Maybe remorse for something—"

"That could be it," Tillman interrupted. "Reed was a mighty square hombre, but he could have made one mistake and regretted it, then killed hisself rather than face facts that were bound to come out someday. Maybe he was thinking of his daughter—or—or something. For all we know, he might have been at the wreck himself that night—"

"The wreck," Quist put in, "occurred about ten o'clock at night. Haldane died around three or four the following morning. Say a difference of five or six hours between the two events. Is it likely that Haldane would hear of that wreck, ride out there, ride back, and then kill himself, all within the space of at most around five hours? And that's allowing him the maximum time to work in too."

Woodward and the sheriff considered. Woodward said at last, reluctantly, "I don't know what to say, Quist. It's only about four miles out to where the wreck occurred. A good horse could cover that distance in twenty minutes easy if pushed—"

"That's right," Tillman boomed. "For that matter, Haldane might have been on the spot when the wreck took place—"

The doctor said weakly, "Maybe it was suicide after all. We could be wrong, Quist—"

"Nonsense!" Quist snapped. "You both know better than that. I say it's murder. I'm not retracting that statement. How about that red line around Haldane's neck, Doc? Have you forgotten that and other things?"

Woodward winced. "So help me, I did forget. You're right, Quist. I should be kicked for ever doubting Reed. Only for that nickel-plated gun . . ." His voice drifted off to silence; then, "It's a mystery."

"I reckon I'll just take that gun along with me," Tillman said, "and keep it in a safe spot. Can't tell, it might prove to be evidence later. By the way, Quist, I understand you had a little fuss with Mustang Neale this morning—"

"Nothing to speak of." Quist shook his head disparagingly.

"By Gawd! I think it was something to speak of. Fact is, I already spoke to Neale the instant Clem told me about it. I looked up Neale *pronto*—found him in the Red Ball Saloon. I warned him, just one more monkey business from him and I'd—Fact is, Neale should have been placed under arrest by Clem. You shouldn't have interfered, Quist—"

"Speaking of warnings, Sheriff," Quist said, "here's something that was left at my hotel room by somebody yesterday." He drew from his

129

pocket the note that had been shoved under his door and handed it to the sheriff.

Frowning, the sheriff took the note, read it through, then swore an oath. "Looks to me like your life might be in danger, Quist. I don't like this a-tall. No idea who wrote it, eh?"

"Not the slightest," Quist said.

"Natural, you wouldn't have, not being acquainted in town," Tillman rumbled. He scrutinized the note again. "Something sounds sort of familiar here." He scowled, forehead screwing into wrinkles. "Sa-a-ay, look here!" He sounded excited now. "There's just one man around here that uses that 'pal' word nearly every time he opens his mouth. See—here—Quist, where this note says 'a man of your talents, *pal,*' and so on. Mustang Neale is always calling people 'pal.' He's the skunk that wrote this note. I'll keep this paper and get after Neale right now—"

Quist plucked the note from Tillman's hand. "*I'll* keep the paper," he said. "If you want to speak to Neale, that's up to you."

The sheriff looked somewhat put out. "Damn whoopin' I'll speak to the dirty so-and-so," he growled belligerently. "Ain't no man like Mustang Neale goin' to write threats in this town and get away with it. Not while I'm sheriff—Say, I just thought of something. Neale's so anxious to get rid of you, maybe he's one of the freight-thieves gang."

"I'm also trying to uncover the murderer of Reed Haldane too," Quist pointed out. And before the sheriff could reply to that, went on, "You were out to the wreck the night it happened, Sheriff. I don't suppose you picked up any evidence of any sort?"

Tillman snorted. "Dark like it was—except for the big fires going—there wa'n't much I could see once I got far from the tracks. Everything was all confused like. Half of this town must have gone out there. There was boxcars blazing, and the engine toppled over on its side. Them thieves sure played all hell with that freight. I hate to see valuable property destructed that way."

"It's the waste that riles a man," Quist agreed. "The sheer vandalism of the business makes me boil. For instance, those oil tanks. There was no need of that."

"Oil tanks?" Tillman frowned. "Oh yeah, sure—"

"Sure, you remember. Hauling those big tanks of machine oil out of the cars and then opening 'em up to run all over. Lord, it still looked like a small lake when I got there."

"Yeah, that was bad." Tillman nodded. "Almost the first thing I noticed was the reflections of the fire in that lake you mention—"

"By the way," Woodward cut in, speaking to the sheriff, "here's the key to this door if you still want it, Matt. Sorry I didn't have it yesterday."

"Don't know's I'll need it," Tillman said. "I'm in here now. Might's well turn it over to Skimpy. I'll just sort of give a last look around—"

"Well, I've got to get going," Woodward said. "It's so near dinnertime now, I'll never get my morning calls to my patients finished. You coming, Quist?"

"Might as well," Quist replied. "There doesn't seem to be anything more for me here. S'long, Sheriff."

"I'll see you around," Tillman replied. He was standing in the center of the room, his eyes roving about the floor, and scarcely lifted his head when he spoke.

Quist and Dr. Woodward made their way out to the bar, closing the door behind them. Woodward said, "One more drink and I'll be on my way. I never could fly on one wing. How about you, Quist?"

Quist refused with thanks. "Another wing and then I'd probably want a third." He smiled. "Lord only knows what that might lead to." He followed Woodward up to the bar. Skimpy approached. The doctor gave his order. Quist asked, "Skimpy, what time did Haldane turn in the night before he was killed?"

The bartender considered. "Lemme see—seems we closed sort of early that night. It must have been around ten-thirty when that cowhand who'd been riding past when it happened arrived here with news of the train wreck. This place emptied right *pronto* at that. Everybody headed hell-bent out to the tracks. Reed and I stuck around a spell looking at the empty barroom, then Reed decides we might as well close the doors. I'd say about eleven o'clock we shut up shop."

"And you went home?"

"I went to the place I sleep," Skimpy corrected. "The Saddlehorn's always seemed more like home to me."

"And Haldane went to bed?"

"So far's I know."

"He didn't send for a saddled horse or anything, did he?"

Skimpy shook his head. "Naw, not Reed. I remember him saying he wasn't interested in no wreck and that it was just morbid curiosity that took folks riding out to the wreck. He said he'd seen enough wrecks in his lifetime 'thout forking a horse to go find one. So I reckon he went to the hay after I left."

"Thanks, Skimpy." Quist turned to Woodward. "Do you still think Haldane rode to the wreck?"

"I'm not sure what to think now, but Skimpy's word is good enough for me."

"And for me," Quist said emphatically. "Well, see you again, Doc." And nodding to Skimpy, he turned from the bar and left the saloon. As he left he heard Sheriff Tillman joining Woodward and giving his order to the barkeep.

133

Quist stood at the edge of the sidewalk a moment in front of the Saddlehorn, mulling certain thoughts in his mind. He glanced across at the sheriff's office, wondering what Clem Vincent had been doing the night of the wreck. And the early morning as well, when Haldane died. "Nothing like asking questions," he concluded, and crossed the roadway. However, the deputy wasn't in the office. The door stood open, so he couldn't be far away. Perhaps Vincent had gone to get his dinner when the sheriff showed up at the office.

Quist hesitated a few moments, glancing over the office. Several three- and four-foot lengths of rawhide dangled from a hook on one wall. Quist glanced over his shoulder, then stepped quickly inside. His examination of the rawhides required but a minute; one length, shorter than the rest, catching his attention. Quist inspected it closely and saw it had been freshly cut at one end. Drawing his Barlow knife, he slashed off another three inches and placed the cutting in his pocket. Then, replacing the rawhides as before, he stepped from the office.

From the sheriff's office he went to the T. N. & A. S. depot and sent a telegram to Carstairs, the company wrecking boss, then returned to Main Street. As he reached the corner of Yucca and Main, he nearly bumped into Mustang Neale, who was going in the opposite direction.

Quist stepped quickly to one side to avoid a collision, then halted and said pleasantly, "I seem doomed to encounter you, Neale. One way or the other."

Neale scowled. "Yaah! I been looking for you, pal."

"So you've found me. So what, Neale?" Quist asked easily. He noted that Neale was standing with his hands well away from his sides.

"Now don't get me wrong, Quist." Neale's strange opaque eyes might have been looking at Quist; again, they may not have. "I ain't tramping no war trail for you. Not right this minute—"

"The sheriff scare you off?" Quist laughed.

"Huh? Oh, Matt. That windbag couldn't scare a fly off'n a bronc's back."

"You said you'd been looking for me. What's your trouble?"

"It's this way, pal." Neale spoke harshly. "This morning you give me some talk about second and third warnings. What'd you mean? I got to know. What in hell was you talking about, pal?"

Quist could see the man was puzzled, bothered, by something unexplainable to his troglodyte mind. The man apparently knew only one trade, that of killing, and only one instinct, self-preservation. Anything out of the ordinary would be certain to confuse him, and until the matter was made clear to his own satisfaction he'd

135

not be able to concentrate on his usual mode of existence.

Quist laughed softly. "Can you write, Neale?"

"What d'you mean? Can I write my name? Certain. I never went to no schools. Why should I waste time with teachers? They can't show me nothing."

"That I can well believe," Quist said. "Can you read?"

"Sure I can read. Do you figure I'm dumb?" Then, lamely, "I don't read no books, pal, if that's what you mean. Ain't never seen no reason to read a book. That stuff is for prairie chickens. But I can read some things real good if I got a mind to it. There was a kid in school I talked to once. He had a book, like they teach from in class. I could read the pages in that better'n the kid."

"First-grade reader, eh?"

Something like surprise came into Neale's face. "Jeez! How'd you know that, pal? Somebody must've been talkin' 'bout me, eh? What t'hell we standin' here chinnin' for? I asked you a question 'bout a warning. Either you got a answer or you ain't."

Quist took the "warning" note from his pocket and spread it in front of Neale's eyes. He could almost hear the wheels turning in Neale's head as he concentrated on the written words. His lips moved noiselessly as certain words were spelled

136

out. Finally he looked up from the paper, his lips twisted in something that was half snarl, half grin. "Jeez, pal! Somebody don't like you, eh? Who sent you this?"

"Didn't you?" Quist asked quietly.

Neale's jaw dropped, then slowly closed. "Me? No, not me. I don't write that good. And I wouldn't waste no time writin' letters to you neither, pal. Hell, I ain't got no pen and ink. What t'hell makes you think I writ this?"

"The sheriff thinks you did. Anyway, that's what he told me. Says you're the only one that uses the word 'pal' around here the way you do—"

An obscene oath interrupted Quist's words. Neale's face darkened. His eyes appeared to grow even more opaque, flatter, with no intelligence in them. "That double-crossin' son of a—" Neale didn't finish. He appeared suddenly nervous and started to back away. "I got to see Matt about this," he said. "You and me can settle our arguments some other time."

"Name the time," Quist invited. But Neale hadn't waited for a reply as he hurried along the plank sidewalks, crowding pedestrians left and right, in the direction of the sheriff's office.

Quist smiled. "No, I didn't think Mustang Neale wrote it," he mused. There was something pitying in his face as he added, "That poor miserable bustard. What sort of system produces

137

a man like that, I wonder? It doesn't say much for conditions in this great land of opportunity."

Quist had started toward his hotel when he heard a voice hail him. Turning, he saw Chris Baxter approaching, a folded newspaper in hand. Quist halted. "You been bird-dogging me again?" he demanded.

"So help me, I haven't," Chris said earnestly. "I was just walking along and I saw you talking to Mustang Neale. He didn't seem like he was on the prod, but I thought it might be good to stick around anyway until you got through talking. Looked like you were showing him a letter. If anybody had asked me, I'd have bet money he couldn't read."

"You'd have lost. Whether he can write or not, I'm not sure. I'm pretty sure he didn't write this, though the use of the word 'pal' makes me think somebody is trying to persuade me Neale is responsible." Quist passed the note across to Baxter.

Baxter read it through, his lips tightening. Then he looked up and returned the note. "Cripes! Greg, this looks bad. You'd better be mighty careful—"

"I'm always careful." Quist smiled. "I don't need notes like that to—"

"But, Judas priest, Greg, maybe you should keep me—and Ramon—near you every minute."

Quist shook his head. "We've already settled that, I thought."

138

"But who do you think wrote that note?"

"Dam'd if I know yet. But I'll find out in time. Whoever did it tried to disguise his writing. You see, it's written in a backhand slant, but every so often the writer forgot and slanted letters the other direction. Might even have been written with the left hand, though it's pretty good for that. Want to do something for me, Chris?"

"All the time."

"Thanks. Take this note, but don't let anyone see the writing. Then prowl the stores that sell stationery and learn if possible who has bought paper like this recently. And that bluish-black ink."

"That shouldn't be much of a job—I mean, prowling the stores. There aren't too many of 'em handling stationery."

"Well, see if you can learn anything. What you carrying that newspaper for?"

"It's the Masquerade City *Gazette*. The T. N. & A. S. is running an advertisement offering a reward of five thousand for information leading to the apprehension of the freight thieves."

"That'd be nice money if you and Ramon could earn it."

Baxter's eyes widened. "Cripes! You think we could?"

"You got as much chance as anybody," Quist said, "providing you and Ramon work together. That money could come handy. I don't imagine you drew down more than ordinary wages from Haldane."

"A mite better than ordinary—but, say, won't you be due for the reward?"

"I'm not entitled to reward money. The T. N. & A. S. pay me a salary. If I'm lucky enough to uncover the freight thieves and you and Ramon help me, I'll be glad to recommend you for the reward."

"That's pretty nice of you, Greg," Chris said gratefully. "The sheriff put up a reward on Mr. Haldane's murder too, you know—"

"More than ever," Quist said, eyes narrowing in thought, "I'm beginning to think the Haldane killing and the freight wreck have some connection—No, I can't say what it is—yet."

"In addition to the reward advertisement," Baxter said, "the *Gazette* prints a long list of the things stolen from the wreck—groceries, guns, clothing, hardware—there's a heck of a long list."

Quist nodded. "The railroad always runs a list like that in papers within a hundred miles of a wreck where freight thieves are back of the business. It warns merchants to be on the lookout for stolen property and sometimes leads to a clue that aids in the apprehension of crooks. You mentioned guns. You likely haven't seen any yet, but there was a shipment of that new Samuels & Tempfield six-shooter on that freight, consigned to Fort Tress. I picked up one of the guns out to the wreck. The thieves had left several scattered around. Just to make things interesting—"

"Hey!" Baxter exclaimed. "I just happened to think of something. Mr. Haldane had one of those guns of that make in his room at the Saddlehorn. I remember noticing it and then forgot about it—"

"I was about to tell you about it. When did you first notice the gun?"

"When we were in the room after Mr. Haldane had—had been shot and found dead."

"Never saw the gun before?"

Baxter shook his head. "Ramon and I both wondered how Mr. Haldane happened to have it. It didn't look to be much good."

"It isn't. But maybe there's a clue there someplace. You see, the sheriff and Doc Woodward sort of feel that the gun proves some sort of connection with the freight thieves—"

"Mr. Haldane?" Baxter exclaimed indignantly. His face reddened angrily. "Whoever says that is a liar!"

Quist's topaz eyes glinted with amusement. "All right, all right, Chris. Don't blow your head off. *I* didn't say it. And I don't believe it either, so don't glare at me that way."

Baxter relaxed. "It just made me damn mad for a moment."

Quist chuckled. "It's a good thing you haven't a temper," he said sarcastically. "Chris, you've

141

got to learn in my business that if you want to think clearly you can't afford to jump to conclusions or lose your temper. Come on, let's find some dinner. My stomach is beginning to think somebody cut my throat."

TEN: Peace Offer

Baxter and Quist emerged from the hotel dining room and stepped out to the street in time to see Ramon Serrano hurrying along the sidewalk. Serrano showed white teeth in a relieved grin. "Have been looking for you, Meester Quist—"

"Greg."

"Greg," Serrano said obediently. "All morning I have circulated this town in hope of learning something to give you the clue. But, no—no one knows from anything. Then, I think, maybe in the Mexican section I will find someone who will talk to me where he might not talk to—to someone else. You see, my Spanish blood lends the confidence"—apologetically—"so everywhere I ask questions—"

"And learned what?" Quist cut in. The three men were standing at the edge of the sidewalk, facing the roadway. A few people passed from time to time.

Serrano threw wide his arms in a gesture of defeat. "Am sorry, but I learn next to nothing. Have told my friends down there to talk to their friends. Just one thing which amounts to little, I suppose. A man named José Mendoza was returning home early the morning that the Señor Haldane was kill'. This Mendoza, he say that he saw Sheriff Tillman riding on Main Street."

"What time was this?" Quist asked.

"Maybee three of the clock in the morning. Maybee a little before or a little beyond."

"Did the sheriff see your friend Mendoza?"

Serrano shook his head. "No, when he see the sheriff, Mendoza jumped quick like a cat in the shadow of a building. You see, the sheriff does not like Mexicans and is alway' ready to abuse them. Does theese mean anything to you, Greg?"

"Not right now. It might later. I don't know. Thanks, Ramon. I think you had an idea, anyway."

Baxter cut in, "Well, I guess I'll start looking for stationery, Greg. See you later." He paused; then, "Ramon, have you seen the *Gazette* that just came out? It offers a reward for the freight thieves. Greg says you and I might have a chance to collect."

"*Socorro*! Is good news."

Somewhat embarrassedly Baxter thrust the newspaper toward Serrano and then hurried off down the street. Serrano looked after him a minute; then, "Sometimes I'm think Chris is one *buen hombre*. Only he is so hot of the temper."

"And you're not?" Quist asked with some amusement.

Serrano appreciated the joke at his own

expense. He grinned. "I, Ramon Serrano, I am alway' cool like the cowcumber. We are a pair of young fools you think, no, Greg?"

"Could be you're commencing to show sense," Quist admitted. "Ramon, where does Shattuck and his Triangle-S crew hang out when they come to town?"

"Sometimes at the Green Bottle bar, most general' at the Red Ball Saloon. You want to see them?"

"I'd like to ask the Shattucks a few questions if possible."

"I will take you. First we try the Red Ball."

Quist and Serrano started along the plank sidewalks, at present in some spots seeping soft resin under the torrid sun's rays, crossed Yucca Street, passed the post office, and pushed through the swinging doors of the Red Ball Saloon.

The Red Ball was a low-ceilinged place with the bar running across the rear wall. There were a number of round wooden tables and straight-backed chairs scattered about the room. A window in the rear wall and a larger one near the entrance furnished such light as there was. Pictures of race horses, burlesque actresses in tights, and prize fighters, clipped from the pink sheets of the *Police Gazette*, were tacked about the walls. The back-bar mirror was fly-specked, and there was none of the orderly arrangement of bottles and pyramided glasses, Quist noticed, such as the Saddlehorn Saloon offered. The Red Ball seemed permeated with the odor of unwashed humanity, stale liquor, and tobacco smoke. The floor didn't appear to have been swept for several days. A beetle-browed bartender presided at the counter, and there were a number of cowhands and townspeople drinking. Mustang Neale was drinking with the cowhands whom Quist judged to be Triangle-S punchers. Neale bent a glowering look on Quist and said something to the cowhands, who immediately stopped their chatter and turned to look at Quist.

Quist and Ramon found a deserted place at the far end of the bar and ordered drinks from the beetle-browed barkeep. Quist had raised his glass to his lips when one of the older cowmen detached himself from his group and approached, saying, "I understand you're Greg Quist?"

Quist put down his glass. "You understand correct."

"I've been wanting to talk to you. I'm Pitt Shattuck." He put out his hand. Quist took it and nodded, waiting. Shattuck went on, "I'd like to get a couple of things straight in your mind."

"I suppose my mind, like any other man's"— Quist smiled—"is subject to correction from time to time. How's for having a drink with us while you talk? You know Ramon Serrano, I think."

Pitt Shattuck nodded to Serrano and received a brief jerk of the head in return. The bartender placed a bottle and glass before Shattuck. Quist looked the man over while the drink was being poured. He was a rather spare type, a bit thick about the middle; probably close to fifty. He seemed in good condition, his face tanned. He had crisp dark hair with streaks of gray through it. His nose was wide-nostriled, the mouth slightly curved down at the corners as though he were embittered at the way life had treated him. There was a sort of worried, harassed look about the man's dark eyes. The gun at his right thigh didn't look as though it had been drawn for some time: Quist noticed a thin dust along the loading gate. Shattuck put down his glass, smacked his lips. He said, "Thanks."

Quist said, "Now what's on your mind?"

"It's this way," Shattuck began. "Everybody knows you're here to find the killer of Reed Haldane—"

"I have certain T. N. & A. S. duties to take care of as well," Quist pointed out.

"Huh? Oh yes, that freight-wreck business." Shattuck laughed shortly. "Somehow, I don't even think of that. You see, it's the Haldane business that concerns me."

"*Por qué*?" Quist asked. "In what way?"

"Undoubtedly," Shattuck went on, "you've heard there's been bad blood between Haldane and the Shattucks."

Quist nodded. "I heard of some trouble twenty

147

years or more back. I've heard certain threats were made—"

"Not by me," Shattuck put in quickly. "Such threats as you might have heard of really didn't amount to anything. They were made by my brother Todd. Todd's inclined to go off half cocked and he gets a mite mouthy after he's had a few drinks, but he doesn't really mean anything. For what happened twenty years ago I can't blame Haldane. He downed my brother in fair fight. My brother was at fault. Blood being thicker than water, I could never like Haldane. At the same time, all I wanted here was to live in peace. I didn't want any trouble."

"Maybe you should have seen to it that your brother kept his mouth shut then," Quist said.

"I've done my best along those lines, but remember, Quist, my brother is a grown man. I can't boss him around like a child—"

"And in case suspicion points toward Todd Shattuck, you want to keep your own skirts clear?" Quist asked.

Shattuck looked pained. "That's not it at all, Quist. The point I'm trying to make is that we had nothing to do with Haldane's death. Todd was out to the ranch that night. That I can swear to. What I'd like you to understand is that we don't want any trouble with you. Our reputation is clear. While Todd has made some threatening talk from time to time, that's all it was—just talk."

"Aren't you sort of overdoing this, Shattuck? To me it sounds as though you are trying awfully hard to protect your brother."

"That's natural, isn't it?"

"Of course it's natural. But you've got to understand, Shattuck, that if I get any evidence that points toward your brother, all your talk won't make the slightest difference. And the same goes for you. Is that clear?"

Shattuck nodded. "That's exactly the way I want it to be. I know we're both under suspicion to some extent, but the fact remains, if there'd been anything definite against us, Matt Tillman would have had us in cells. You talk to Tillman—"

Quist laughed softly. "I'm afraid that Tillman's word doesn't impress me too much."

"I was afraid of that," Shattuck said soberly. "Tillman's considerable of a windbag, but he's honest, Quist. Actually, he's a pretty good man on his job."

"All right, so he's a good man on his job. But his job isn't my job. I prefer to look into things myself and decide things for myself. So alibi-ing your brother, Shattuck, doesn't impress me one way or the other. In my eyes you're both objects of suspicion until proved otherwise. I just can't afford to take Tillman's word for anything."

Shattuck sighed. "You're a pretty hard man, Quist."

"Not so hard as sensible."

"I suppose it seems that way to you. T'tell the truth, this is just about what I expected. I'm not surprised you doubt the alibis offered by Todd and me—"

"I've not yet said I doubted 'em. I just think they're open to examination. For all I know to the contrary, you and your brother are pure as the lilies in the dell—but I somehow doubt it. Whether either of you killed Haldane or not, I just don't know." Quist paused. "But, by the Almighty, I'm going to find out before I get through here."

"That's exactly what I want," Shattuck said frankly. "Suppose you question every man who was at the ranch that night and see what they say. They'll tell you both Todd and I were at home."

"I imagine they would. They work for you."

"By Gawd, I've never seen such a skeptic. Do you think my men would be li'ble to lie for the sake of the money I pay 'em?"

Quist chuckled. "I think it more than possible. I figure I'd just be wasting my time in such questioning. And damned if I know what you expected to gain by talking to me this way."

"I'll tell you what I want," Shattuck said. "I want you to find Haldane's murderer. Only in that way will Todd and I be above suspicion. I'd like to be able to live here in peace. I don't want any more trouble. And if I can do anything—

anything—to help you in your search for the killer, I want you to call on me."

"Well," Quist said softly, and again, "Well. Here I'd been expecting I might have trouble with your outfit, and you come to me with a peace offer."

"That's exactly what I intend," Shattuck said earnestly. "The day you uncover Haldane's killer I stand ready to hand you five hundred dollars—"

"Even if the killer proves to be your brother?"

Shattuck gave a short disparaging laugh. "That's one thing you'll never prove," he said confidently. "Oh, I know, a lot of people hereabouts don't like Todd, and they'd like to see him in trouble. Certain things he's said won't be forgotten. I'll even go so far as to state that if he'd had the chance he might have tried to kill Haldane, but I've kept a pretty firm check on him. I hope you'll believe me in all this."

"Can you think of any reason why I should?" Quist asked.

Shattuck looked disappointed. "I suppose I see your attitude," he conceded. "I shouldn't expect anything else. But believe me, Quist, I'd like to be friendly with you, and I'm ready to throw my whole crew on your side if it could prove of help in any way. I'm doing my best to keep things peaceful. For instance, Mustang Neale and you have had a couple of run-ins. I've ordered Neale to behave himself. I've told him I want to help, not hinder you."

"And will Neale obey orders?"

Shattuck hesitated. "I'll be square with you. No man can ever say what Neale will do. But I've slowed him up for the time being."

"Very kind of you, I'm sure," Quist said caustically. "Personally, I should think you'd get rid of a man like that, Shattuck."

Shattuck drew a deep breath. "I don't like to fire anybody. And Neale's a good worker—"

"At what?"

"Handling cows. What else?"

"Whose cows?" Quist asked sarcastically.

Shattuck's face darkened. "I don't like that sort of joshing, Quist. No one's ever accused the Triangle-S of doing any rustling—"

Anything further he might have intended to say was interrupted by an individual who came barging angrily through the swinging doors of the Red Ball calling loudly for Pitt Shattuck. Looking at the newcomer, Quist guessed that he was Pitt's younger brother, Todd. Todd wasn't quite as heavy as Pitt, he was considerably younger, but both men had similar physical characteristics. He came hurrying across the barroom.

"Pitt!" he exclaimed. "You've got to—"

"Just a minute, Todd," the elder Shattuck cut in. "I'd like to have you shake hands with Greg Quist. Quist, this is my brother Todd."

Todd Shattuck stiffened, then nodded shortly to Quist. He didn't offer his hand, nor did Quist, though he said rather sneeringly, "Ah, the big detective, eh? Hope you're finding enough to keep you busy, Quist."

"If I haven't so far, I will before long," Quist said quietly.

Todd Shattuck ignored the reply. "I've got to talk to you a minute, Pitt." He drew his brother off to one side and spoke briefly, low-voiced. Pitt's face darkened angrily. Quist caught a word that sounded like "Porky" but lost the words that followed. Then, Pitt's voice, ". . . I told him to stay at the ranch . . . sleep it off . . ." And Todd breaking in, "He refused to listen to me. You got to do something right . . ." He lowered his voice again.

"I'll take care of it," Pitt snapped. He left Todd and turned back to Quist. "One of my cowhands has taken on a load of liquor and is making a nuisance of himself around town. He was drunk when we left the ranch. I told him to go to his bunk and stay there, but he—"

"For gesis sake, Pitt, get moving," Todd said nervously. "That fool bustard will spill—" He broke off and cast a quick glance at Quist, then finished lamely, "He'll spill catsup all over. You see, this Porky Gerard is a good man, but he goes on a tear ever' so often. Then it seems like he can never get enough to eat. He's down to the K. C. Chop House now, waving a bottle of catsup around and—"

"Is that anything to get so excited about?" Quist asked quietly.

"Hell! You don't know Porky—"

"I'll see you later, Quist," Pitt Shattuck said as he started toward the swinging doors to the street.

Quist turned to Ramon. "You know this Porky hombre, Ramon?"

Serrano nodded. "Got an appetite like the horse, Greg. Is always eating. Nevair yet did I see him without the sandwich or the piece of cake or a pie. Always is eating."

"And now he's pie-eyed, I take it." Quist laughed. Ramon looked at him reproachfully. Todd Shattuck had already taken up a position with the other cowhands farther down the bar. None of the Triangle-S men seemed to find any humor in the situation. That, to Quist, seemed rather puzzling. Why get so upset about a cowpuncher who gets boiled and overeats? Something funny was going on here.

There was a sudden commotion beyond the swinging doors, then an extremely stout man in cowpuncher togs lurched through the entrance, apparently but little impeded by Pitt Shattuck, who was clinging desperately to one arm. But Shattuck was outweighed and, once the cowhand was inside the saloon, released his hold and looked helplessly around. The fat cowhand had little piglike eyes and taffy-colored hair. He wasn't just fat around the middle; he was big all

154

over. Under one arm he carried a square tin box.

For a moment Porky Gerard swayed uncertainly just within the entrance, beaming jovially on all present. "Thash better, Pitt," he hiccupped. "Ish hard work . . . *hic!* . . . holdin' you up . . ."

"You go on back to the ranch." Pitt's voice trembled with anger.

"Whash mad 'bout, Pitt? Ain' we all . . . *hic!* . . . frien's together? . . . Why'd you all go . . . *hic!* . . . off an' leave me behin'? Here . . . have . . . cracker."

He extended the open box toward Pitt, but Pitt swore at him. Gerard laughed. In a sort of maudlin, singsong voice he proclaimed, "Today is the day . . . *hic!* . . . we give . . . *hic!* . . . crackers away with a drink of . . . *hic!* . . . good whiskee . . . Have cracker . . . fellowsh . . . good for . . . *hic!* . . . ails you."

He staggered along the bar, offering his box to all. The punchers swore at him and told him to go home. The townspeople just laughed. Finally Gerard reached Quist. "Have one of my crack-ersh," he invited, extending the box.

Quist grinned and accepted one of the crackers, which proved to be a square thin piece of pastry with raisins baked in. The box was of brass-colored tin, equipped with a top and hinges, the sort seen in grocery and general stores, and about nine inches square. In the front was an isinglass window to which was pasted a small label proclaiming the contents to be Sultan Crackers. Ramon also accepted a cracker.

The fat Gerard stood teetering before Quist, waiting for a verdict. "You . . . *hic!* . . . like 'em?" he asked.

Quist chewed and nodded. "Dang good crackers. Where'd you buy them?"

Owlishly Porky Gerard considered the question. "Where'd . . . I buy 'em . . . lemme see . . ." Abruptly he turned belligerent. "What in . . . *hic!* . . . you care . . . where I buy 'em? . . . Maybe . . . didn' . . . buy 'em. You don't have . . . to . . . *hic!* . . . eat my crackers . . . don't like 'em . . ."

"But I do like them. I want to get some," Quist said placatingly.

He'd noticed that the Shattucks and the other cowhands were watching him and Gerard warily now. There was some angry muttering going on among them.

"Oh . . . you like 'em all right . . . eh?" Gerard said thickly. His bloodshot pig eyes surveyed Quist, then his manner softened. "You like 'em . . . *hic!* . . . you frien' of mine . . . Ain't nothin' like . . . *hic!* . . . good food . . . cemen' frien'ship . . ." He swayed back and would have fallen if Quist hadn't grabbed his arm.

"Where'd you buy these crackers?" Quist persisted.

Gerard considered the question. One hand

156

waved uncertainly. "Don' remember," he admitted finally. "Gen'al store . . . guess. *Hic!* Thash it . . . gen'al store . . ."

Quist heard Pitt Shattuck say sharply, "Don't you, Todd!"

Todd jerked out, "The utter damn' fool!" Furiously he flung himself across the floor, lifted his Colt's six-shooter, and brought the heavy barrel down on Porky Gerard's head. Gerard stiffened. His jaw dropped. His eyes became crossed. Quite abruptly he pitched forward on his face. The open box of crackers hit the floor; crackers scattered in all directions.

"The utter damn' fool!" Todd Shattuck said again. He glared at Quist.

Quist said quietly, "I'd say that was uncalled for. The poor bustard wasn't doing any harm."

"That's none of your business," Todd snapped. He still held the gun in his hand. "Quist, why in hell don't you get out of here and mind your own business? We settle things our own way—"

And that was as far as he got. Quist closed fast, his left hand clamping on Todd Shattuck's wrist, forcing the gun well away from him. His right hand darted beneath his coat, drawing the heavy .44-caliber gun from its shoulder holster. Within the space of less than a minute a second man struck the floor, the victim of a heavy gun barrel placed with some accuracy and force against his head. Todd Shattuck's six-shooter went clattering across the barroom floor as he pitched down and lay without movement.

Quist's weapon was now covering the men at the bar. Serrano had drawn his gun.

"I still maintain," Quist said pleasantly to the room at large, "that Todd's action was uncalled for. Anybody in the mood to disagree with me?"

ELEVEN: Threat

A dead silence permeated the barroom. None of the Triangle-S crowd made a move to draw weapons. Pitt Shattuck's face was white. He glanced at his brother stretched unconscious on the floor, then said, "We don't want any trouble with you, Quist. You can put that gun away."

Quist said, "Thanks," in a dry voice and slipped the six-shooter back in its holster. Serrano did the same with his Colt's.

Shattuck said angrily, "I tried to stop Todd. He's impulsive."

"I noticed that." Quist nodded. "Maybe he'll think twice after this."

"But how about your own actions?" Pitt demanded. "Do you think that was right? Todd wouldn't—"

"Just put it down that I'm impulsive too," Quist said whimsically. His voice became harsh. "Look, Shattuck, what in hell would you expect me to do? Your brother had his gun out. He was making war talk. What was I to do—offer him a cracker?"

Shattuck said wearily, "Oh hell, I guess your hand was forced, Quist."

"At least," Quist pointed out, "I didn't come up behind Todd, like he did with this poor drunken gut-stuffer. If Todd's actions are any indication, I don't think much of the peace offer you made a while back."

"I'm sorry it happened," Pitt said abjectly. "Todd was at fault—and—and that damn fool Gerard."

"Gerard didn't hurt me any," Quist said coldly. He added cryptically, "Maybe he even helped."

"What do you mean by that?" Pitt asked sharply.

Quist replied, "I've a hunch your brother and I wouldn't get along. Gerard just brought things to a head a little sooner than they'd have happened normally. Now Todd knows where I stand. I hope you do too." Then to Ramon, "Come on, let's get out of here."

As they left the saloon, they heard Pitt giving orders to "throw some water on those two damn fools and get 'em back to the ranch."

Outside, Quist smiled. "Anyway, Ramon, I know where you stand."

Serrano frowned. "What is it you say, Greg?"

"I know you won't run out on a scrap. You had your gun out almost as quick as mine."

Ramon beamed. "Is nothing. I know, perhaps, that Triangle-S crew. If they get the jump on you, they can be ver-r-y rough—"

"And you were making sure they didn't get the jump on us, eh?"

160

"To speak in truth, Greg," Ramon confessed, "I made the draw before I hav' time to think. I did not know how occupy' you would be."

"Anyway, that gang know where we stand now. And thanks for the help. Come on, I want to go across to the sheriff's office."

They crossed the street and found Deputy Clem Vincent at the desk. Quist asked, "Tillman not around?"

Vincent shook his head. "He left on the one thirty-eight."

"The sheriff gone away?"

"To Rawnston in the next county. He makes the trip every so often to, as he says, 'visit my dear old mother and bring some cheer to her heart.' " The deputy's voice sounded mocking.

Quist smiled. "It's wonderful what mother love will do for a man. So the sheriff has a mother in Rawnston. I wonder what she's like. Probably some frail wisp of a woman who bullies him unmercifully. He's the type for that sort of thing. When will he be back?"

"Couple of days, likely. He never stays long."

"Would it matter if he did?" Quist grinned.

"Not with a good deputy in charge." Vincent laughed. "Do you have to see the sheriff? Anything I can do?"

"I want to report an accident. Or maybe it wasn't an accident," Quist said. "I just had a little run-in with the Triangle-S boys at the Red

161

Ball . . ." He went on to tell what had happened.

Vincent sobered as he heard the story. "That damn Todd," he said angrily, "will yet get his comeuppance—rather, it looks like he got it. Served him right. Poor Porky. All's he ever asked, I think, was plenty to eat. You want to lodge a complaint, Quist?"

"I've got nothing to complain of," Quist said. "I'm just making a report in case they do any beefing."

"I don't think you'll hear anything more of it," Vincent said. "Apparently you stopped the Triangle-S in its tracks. There's no need of me taking any action. I could warn 'em, but they've been warned before by Tillman, and it never did any good if they felt like riding roughshod over anyone. Until I have more authority—" He broke off. "I guess I'll just slip across the street and see what's said."

Rising from the chair, he left the office and headed toward the Red Ball. Ramon and Quist sat down to await his return. They rolled and lighted cigarettes. Quist's eyes roved about the room and settled on the rawhides looped over one hook on the wall. He rose to his feet, examined the strips of thin leather, and replaced them. "There," he told Ramon, "is one of the greatest inventions in the West—the rawhide. You can mend practically anything with it, from fences to saddles. The first Texans that drove up the trail to Abilene used

162

to be known as Rawhiders because they used rawhides for practically everything and anything. It's certainly handy stuff to have around."

"Sometimes maybe too handy?"

"What do you mean, Ramon?"

"I am thinking of the garrote that was used on Mr. Haldane. Could a rawhide have been used?"

"You're getting smarter all the time, Ramon. Yes, it could have been—"

"But not one of those on the hook—no?"

"No—but one very similar. Someday we'll learn—"

Quist broke off as Clem Vincent re-entered the office. Quist looked inquiringly at him. Vincent said, "There won't be any trouble. I got the story from Pitt. He states that Todd was in the wrong and you were within your rights. He says he's going to give Todd a good talking to. Todd and Porky were both slumped in chairs, looking right groggy, when I was there. The outfit was preparing to leave—they're all blaming Porky for the whole business. Said he was getting obnoxious with you."

"Not to speak of. I hope you got one of Porky's crackers." Quist laughed.

"There weren't any crackers in sight when I was there," the deputy said. "I guess the barkeep had done some sweeping up."

"Lord knows the place needed it," Quist said.

"Pitt Shattuck was sort of peeved," Vincent

went on. "He said he tried to be friendly—offered any help he could give in running down Haldane's killer—and that you acted like you didn't care if you had his help or not."

Quist grunted derisively. "All right, Clem, put yourself in my place. If you were running down the murderer of Haldane, would you welcome Shattuck's help, considering all that's gone before?"

"Did *I* say you were wrong?" Vincent laughed. "It's just that Shattuck got the impression that you don't trust anybody much."

"Shattuck's smarter than I thought. How far does Sheriff Tillman trust him?"

"No more than you, I reckon. I know the minute he heard Reed Haldane had been murdered he sent me to round up the two Shattucks."

"So you told me. That night the sheriff went out to the wreck, what were you doing, Clem?"

"Nothing much. With practically everybody that could ride going out to look at the wreck, the town was plumb deserted—consequently peaceful. I strolled around town for a spell. There wasn't hardly anybody in the saloons. Everything was quiet, so I turned in to my cot there"—jerking one thumb in the direction of the cot against the wall.

"Didn't you wait up for Tillman's return?"

"There wasn't any need that I could see.

With Matt away so much, I catch my shut-eye whenever I can."

"What time did he get back to town?"

"Shortly past daybreak."

"Did he wake you up here?"

Vincent shook his head. "No, I guess he went right to his boardinghouse. It wasn't until well along toward two o'clock that he showed up here. I remember he mentioned that the sun was nigh up before he got to bed."

"Did he say much about conditions at the wreck, mention he saw anything suspicious—things like that?"

"Not as I remember. Matt just mentioned that everything was knocked galley-west and that such stuff as wasn't wrecked all to hell was burning. Of course he did the usual cursing of freight thieves, but Matt's cursing never apprehended any criminals."

"How about his other actions?" Quist asked.

Vincent smiled. "I'm not sure, but I guess he had a pretty good rep earlier in life."

"He should have quit sheriffin' before he got this old then," Quist said. "Well, I reckon I'd better push on. You ready, Ramon?"

"Whenever you say the word, Greg."

They said good-by to the deputy and moved out to the street. Across the roadway, the two Shattucks and the other Triangle-S hands were just emerging from the Red Ball. Both Todd and

Porky Gerard moved as though they weren't quite steady on their legs. Gerard had to be helped into a saddle. Todd was about to mount when he happened to see Quist. At once he removed his foot from the stirrup and came across the road. Pitt called angrily, "Todd, you come back here."

Todd didn't reply, but continued on toward Quist. Quist said, "You want to see me, Todd?"

"No more than I have to," Todd snarled, coming to a halt a few feet away. "I just want to tell you a couple of things, Quist."

Quist smothered a yawn. "Speak your piece."

"I'm not forgetting what you done back in the Red Ball——" Todd commenced.

"I intended you'd remember it." Quist smiled thinly. "Hoped it might teach you a lesson for some other time."

Todd swore—but not at Quist. "That's whatever." He scowled. "I'm just telling you now that I'm not forgetting. Nobody ever done anything to me without paying for it. My time will come—and yours."

"Can I put that down as a threat?" Quist asked quietly.

"I don't give a blasted damn what you put it down as," Todd exploded. Then, defiantly, "Yeah, call it a threat if you like. And what you aiming to do about it?"

He backed away a step, one arm moving impul-

166

sively toward his gun, then he hesitated as Quist started to laugh—started to laugh and drew a small black notebook and stub of pencil from his pocket. As though paying no attention to Todd, Quist pretended to write in the book.

Todd looked puzzled. "What in hell you doing?"

"Putting down your name, Todd, just putting down your name."

"What's the idea?" Todd demanded.

"It's this way," Quist explained gravely. "I've already had one warning note and threats from Mustang Neale. Business seems to be piling up, but I can't take care of you right now. At the same time, I didn't want you to miss your turn. With my notebook to remind me, Todd, I'll remember that you're third on my list. When the right time comes, you'll be taken care of. Try to remember that."

Todd's jaw dropped, then his face reddened. "Aw-w," he sputtered, "you don't get my nerve with any such talk." He backed away a step, not liking the contempt in Quist's face. Quist was laughing now, but the laugh had nothing to do with his eyes.

From across the street Pitt called anxiously, "You, Todd, come on now. We're going home."

Quist raised his voice. "I'm not sure if Todd is or not, Pitt. I'm inviting him to stay if he gets the urge."

Todd backed another step. "Aw—aw, you go to hell, Quist," he blurted impotently, then turned and hurried toward his horse. A moment later the Triangle-S men were riding out of Masquerade City.

Ramon laughed softly. "I'm think you took all the wind from his sailing—no?"

"Could be." Quist nodded. "I've a hunch he's mostly wind anyway."

They finished crossing the road and started west along Main Street. As they were passing the K. C. Chop House, Quist said, "I could use a cup of coffee. How about you, Ramon?"

"Is good," Ramon agreed. They entered the restaurant, which was deserted at the moment, and seated themselves at the long counter that ran along one wall. The proprietor served them with cups of coffee and triangles of apple pie. He stood near in the hope of further orders.

Quist drank half his coffee, then rolled and lighted a cigarette. He said to the proprietor, "Had a mite of excitement here a spell ago, I understand."

The proprietor frowned and looked inquiringly at Quist. "I don't know where you got that idea, mister. There ain't never any excitement in running a restaurant—nothing to do except stand and watch folks stuffing their faces all day—no offense meant, you understand."

"And none taken." Quist smiled. "I understand

168

Porky Gerard was in here, drunk and spilling catsup around."

"Thank Gawd he wasn't!" the man said vehemently.

"What's wrong with Porky?"

"If you knew him you wouldn't ask. That's one man I hate to see come in my place. He eats so much bread and butter, he takes all the profit off my meals, cleans out my sugar bowl, empties all my condiment bottles. He just plain eats like a hawg."

"And he wasn't in here today?" Quist pursued.

"I didn't even know he was in town. Maybe I'd be smart to close up for a few hours."

"Don't worry. He left a little spell back."

"That's a lot to be thankful for."

Again on the street a few minutes later, Quist said softly, "I figure Todd Shattuck is just a fibber. What do you think, Ramon?"

Serrano nodded. "But why, Greg, should he say that Porky was at the K. C. Chop House if is not true?"

"That's something I've got to figure out. You got any ideas on the subject?"

Serrano scowled in thought. Finally he shook his head. "I am dumb like the dishwater, Greg."

They walked on a few more paces. Suddenly Quist said, "Let's cut over to the depot. I want to send a telegram."

Returning from the railroad station a short time

later, Quist announced he was going to sit in the shade of the hotel porch and try to get a few things straightened out in his mind. He got bottles of beer from the hotel bar and he and Ramon deposited themselves in a couple of chairs with their feet on the hotel porch railing. Quist was slumped down in his chair, hat tilted over one eye. He scarcely touched his beer but appeared to be gazing off into nothingness. Serrano spoke from time to time but received only monosyllable replies.

Abruptly Quist roused himself. "Damn it, I'm hungry, and it's not near time for supper yet. I should have eaten more at the K. C. Chop House."

"I could get you a sandwich," Serrano offered.

"That's a right idea—No, wait. Those Sultan Crackers that Porky Gerard had tasted right good. I'd sooner have a pound of those. I forgot where he said he got 'em."

"I will find the crackers." Serrano got to his feet, descended the steps from the hotel porch, and hurried off down the street.

He was scarcely out of sight when Quist straightened, chuckling, in his chair. "Now Ramon's got something to occupy his mind, maybe I can get something done." He started to settle back in his chair, then swore suddenly. "Darn'd if I know where *my* mind is," he grumbled. "I should have thought of that when I was down there before." He settled his hat firmly on his head, rose, and started in the direction of the railroad depot.

At the depot he sent a second telegram to the same address he'd used a short time before, then paused a minute at the ticket window. "What time does the train get into Rawnston?"

"Depends on what train you mean. Rawnston isn't on the T. N. & A. S. line, you know. That's the Rock Buttes road. Anybody leaving here has to change at Pakenham. There's about an hour-and-a-half wait-over. For instance, Sheriff Tillman bought a ticket for Rawnston on the one thirty-eight today. He'll get into Pakenham at four-three this afternoon, but the Rock Buttes doesn't leave for Rawnston until five-forty. That'll get the sheriff into Rawnston at seven-two tonight."

"Makes a sort of roundabout route, doesn't it? With a good relay of horses a man could make almost as fast time."

The ticket agent grinned. "Can you imagine Tillman making fast time—or riding horses that distance?"

"I reckon not." Quist chuckled. "Thanks for the information."

Quist returned to the hotel porch and again settled down, deep in thought. Once he entered the hotel bar for another bottle of beer, then returned to his chair. The sun swung farther to the west, but Quist's problem was still far from the solving point. It must have been nearing six o'clock when he noticed both Ramon and Chris Baxter approaching along the sidewalk, their faces the picture of gloom. Slowly they ascended to the hotel porch and seated themselves on the railing, facing Quist. A few people passed on the sidewalk from time to time; there was no one else on the hotel veranda.

Quist eyed the pair gravely. "Where's the funeral?" he asked.

Chris spoke first. "I ran into Ramon a block back," he said. "We've been comparing notes and we've decided we're just about the most hopeless pair of assistants you've ever had. We get sent on simple little errands, and all we can report is failure."

"*Por qué?*" Quist asked.

Serrano said dramatically, "All afternoon I have comb' this town like one *demente* in the search for Sultan Cracker. Soda cracker, yes. Butter crackers, yes. Crackers weeth salt, yes. Crackers weeth chop' nuts, yes. But of crackers weeth raisins—Sultan Crackers—no! Every storekeeper in Masquerade City thinks I am crazee, because I do not accept the substitute. No one has the Sultan Cracker. No one has evair placed in stock the Sultan Cracker. Is not known in town. Am sorry, Greg."

Quist chuckled. "Cheer up! I forgot I was

172

hungry for a spell." He turned inquisitively to Chris.

Baxter said, "I've been up against pretty much the same thing." He extended the warning note to Quist. "I've tried everywhere to find paper to match that, even in places that wouldn't be expected to carry stationery. There's no paper like that in this town. As to the inks, I couldn't say. Lots of places keep ink, of course, but it is hard to tell one ink from another. Maybe the ink came from here—I don't know. But that paper never came from any dealer in this town, I'm right sure."

"And so you've flopped on your job?" Quist's eyes twinkled.

"What else can you call heem?" Serrano said despondently.

Quist laughed. "Actually, you've both told me what I want to know. You've narrowed the search for me. I could have spent hours tramping around on this same business. While you did that work I've had a chance to do some thinking. Much obliged, pards."

Puzzled, Chris and Ramon looked at each other, then at Quist. Was he joshing them or just letting them down easy?

Quist said, "Chris, I suppose Ramon told you what happened at the Red Ball today." Chris nodded. Quist went on, "We proved that Todd Shattuck did some fibbing. Now Ramon has

173

proved that Porky Gerard was a liar too. Porky said he got those crackers in town. We know now that he didn't—"

"But why are those crackers so important?" Baxter cut in.

"You'll understand shortly. As to the paper you couldn't match, all I have to do now is look around for someone who gets his paper out of town. Like I say, that narrows my search. Chris, do you know Rawnston at all?"

"Not much. I've only been there once. It's quite a bit bigger than Masquerade City."

Quist nodded. "You're going there tonight. You can't get a train until after eleven, so you'll have plenty of time to get out your best city clothes and get ready—"

"But—but what for?"

"I'm going to give you a copy of the waybill describing the various articles that were stolen from that freight wreck. I want you to go around to various merchants and ask if they're interested in buying such articles, with delivery later, at a low price—"

"My gosh, Greg!" Baxter blurted. "I'll be glad to do it, but I don't know the town. Wouldn't have any idea which merchants to approach first—"

"Don't worry about that. I've a friend up there, Tom Fitzgerald—operative for the Redmondton Detective Agency. I've wired him to meet you at the station. He'll help you all possible. And if

174

you should run across Sheriff Tillman up there, try to see him first. He'd just blow the news all over town if he got an inkling what you were doing in Rawnston."

"Sure, I'll go," Baxter said hesitatingly, "but suppose I get arrested for trying to sell stolen property."

"In that case," Quist said gravely, "Ramon and I will visit you at the prison." He exploded into laughter at the look on Baxter's face. "I'll take care of any jams you get in."

"Greg!" Ramon looked excited. "Would eet be possible that Sultan Cracker' are on that waybill list?"

"Could be." Quist nodded.

"Then Porky Gerard is a freight thief?"

"Don't jump to conclusions, Ramon. I don't know. All I do know is that you hombres seem to be learning right fast. That's the way I like it; you save me lots of work. But don't ever condemn any man without proof. That way lies failure. I know."

TWELVE: A Double Problem

Baxter left for Rawnston that night, and the following morning when Quist left his hotel he headed first for the T. N. & A. S. depot. Two telegrams awaited him. The first, from Carstairs, the railroad wrecking boss, furnished the information that he had not seen Tillman the night of the freight wreck. The second telegram was signed "Tom Fitzgerald" and read, "NO ONE ANSWERING TO YOUR DESCRIPTION ARRIVED IN RAWNSTON ON THE 7:02. WILL BE ON LOOKOUT FOR SECOND PARTY WHEN HE ARRIVES AND GIVE ALL AID POSSIBLE."

Quist frowned. "So maybe Tillman didn't go to Rawnston to see his dear old mother after all. If not Rawnston, where did he go? Hell's bells! This upsets my calculations. Oh well, I'll learn eventually."

He scratched a match, touched it to both telegrams, and when they had burned to ashes headed back toward the hotel. Here he found Ramon waiting for him on the corner.

"And what do I do today?" Ramon asked.

"First, come on in and eat some breakfast with me. I'm starved."

"*Gracias*. But please, Greg, do not mention the Sultan Cracker. Eggs, yes. Ham, yes. Coffee, *sí*, *sí*! But of Sultan Cracker' I have heard enough for the present."

"And some fried spuds to go with the other fodder, eh, Ramon?" Quist laughed. "After breakfast I'm aiming to pick up that buckskin horse and ride out to see Francisca Haldane."

"*Bueno*!"—eagerly. "I will be glad to show you the way." Smilingly Quist shook his head. Ramon's shoulders slumped. He said ruefully, "I am forgot that I hear the Señor Quist already knows his way with women."

Quist scowled. "You don't want to believe everything you hear. That's just a lot of talk, Ramon. I can find my way out to the Rafter-RH all right. I want you to stay in town and keep plugging. Just amble around and ask questions. You might pick up some information."

Ramon shrugged. "So far I seem not so much good at that."

"You've been more help than you realize. You'll understand later."

"Maybe I can keep the eye on Todd Shattuck."

"Is he in town"—Quist frowned slightly—"so early?"

"Todd and two Triangle-S riders passed but a moment before you arrive' here. One of the riders was Porky Gerard. That *pobre* Porky is not look so good this morning—but he is

178

eating—as usual—with the apple in his fist."

"Maybe I can avoid some trouble by getting out of town for a day," Quist said reflectively. "Come on, let's get that breakfast." Taking Ramon's arm, he guided him into the hotel.

An hour later Quist was mounted on the buckskin gelding, riding west out of Masquerade City. Crossing the plank bridge over the Rio Mascarada at the edge of town, Quist struck out toward the northwest on a well-defined, hoof-chopped and wheel-rutted trail. The bright sun made it too warm for fast riding; besides, Quist wanted to get a few matters straightened out in his mind, so he didn't push the buckskin hard.

Overhead only a handful of wispy white clouds chased each other across a sky so blue it appeared almost black. Quist glanced toward the towering peaks of the Masquerade Range. In the clear bright light, bringing sharply etched deep shadows, the two headlike buttes looked more than ever like masked faces. Mesquite grew thickly on either side of the trail, the feathery green branches waving easily in the slight breeze that lifted across the range. Clumps of prickly pear were passed, their huge pads sending out brilliant yellow flowers.

Quist mused, "Queer that such spiny, rough plants like a cactus should produce such delicate blooms."

Now and then he saw small clumps of peyote—

the cactus narcotic—huddled low at the edge of the road where it could receive the shade of nearby mesquite, pushing out its tiny pink blooms. A few barrel cacti were seen and the ever-present sage. Occasionally the trail was shouldered aside in a graceful arc by a rugged outcropping of granite. Then, as the country became more rolling, the mesquite thinned out considerably and gave way to lush grass lands. Quist commenced to spot small bunches of cows, the Rafter-RH design showing plainly on their left ribs. Off to his left where a line of marching cottonwoods marked the Rio Mascarada, the cows were more thickly bunched.

"Look like nice grazing country," Quist commented. "Those cows appear right sleek. Haldane has—had—a nice spread here. I suppose Francisca inherits. And that's something else I must ask her about."

It was shortly past noon when, topping a slight rise of land, Quist found himself gazing down a long slope toward a clump of live-oak trees. Nestled among the trees were the buildings of the Rafter-RH—the ranch house proper, and some distance back of it the bunkhouse with adjoining mess shanty, corrals, stable, barns, and blacksmith shop. To Quist's ears came faintly the clanking of the windmill as its vanes turned easily in the breeze. He touched spurs to the buckskin and loped down the long grade.

Not seeing anyone on the ranch-house gallery, Quist rounded the building and continued on in the direction of the bunkhouse and mess shanty. As he neared the combination rock-and-adobe structure, a grizzled individual in Levi's and suspenders appeared in the doorway.

"Howdy, stranger," he greeted Quist. "We heard you coming. Dinner's on the table right now, case'n you'd like a snack."

"I'd like," Quist accepted as he swung down from the saddle, "though I warn you, it'll take more than a snack to satisfy the appetite I've worked up on my way here. I'm Greg Quist."

"T'hell you say. Cripes! We've heard of you. Francisca was saying—By the way, I'm foreman here. Brose Tucker's my moniker." The two men shook hands. Tucker turned his grizzled head toward the doorway and bawled, "Slim, come out here."

A young cowhand appeared from the mess shanty, gulping down food. "Slim, this is Greg Quist. Take care of his horse. See it gets feed and water." Quist shook hands with Slim, who walked off leading the horse, then accompanied Tucker into the building. Here Quist was introduced to the other hands seated at a long table which ran almost the length of the bunkhouse. Food was already on the table, and Quist found a seat on the bench near Tucker. The ranch cook came in bearing more food and glanced dourly at Quist,

muttering—as is the manner of all ranch cooks—
something about there never being any end to the
hungry mouths to be fed. But there was a twinkle
in his eyes when he said it.

Various names were mentioned by Tucker.
Quist nodded pleasantly to the punchers and
started to eat. While he consumed food he looked
them over and decided they looked entirely
capable. Little was said until dinner was concluded. Slim returned and sat down to finish his
food. Cigarettes were lighted and more coffee
poured.

Tucker said, "I reckon you came out to see
Francisca." Quist nodded. Tucker went on,
"Francisca said you were taking a hand in trying
to learn who killed Reed." He scowled angrily.
"There wa'n't a better man ever lived; and them
fools trying to make folks think he committed
suicide. None of us believed that, but if it hadn't
been for you, Quist, we'd have had to take it and
like it, 'cause we didn't have nothing to offer
different. Lucky you arrived when you did—" He
broke off and spoke to another of the cowhands.
"Hub, when you finish your coffee, you might
slope up and tell Francisca that Greg Quist is
here." He turned back to Quist. "Never could
understand why, but female folks always wants a
chance to tidy up before visitors arrive."

"Never understood it myself." Quist grinned.
He changed the subject to Haldane's murder and

182

listened to various comments from the punchers. He introduced questions into the discussion but, by the time the conversation was finished, had to admit he had learned nothing new. None of the Rafter-RH crew knew of any enemy, with the exception of Todd Shattuck, who might have killed Haldane, but Shattuck had been making threats for so long without doing anything that the crew couldn't even feel convinced of his guilt, particularly in view of Pitt's alibi for his brother. One and all stated that Pitt Shattuck had apparently tried to keep the peace.

Silence began to settle over the table. Brose Tucker growled, "It's certainly a puzzle, and you'll have the thanks of every man here, Quist, if you can lay hand on that killer."

"It's a problem all right," Quist agreed. "But I've a hunch something will break soon to give me a lead."

"But there's nothing yet, eh?" Tucker pursued.

"Nothing I want to put into words," Quist evaded.

One by one the men commenced to leave the table to go about their work. Hoofs sounded outside the building as riders headed out toward the range. A couple of men commented they'd better get back to the whitewashing they were doing. One hand said something about certain work in the blacksmith shop that demanded his attention.

A few minutes later Quist made his way through the oak trees and arrived at the house to find Francisca seated on the gallery, attractive in fresh green-checked gingham; her lustrous dark hair was piled high on her head, and she had a certain scrubbed look that made Quist think she had just stepped from a bath.

"Greg—" The girl stopped in some confusion. "I mean, Mr. Quist. Darn! I'm so used to hearing Ramon and Chris call you Greg—"

"Why not? Greg's the name my friends call me. I hope we're friends, Francisca."

"I've felt that," the girl said sincerely, "since the first night I knew you. Golly! I was commencing to think you never were coming to see me. I've ridden to town twice but didn't see you."

"I'm sorry. I've been busy. I was away from Masquerade City for a couple of days—longer, in fact. I haven't come out here before because I figured you'd like a time to—well, sort of adjust yourself to what's happened. Didn't want to bother you more than necessary—but there are some questions I want to ask you."

The girl indicated a rocking chair at her side, and Quist sat down. "Ask anything you like. I'll be glad to answer."

Quist rolled and lighted a cigarette. "Suppose I asked who was courting you now and what progress they're making."

Francisca flushed. "There are a few subjects

184

we'd better not go into, Greg—not that they're important, of course—"

"On the contrary." Quist chuckled. "You don't know. I might even be wondering if there was a chance for me to join the group nightly serenading under your window."

The girl was laughing now, her long-lashed eyes dancing. "Greg, you're teasing me. Here I've been expecting serious questions about—about Dad"—the smile died from her face and then returned—"and you've taken me off guard with a line of palaver." She studied his face, liking what she saw, intrigued by the shrewd, yet kindly topaz eyes. She thought of a phrase of her father's when speaking of men he liked: "A man to ride the river with." That was Greg Quist; the girl knew it instantly and knew she could trust him to any extent. What she hadn't realized was that Quist had chosen his opening remarks to place her at ease and thus make easier for her the questions he would have to ask later.

"If you don't mind," Quist said after a minute, "I'd like to go through your father's papers later. You see, I'm sort of out on a limb and I'm trying to catch up. I want to learn who his acquaintances were, if he'd received threatening letters, things like that."

"His desk and safe are in the house," the girl said. "I thought you might want to look through

185

things and I've arranged them on his desk. I felt you'd come to see me sooner or later." She hesitated. "There's something I suppose I should tell you if you want to learn his past life. There was trouble with the Shattucks years ago. My mother—"

Quist interrupted her. "You won't have to go into that, Francisca. I've had a talk with Doc Woodward. He gave me the details in that direction." The girl looked relieved. Quist went on, "I also understand that Todd Shattuck has made various threats from time to time. How well do you know Todd?"

Francisca hesitated; then, "There was a time when he didn't make threats. He came here several times to visit. When Dad heard of it he naturally enough didn't care for the idea. Though he didn't forbid me to see Todd. You see, Todd once asked me to marry him. I've never told anybody about that before—"

"I can understand it would have raised the devil," Quist cut in dryly. "You didn't care enough for him, of course."

"Of course not," the girl said promptly. "He told me I'd be sorry I refused him. Later he renewed the threats against Dad."

"How long ago was this?"

"Nearly two years back. I've always felt that Todd talked more than acted. He liked to boast. I could never take him seriously, though, until recently. After what happened, I don't know what to think."

"He has his brother's alibi," Quist reminded the girl, "so for the present let's forget him. What other enemies did your father have aside from the Shattucks?"

"None that I can think of. And he always told me everything. Practically everyone liked Dad."

"He had lots of friends then?"

Tiny frown wrinkles appeared on the girl's forehead. "I wouldn't say he had lots of friends. Call them genial acquaintances. I don't think anyone ever got close to him except Dr. Woodward. You could call him a real friend. You see, Dad was pretty quiet. He didn't talk much, just listened. He liked to be around the Saddlehorn. There was talk there most of the time. Dad always said he had lots to forget. Of course Brose Tucker could be considered a pretty close friend. Dad knew him for years. And he thought heaps of all the men in the crew. They've worked for the Rafter-RH a long time."

"What about women?" Quist's color deepened. "I mean, your father never considered marrying again?"

Francisca shook her head. "In the first place, he wasn't what you'd call a ladies' man. In the second, he told me there'd never been anyone but Mother. He suffered more over her and what he'd done than anyone ever knew. I heard him say once that remorse was the worst sort of agony a man could undergo."

"I suppose you're acquainted with his will. Did he leave enough money to anyone to warrant his—?" Quist hesitated.

"You mean, would anybody stand to benefit by his death?" the girl said calmly. "There's a copy of his will on the desk for you to see. Of course it will have to go through probate. I'm to receive the bulk of the estate. Chris and Ramon each are to get five thousand dollars. Brose Tucker and the crew are to get something too. And Dr. Woodward is down for a thousand, as an evidence of Dad's regard. Skimpy Degnan is to receive a share in the Saddlehorn. He'll be running it for me. Later I think I'll make him half owner or sell out. I can't somehow imagine myself running a saloon."

"A decently run bar has its place in civilization," Quist said. "It's not the use but the misuse of liquor that's bad. Well, let's go inside and look at those papers."

They rose and entered the house. "What you said about bars," Francisca said, "reminds me I've not been very hospitable." She called, "Josefa," and a middle-aged Mexican woman appeared from the back of the house. Francisca spoke in Spanish, and the woman nodded and disappeared.

"I was wondering if you lived alone in this big

place," Quist commented. He glanced around. The main room of the ranch house in which he stood looked extremely livable. Indian rugs were scattered about the oak flooring. The furniture was comfortable. A mounted deer head raised antlers above the fireplace.

"Josefa was hired by Dad when I first came here," Francisca said. "Actually, I could care for this house by myself, but she's good company and it's nice to have her here."

Josefa reappeared carrying a tray on which stood glasses, water, a bottle of Old Crow bourbon, and a bottle of sarsaparilla, then once more withdrew. Francisca served drinks. "The way to a man's heart"—Quist smiled—"is through his stomach."

"I always thought that saying referred to food," the girl said.

"There's sugar in alcohol. Sugar's a food." Quist laughed. "I've known times when I was awfully hungry."

"That's one way of looking at it. Incidentally, I've told Josefa you'd be staying for supper with me tonight. Now don't tell me you can't, Greg. A girl gets mighty lonesome sometimes."

"Are you sure it's necessary?" Quist asked.

Francisca lowered her eyes. "Under present conditions—yes."

Quist studied her a moment, then changed the subject. "Let's get to those papers." He settled

189

himself at the desk. Francisca took a chair nearby where she could go over the papers with him and answer questions.

Francisca indicated the small iron safe next to the desk. "I can open that if you like," she offered, "but all it contains at present are some stocks and bonds and money for current expenses."

"I reckon that won't be necessary," Quist replied, and applied himself to the mass of papers on the desk. The hours passed swiftly, with small conversation between the two. Cigarette smoke curled through the room; once Francisca did things with the bottles and glasses. Almost before they realized it, the sun had passed far to the west and was dropping below the peaks of the Masquerade Mountains.

Quist put down the last paper. There hadn't been many letters, and those were apparently, in the main, communications from slight acquaintances of distant date; there were receipts, deeds for property, papers relative to business deals at one time or another, but none of the concrete evidence that Quist sought. "Not one blessed thing," Quist stated as he pushed back the stack of papers.

Francisca looked disappointed. "So you've wasted the whole afternoon, and I did so want to be of help."

Quist's topaz eyes moved swiftly toward the girl. He smiled. "Wasted?" he said dryly. "With

190

you seated beside me half the day? I can't remember a more pleasurable afternoon. I can think of men—two in particular—who'd really envy me this day. And who could blame them?"

Francisca colored. "Greg"—she smiled—"I think you have a mighty smooth tongue, but I must admit a girl likes to hear such things anyway. I think you've been pretty good for me this afternoon too. Somehow, you make me think everything isn't so hopeless as I thought at first right after—after Dad—"

Quist cut in, "I think I heard Josefa call you."

"For supper," the girl said. "Come on out to the dining room, Greg."

While they were eating, served by the Mexican woman, Francisca asked, "And you didn't learn one thing from all those papers?"

"I think I did," Quist told her. "The very fact I found no leads to other parts of the country proves that the skulduggery is local. I've narrowed my search just that much more." He drained his coffee cup and watched it being refilled by Josefa; then, "You've said your father never mentioned any threats made against him except those of Todd Shattuck's—"

"And he wouldn't have told me of those," Francisca cut in. "I heard about them one day in town. When I asked him about it, he admitted the truth of it but said it was nothing to worry about, as Pitt could hold his brother in check, he thought, and besides, he had Ramon and Chris with him most of the time. He honestly felt that Pitt wanted no trouble."

"Did he ever say anything about the Shattuck outfit—any man there who might—?"

"No," the girl said. "The only time I remember him mentioning the Triangle-S in that way was to wonder why Pitt maintained such a large crew, particularly when his herd was so depleted by the drought some years back and never rebuilt. Dad said he could understand the size of the crew if there was a lot of rustling around here, but there's scarcely any. And the crew seemed to find so much time to hang around town when you'd think they'd be working out on the range."

"Hmm," Quist mused. "Maybe that is something to think about." The girl looked questioningly at him, but he didn't augment the remark.

Dusk had arrived before dinner was concluded. It was dark by the time Quist prepared to leave. The girl mentioned something about hating to see him leave at night and said there were plenty of extra bunks at the bunkhouse. They had stepped out on the gallery by this time. Quist stood beside the girl, sombrero in hand.

"I'd like to stay," he admitted, "but I want to get back to town tonight and see if anything's turned up."

"There's a fifteen-mile ride ahead of you, Greg—and at night." She shivered slightly.

192

"Now don't talk foolish." Quist laughed. "You'll spoil things. I've really had a nice day and a good dinner. Things that have happened lately have made you nervous, Francisca. All this will pass. Even the pain of your father's death, after a time. It's all not as hopeless as you think. This problem will iron itself out—" He broke off as something like a muffled sob escaped the girl's lips. Quist swore under his breath, put on his sombrero, and, placing both hands on the girl's shoulders, turned her around so he could see her face, which looked luminous in the faint light from the house windows. He could see the dark eyes were moist.

"Look here," Quist went on, "will you take my word for it that everything is coming out right? One of these days you'll have forgotten how upset you were, and you'll be married and all will be well—"

"Married," the girl said bitterly. What else she said Quist didn't quite catch; then, half sobbingly, "You speak of having a problem. Suppose you had a double problem and didn't know what to do."

"Double problem?" Quist frowned, his hands still on the girl's shoulders. "That I don't get."

"It's—it's—those two."

"What two?"

"Ramon and Chris. They—they both want to marry me."

"I can't say I blame 'em."

"Oh, Greg, you don't understand. They were both here—at different times—that day the sandstorm started. I've promised both—Oh, Greg, all I can see is trouble ahead. Right now there's a sort of truce. Each feels magnanimous, and until things are settled they'll co-operate but later they'll start fighting again. I just can't bear it. They've always fought, but this time it will be worse—"

"Francisca, listen to me. This can be fixed later. One of them you surely care the most for. How much do you care—?"

"Everything, Greg. You don't understand—"

"Francisca, you're making a mountain out of a gopher hole. They're both level-headed. The loser will want only your happiness—"

"There's the trouble, Greg. I don't know which one I—"

"Dammit, you're not in love." Quist stared at her.

"But I am, I am," the girl insisted. "I want both of them."

"Do you realize, Francisca, how insane that sounds? Surely you can't love both. That's ridiculous!"

"I know it sounds like that to you, a man. But, Greg, isn't it possible a man could love two women?"

Quist started to say, "That's different," then

checked himself. He considered a moment and said finally, "Yes, I think he could. Love them for different qualities. But he couldn't have both. Not at the same time."

"Would you deny a woman an equal choice in such matters?"

Quist frowned. "That's just the point I'm trying to make, girl. You'll have to make a choice."

"But I can't, I simply can't. Any choice I make will result in trouble between them. Oh, Greg, I'm such a silly fool, but I just can't decide. When I'm with Chris, I'm certain he's the one. And then I see Ramon, and you can't understand the attraction he has for me—how I'm drawn to him. Somehow, he just fascinates me. Except when I'm with Chris. Oh, darn! Everything is so topsy-turvy-y-y . . . ." The words ended in a frustrated sob and she swayed toward Quist.

Quist drew her close, feeling her teary face against his own, speaking soft words of consolation. Finally she ceased sobbing and she drew a long convulsive sigh but remained within his arms, as though only there did she feel a certain peace. Quist said dryly at last, "Have you ever considered tossing a coin or telling those two to draw straws?"

Something very like a giggle escaped Francisca's lips. "I'm such an idiot, I may yet be forced to do something like that. Or ask *you* to marry me. Of course you'd refuse. But can't you see, Greg, that would settle everything for me? I'm learning more every minute that you're a very solid sort of person—"

"Nonsense! And it would settle nothing. You don't realize what you're saying."

"Perhaps I do, more than you realize. Oh, fiddlesticks! I'm sorry, Greg, for messing things up this way. It was just that—that you were so kind and considerate that night I came to your room. I've felt ever since that all I had to do was dump my troubles on your shoulders and you'd take care of everything." She took his face between her hands, raised her body on tiptoe, and he felt her warm lips on his. His arms tightened about her for a moment, then he drew back.

"That's not the way to settle things, Francisca," he said, and his voice wasn't quite steady. "You know that as well as I do."

"I'm not so sure," and her words were almost a wail.

"I am. You're not seeing straight right now. You don't know whether you're coming or going, do you? You miss your father and because I'm quite a bit older than you, you're trying to transfer your affections to me. It won't work, Francisca, believe me. You're upset over all that's happened; you're building up fears of what may happen. Now you listen to me. Nothing, where Chris and Ramon are concerned, has to be settled right now. And when their time comes,

196

your other problems will have been ironed out. Now, you slope into the house and quit worrying. Leave all the fretting to me, and take my word for it, everything—*everything*—is going to work out right for you."

Five minutes later, as he passed beneath the limbs of the oak trees on the way to the corrals, Quist muttered, "What a liar I'll be if things don't come as I promised. Francisca sure does have a double problem. I reckon I've got it easy. All I have to do is uncover her father's killer and trap a passel of freight thieves."

THIRTEEN: Gunfire!

For five miles Quist pushed the buckskin along the trail in an easy lope, leaving largely to the horse the business of keeping to the road. It was too dark to see much of anything, the moon not yet having lifted above the eastern horizon. There was nothing but starlight to show the way, and that hadn't yet reached its brightest intensity. Now and then Quist felt the buckskin swerve to pass a low-hanging cottonwood limb or round an outjutting of sandstone at the edge of the trail, even before his eyes pierced the gloom to pick out such objects, but the horse drummed steadily through the darkness.

After a time Quist felt the animal negotiating a gradual downgrade and remembered the arroyo he'd crossed earlier that day. Ahead lay an old river bed, dry at present, but cluttered with chunks of broken rock. The trail dipped between thick clumps of brush on one side and led up through twin stands of mesquite bush on the other. Quist was halfway across the arroyo, his pony stepping carefully across the cluttered chunks of rock in the ancient stream bed, when it happened.

What caused Quist to swerve his body to one

side at that particular moment he was never certain. Perhaps he moved his body to shift weight while the horse maneuvered some particularly difficult crossing of broken rock. It may have been sheer instinct, that functioning of a man's sixth sense in time of danger. At any rate, the movement more than likely saved Quist's life.

He had a brief glimpse of a stabbing lance of orange gunfire, then heard the savage detonation of a .45, even as the bullet winged dangerously close past his body. The next shot also missed.

Quist was already swinging down from his saddle as the second explosion came from the mesquite bush. He fired once as his feet left the stirrups. A second time as they struck the river bed. And then a third shot roared from his heavy .44 while he crouched low near his horse's belly. The first shot had been directed toward the flash he'd seen. The other two were spaced about a yard to either side, one somewhat high, the other low, in the conjecture that the assailant had moved since firing the first shot, and to keep him so busy he'd not have time for a steady third shot.

And then at Quist's third shot he had the satisfaction of knowing that his theory had proved correct: there came a sharp anguished cry from the mesquite and the sound of a falling body. Then complete silence after a brief thrashing about in the underbrush.

Quist waited a moment while the echoes of the shots died away. His nostrils twitched from the acrid odor of burned powder. The buckskin horse had stood without movement, for which Quist was thankful. Neither had there been any further movement from the mesquite. Finally Quist drew a deep breath and, his ears still attuned to the slightest sound at the far side of the arroyo, he plugged out his empty shells and reloaded in the darkness. Then, taking his horse's reins, he started in the direction from which the hidden would-be assassin had fired.

Abruptly a horse whinnied nearby. Quist stiffened a moment, then pushed through the thickly growing mesquite. Within a few moments he had found his assailant's horse tethered to a limb of one of the trees. Dropping his own reins, Quist began a cautious search through the brush, the .44 clutched in his right hand.

By the time he found the body Quist knew there was no need for such caution. He slipped the six-shooter back into its holster and knelt beside the still figure of the dead man. Then he reached for the man's pulse. There wasn't any. A further exploring of the body brought only a warm stickiness to his fingers. Quist swore softly in the gloom. After a minute he scratched a match, then he swore some more.

"You poor misguided bustard." Quist spoke in a level flat tone. "So this is the way you tried to square yourself with your gang. I wonder now, was this your own idea or did they force it on you?"

The dead man was Porky Gerard, the Triangle-S glutton.

Quist struck further matches. He found half a dried apple pie on a tin plate and three apple cores. Even while Gerard had waited for Quist to come along the trail the obese cowpuncher had been satisfying his appetite. Carefully Quist went through the man's pockets and as carefully replaced everything. There was nothing to furnish a clue—just a Barlow knife, a soiled bandanna, some cards from saloons and gambling houses, tobacco and cigarette papers, a small sum of money. That was all. "Not even a letter from some woman," Quist mused. "You poor misguided cuss."

He found Gerard's gun where it had dropped from his hand, a few feet away, and shoved it into the dead man's holster. Next Quist brought up the dead man's horse and lifted its owner head down across the saddle, lashing the still-warm form in place with Gerard's lariat. That done, he took the reins and, mounting the buckskin, started for Masquerade City. . . .

It was close to one in the morning when Quist led the horse with its grisly burden into Masquerade City. The moon was up now, moving serenely through the scattered clouds that had gathered in the sky. Mostly the buildings along Main Street were dark, though here and there a light shone. A dim, feeble yellow glow emanated from the hotel office. One or two saloons were open. Quist noticed as he passed that the Saddlehorn was dark, though light and voices still issued from the Red Ball Saloon. There were no pedestrians abroad.

Deputy Clem Vincent had apparently turned into his cot. The sheriff's office was dark when Quist drew rein before the building. He stepped softly to the porch and rapped lightly on the door. There came movement from within, then a man's feet struck the floor. Vincent said, "Who is it?" He sounded wide awake. Quist told him who it was. An instant later Vincent opened the door. Though in his underwear, he already had donned his boots and sombrero. "What's up?" he asked.

Quist pushed into the office. "Don't bother with your lamp. I'll give it to you while you get dressed." He talked quietly while the deputy got into his clothing and buckled on his gun. Once Vincent said, "Geez! Porky Gerard! I can't believe it. He never gave anybody any trouble. Big fat good-natured cuss. All's he cared about was a full dinner pail—"

"I'm giving it to you as it happened," Quist said harshly. "Do you think I wanted to kill the poor slob?"

"Hell, no, Greg. Don't get me wrong. To do

different than you done would have been suicide. You had to shoot—"

"You going to get any ideas about putting me under arrest?"

"Don't talk foolish. There'll probably have to be an inquest, of course, but I can't see anything for you to worry over."

"I'm not worried," Quist said shortly.

Vincent was dressed now. The two men made their way out of the office, Vincent closing the door behind him. He said, "In case you want to get to bed, I'll lead that horse down to Hume's Undertaking Parlors. Then I'll look into the Red Ball. There's probably somebody from the Triangle-S still there—I know the Shattucks were in town earlier—and give 'em news of what's happened."

Quist said grimly, "You go ahead and deliver that body. I'm aiming to drop into the Red Ball myself and break the news—"

"Now look here," Vincent said earnestly, "you'd best wait for me to be with you. I don't want any more shootings to start tonight."

"No more do I. And don't worry about me."

The deputy hesitated, then took the reins of the dead man's horse. "I'll be right back," he said a bit nervously. "Only that I don't like to leave this body here—"

Quist didn't wait to hear what else the deputy would say but started across the street toward

204

the Red Ball Saloon. Pushing through the swinging doors, he noticed that every man at the bar instantly turned his gaze toward the entrance. Quist told himself: They're waiting for, expecting, something, all right.

Both Shattucks stood midway of the bar with half a dozen of their hands. Much nearer to the entrance, standing by himself, was Ramon Serrano, three untouched bottles of beer before him. Relief lighted his eyes at Quist's appearance. He said quietly enough, "It's good to see you back, Greg."

Quist nodded but kept his eyes on the Shattucks. Pitt Shattuck was the only one who spoke, saying civilly enough, "Evening, Quist." The others just scowled, particularly Todd, who appeared baffled, disappointed. Quist nodded again and said, "Shattuck, you may or may not have had anything to do with it, but at this moment Clem Vincent is on his way to the undertaker's with Porky Gerard's body."

Silence greeted the announcement, then abruptly various comments were heard; one or two men even sounded surprised. Pitt Shattuck exclaimed, "My God! What happened to Porky?"

"What'd Porky do," Todd sneered, "try to swallow a beef whole?"

"—and what the hell do you mean, Quist," Pitt finished, "by saying I may have had something to do with it?"

Quist snapped, "Exactly what I said. Gerard worked for you. He tried to dry-gulch me tonight. It wasn't his night for luck."

"Where—where was this?" Pitt stammered.

"If you don't know, you can get the story from Vincent. I'm not going to repeat it again," Quist said coldly.

"But—but I don't understand," Pitt persisted. "Why should Porky try to kill you? You never had trouble with him, did you?"

"I sort of doubt," Quist said tersely, "it was Gerard's idea."

"You mean somebody put him up to it?"

"That's exactly what I mean. Gerard had to square himself."

"But for what? What had he done?"

"If you don't know, think it over. Or ask that punk brother of yours. He was the one that jumped Porky the other day."

"Now, you look here, Quist," Todd burst out furiously. "I don't like what you're saying—"

"And I don't like what you're trying to say," Quist said harshly. "And now that I think it over, I don't like anything about you. Personally, I think you're yellow and sent Gerard to do a job you were afraid to try yourself—"

"That's a goddamn lie. We don't have to stand for your bushwah, Quist, and furthermore—"

"You'll stand for it and like it, Shattuck." Quist laughed contemptuously. "And get it straight in your mind that I don't want any more bush-whacking tricks tried on me. So help me, if anybody else tries to plug me from cover, I'm going to hold you responsible, Todd Shattuck, and"—the topaz eyes narrowed—"you'll be awfully regretful you didn't behave yourself before I get through with you—"

"But see here"—Pitt rushed to his brother's defense—"anybody might try to ambush you, Quist, and you couldn't blame Todd—"

"That's just the point I'm making," Quist said ironically. "Anybody might try to ambush me—but not your brother. That saffron streak up his back stops him. But he could do a lot of scheming."

"Damn you, Quist, I believe you're looking for trouble," Todd half yelled.

"Of course I am." Quist nodded. "Have you just reached that conclusion, or have you been too yellow to think about it before? What in hell do you think I'm driving at you for, Todd Shattuck? I'm just hoping you'll make a move toward that gun—that gun you were so quick to use on Gerard when he did something you didn't like. Go ahead, pull that iron and go to work if you don't like what I'm telling you. Go on! Pull it!"

Todd Shattuck backed away, his face white, arms well out from his sides. "You—you don't force me into no fight—Quist," he quavered.

Quist turned disgustedly away and faced the other Triangle-S men. "Any of you hombres feel like taking up for Porky?" he demanded, his eyes like topaz ice.

No one spoke. Mustang Neale licked dry lips and looked as though he might be tempted, but he relaxed when Pitt Shattuck spoke nervously. "Nobody here wants trouble with you, Quist. You're off on the wrong track—"

At that moment Deputy Clem Vincent came plunging through the swinging doors. Quist laughed suddenly. "What did you do, Clem, run all the way? No need to hurry. I told you not to worry about me. No one here has the guts to start anything. Clem, give these boys the story as I told it to you, though I think they know it, right up to the point where Gerard quit eating and reached for his gun. Ramon"—turning to Serrano—"let's get out of here."

"At any time I am ready, Greg."

On the street a minute later, Quist gave details on the attempted ambushing. Ramon said, "That was the narrow escape, Greg."

Quist shrugged. "I've had narrower. Did you learn anything today?"

Ramon shook his head. "Mostly I keep the eye on Todd Shattuck to see if he ride after you. I never dream that Porky would go. But I have stick like a burr to Todd, in case he suddenly leave to find you. So all day I have been on his tail."

"Must have been sort of uncomfortable for you in the Red Ball with all those Triangle-S hands. It's a wonder they didn't try to get rough."

"Such intention' they have, I'm believe, but Pitt Shattuck order them to leave me alone. To the remarks they make I turn the deaf ear, and so long as I continue to buy beer, the barkeep cannot order me out. What now, Greg?"

"I'm going to the hotel and see if my bed is as soft as it was last night. You'd better hit the hay too."

Quist started to walk down the street, Ramon still at his side. Ramon said at last, "And how did you find the Rafter-RH?"

"I followed the trail until I got there." Quist smiled.

"I mean, how was evairything?"

"Everything was fine. No, I didn't pick up any clues as to Haldane's killer."

There was a long silence. Finally Ramon said hesitatingly, "And how was Francisca?"

"Physically, like a million dollars. Mentally— well, that poor girl is pretty upset over something. It's going to take a time to get her straightened out. She needs time to think. Don't crowd her too much, Ramon."

"Me? Crowd Francisca. I do not know what you mean, Greg."

"Buffalo chips! I know how you stand in that direction, Ramon. Now let me go on alone without more questioning. I'm weary, and you should be too. Get on to bed and store up some rest. If I'm not mistaken, we'll be mighty busy before too many more days pass, and you'd better keep your powder dry."

FOURTEEN: An Averted Fire

The following day Dr. Yost Woodward held an inquest over Porky Gerard's body, and the resulting verdict of his coroner's jury completely exonerated Quist of all blame in the death of the fat cowpuncher when it brought in its decision: "Justifiable homicide." The day after that the funeral was held and attended by the Triangle-S crew in a body, more as a matter of form, Quist suspected, than because of any particular regard the men held for Porky. Later, when the punchers returned from Boot Hill Cemetery south of town, they headed directly for the Red Ball Saloon and proceeded after some three rounds of drinks to voice threats of vengeance against Quist for the death of their comrade. News of the threats eventually reached Quist, but he shrugged it off. Such talk, he concluded, was rather hypocritical on the part of the Triangle-S men. True, they might have wanted Porky out of the way, but their threats weren't based on any particular love for Gerard.

Shortly past noon of that same day Sheriff Matt Tillman returned, and when he ran into Quist in front of Johnson's Feed & Hay Store he said grouchily, "Hear there's been some trouble while I was up in Rawnston. That's just why I hate to leave here a minute. The instant my back is turned—"

"Trouble?" Quist assumed a surprised look.

"I'd call it trouble," Tillman said pompously. "You had a fracas in the Red Ball. Gun-whipped Todd Shattuck, as I get it. Then two nights ago, dammit, you killed Porky Gerard."

Quist said, "I regretted more than most people, I believe, the killing of Gerard, but as I see it, there was nothing else I could have done. If you'd been at the inquest—"

"Cripes A'mighty, Greg! I'm not blaming you. The only thing that puzzles me is why Gerard tried to bushwhack you. You and him never had words, did you?"

"Not fighting words. I saw him one day in the Red Ball. He was drunk—"

"Yeah, I heard about that from Clem." Tillman considered. "I just can't understand it."

"I've a hunch one of the Shattuck crowd put him up to it."

"That could be," Tillman agreed. "It'd be Todd, of course, after you knocking him down with your gun. But I ain't no way to prove that, of course. Just the same, I think I'll put a bug in Todd's ear and warn him to go easy. Ain't no man going to come that sort of game on a friend of mine, not while I'm sheriff of Mascarada County."

The sheriff scowled ferociously and spat a long stream of tobacco juice. He looked even sloppier than usual today, even though he'd been shaved within the past twenty-four hours. His wide straggly mustaches were stained deeply with tobacco juice. His collarless once-white shirt was a dingy gray. A bit of dried egg yolk clung to his skimpy vest. The upper button of his trousers was missing, allowing his ponderous paunch to sag over the edge, as though it were weighted down by the six-shooter that dangled loosely at his right thigh. He spat again. "B'Gawd, Greg, I just wish you could get me some proof to act on. I'd toss that Todd bustard in a cell so fast it'd make his head swim."

"That I'd really like to see," Quist responded. "Who knows, maybe I'll get a break soon."

"If you do, you'll let me know, won't you?" Tillman asked eagerly.

"Any time I get anything to act on, you'll know it, Matt," Quist replied. "I'd need your authority in case there were arrests to be made. Heard you've been visiting your mother. How were things up in Rawnston?"

Tillman brightened, saying with some enthusiasm, "Now there's one sweet old lady, Greg. I wish you could know her. Eighty years old and bright as a dollar. Even got most of her teeth. Never wears specs except for reading. Had a new pair of socks knit for me. I'm savin' 'em for dress-up. Bosses me around like I was a ten-year-old. Generally I take her out and buy her some doodads in the stores, but mostly, this time, we stayed indoors. Would you believe it? It rained like hell while I was in Rawnston, reg'lar cloudburst, and then kept coming down. Still raining when I left. I got soaked."

"Been nice weather here," Quist observed. "Rawnston your home town?"

The sheriff shook his head. "Nope, my mother just moved up there a few years back. My uncle Charlie—he's getting right feeble—needed caring for—and Mom took on the job. She was sure pleased to hear I knew you. She'd read a lot about you in the newspapers one time or another and was holding you up as a model for me—"

"That's tough on you." Quist grinned.

"It'd be tough for me to try to live up to your exploits," Tillman conceded. "But you know how a mother is, thinks her own offspring is capable of doing anything anybody else does. But I sure wish she could meet you. It'd bring joy to her life. An old lady her age needs something like that just to keep her plugging from day to day—"

"Tell you what," Quist cut in, "when I leave here, I may have to spend some time north of here. Maybe I could find time to drop in on your mother and say hello."

"Would you do that?" Tillman beamed. "B'Gawd, that'd tickle her to death."

"Glad to do it," Quist said. "Let me have her address."

Tillman reached for a much-thumbed notebook in his pocket, then paused. "I'll do better than that, Greg. I never can remember the number of that street, but when you leave I'll go with you. Take you right to the house. How'll that be?"

"I think it's a fine idea, Matt. Let's hope we can make it soon, eh?"

"The sooner the better. When that time comes I'll know you've cleared up all the trouble here. I like to see crime washed up fast in Mascarada County. Looks better on my record. I have to think of the people, my constituents." He winked at Quist. "Election will be on us before we know it."

They talked a few minutes longer before parting, Quist heading for the Saddlehorn Saloon with the thought that a bottle of beer might do something toward alleviating the heat of the day. There were only two cowhands and one of the town's citizens at the bar when Quist stepped into the place. Neither of the cowhands was a Triangle-S man.

Quist gave his order to Skimpy Degnan and lounged against the bar enjoying his drink. The two cowmen departed and a few minutes later the third customer also left for the street. Skimpy employed a bar rag to mop up certain wet rings from the mahogany. "I suppose you're picking

215

up clues by the handful these days, Mr. Quist."

"I wish I could, Skimpy."

"I'll be mighty pleased once you've run down Reed's killer."

"That makes two of us with the same idea. Business sort of dull today?"

"Sort of." Skimpy nodded. "I'm pretty busy right after dinner. Then things let off. Long toward evening the Saddlehorn gets a stronger play, and after supper."

"I never see any Triangle-S hands in here."

"Not likely to, either." Skimpy put away his rag and took up a position opposite Quist, placing another bottle on the bar. "That's on the house."

Quist said, "Thanks"; then, "I suppose the trouble between Haldane and the Shattucks keeps Triangle-S men from coming in."

The barkeep nodded. "I understand Shattuck give 'em orders to stay out of here. Mr. Haldane let it be known he didn't want their trade neither. But that was after—"

"After?"

Skimpy explained. "Like you've probably noticed, the Triangle-S is a pretty rough crew. 'Bout three years back a bunch of 'em came in here and started roughhousing. Mr. Haldane asked them to leave. They just laughed at him, so he went across the street and got Sheriff Tillman to take care of the business. Tillman run 'em out in a hurry and, furthermore, told Shattuck to keep 'em away from here. We never had no trouble with 'em since." Skimpy paused. "Fact is, I guess that's just about the last time the sheriff was in here, too, while Reed was alive."

"That so?" Quist didn't appear greatly interested as he sipped his beer. "Don't tell me Haldane and the sheriff had trouble too."

Skimpy shook his head. "It wa'n't what you'd call real trouble. Reed was talking to Doc Woodward one time and he mentioned he thought a change in the sheriff's office might be a good thing. Tillman happened to overhear it, and he took exception, as they say. Him and Reed had a few words over the matter, and he told Tillman an efficient law officer 'stead of a fatheaded windbag would be an improvement in Mascarada County. Finally Doc Woodward got the two of 'em calmed down, and Reed apologized, and Tillman said he was sorry for things he'd said. Said he guessed he was too thin-skinned. Thin-skinned like an elephant, I calls it."

"And that's all there was to it?" Quist asked idly.

"That's all. Things were patched up, and whenever they met they was friendly. Reed told me he was sorry the sheriff had heard him, as he didn't want any feelings hurt. The whole business was just over the way Tillman never gets to his office until around noon. That always sort of griped Reed."

"When was this?" Quist asked.

"Long time back—nearly three years, I guess. But I noticed that the sheriff never came in here since." Skimpy shook his head reminiscently. "Anybody can see that Tillman's run to seed the past few years. I can remember him when he used to be a pretty good man. Now all he does is push wind through his teeth."

The swinging doors at the entrance were pushed aside and Dr. Woodward came in. He looked dusty and warm. He took a place at the bar and set his black bag on top. "Whew! That beer looks good, Greg. Skimpy, open a bottle for me *pronto*!"

The drink was put out and Woodward downed half a glassful, then set it on the bar with a long sigh of satisfaction.

"You look like you'd been swallowing dust, Doc," Quist commented.

"Plenty. Too much, in fact. I had to make a call at the Triangle-S and change a dressing for Floursack Regan."

"Sounds like he might have dough." Quist laughed.

"He does—most of the time. Regan's the Triangle-S cook."

"What's wrong with him?"

"Sprained his right ankle several days back. Fell off a stepladder. I should have been called in sooner, but Regan tried to fix the ankle himself with horse liniment. He can just make to hobble around now. It isn't just the sprain. When he fell he dropped a knife he was holding and it slashed a nasty cut in his knee too. Oh, he'll be fit as a fiddle in a few days, I imagine, but his knee's going to be right stiff until that cut heals up. The knife opened up nearly to the bone."

Another customer entered and Skimpy moved down the bar to serve him. Woodward said, "I had quite a talk with Pitt Shattuck while I was out there."

"I hope he had something interesting to say."

"Nothing what you might call important," Woodward replied. "He was just commenting on the trouble you'd had with Todd—and the shooting of Gerard—things like that. He told me how much he regretted all this, that he felt he'd gotten off on the wrong foot with you and he wishes that you and he could be friendly. He says he feels sure you suspect him of having a hand in Reed's death. He hopes you'll find the killer soon so as to clear his record."

"Maybe I will," Quist said quietly.

Woodward looked startled. "You mean you know who the killer is, Greg?"

"I'd hate to have it repeated, but the way things are shaping up, Doc, I'm starting to get hopes. If I can just find out one or two things more, the case is in the bag. But for cripes' sake, don't tell anybody I said that."

"You can rely on me, Greg. At the same time you arouse my curiosity like the devil. You can't give me any hints?"

Quist smiled and shook his head. "I've got to dovetail a couple of facts before I'm actually sure, Doc. In case I was wrong I wouldn't want you remembering I went off half cocked. But I'm pretty sure I'm not wrong."

"In that case"—Woodward laughed—"I'll just have to continue being devoured by curiosity. Damn you, Greg Quist, I'll not be able to keep my mind on my afternoon calls now. And I'd better get started making them too." Still laughing, he picked up his black bag and departed from the saloon.

That evening Ramon Serrano joined Quist at supper in the hotel dining room. Over roast beef, mashed potatoes and gravy, canned peas, dried-apricot pie, and coffee the two conversed steadily for some time. Finally Quist said, "Pick up anything out of the ordinary this afternoon, Ramon?"

Serrano frowned. "Nothing that seem' of import, Greg—but I am not of sureness if there is some connection in a thing that has happen'."

Quist forked a mouthful of beef between his lips, chewed a moment, and said, "Suppose you let me be the judge."

"Today I am spending my time in the Mexican district and I hear of something. A very old

220

Mexican—is name' Diego Santandar—have disappear' from the home of relatives where he came but recently from Old Mexico to stay for the visit. He had planned to open here a restaurant of Mexican food—*tortillas*, *chili*, *frijoles*, *enchiladas*—and now is gone. When last seen he was talking with Pitt Shattuck in the Mexico City Saloon—"

"I don't know the place."

"Is the bar for *Mejicanos*—on the north side of Main Street, about half a dozen doors west of Apache Street."

"Oh yes, I remember—"

"But why should he be talking with Pitt Shattuck?"

Quist said lazily, "If Santandar came here to open a restaurant, he can cook. The Triangle-S cook had an accident. Shattuck needs a cook for his outfit. So he hired Diego Santandar."

Serrano's eyes widened. "*Dios mío*! You know everytheeng, Greg. So there is no mystery." Serrano paused. "But why should not Santandar tell his relatives where he is go before he leaves?"

"That's one of the things I don't know, Ramon." Quist scowled. "And why should Shattuck hire a Mexican for the job—or hire an extra cook at all? The regular cook—Floursack Regan—can hobble around all right, Doc Woodward told me."

"Could it be," Ramon asked shrewdly, "in case of some underhand' business, Shattuck think' a

Mexican might be more secretive—or the more easy frighten' to silence?"

Quist shrugged his wide shoulders. His topaz eyes narrowed in thought. "Could be you've hit it," he said. "At any rate, Ramon, you can let word circulate among your Mexican friends that you think you know where Santandar is. That may save them some worry."

"I will do that. Still, I do not understan' why this Santandar should go off without leaving the word."

"Maybe Shattuck didn't give him time." Quist drained his coffee cup. "Through? Let's get out of here."

It was nearly dark when the two stepped outside. They stood at the edge of the sidewalk talking a minute, then Serrano started for the Mexican district.

Quist stood on the sidewalk, gloomily turning over various speculations in his mind. Far to the west the highest peaks of the Masquerades were silhouetted faintly against a fading sky of old ivory. Almost directly overhead a few stars were struggling to life. Various rectangles of yellow light shone here and there along Main Street, but for the most part the shops and stores were closed. Quist twisted a cigarette and lighted it, then headed for the depot. There he found no telegrams had come in for him, and he returned to Main Street once more. A few ponies and rigs were strung along the hitch racks. There weren't too many pedestrians on the street. Mostly people were home at supper at this hour.

At the corner of Yucca and Main, Quist paused, still lost in thought. Finally he reached a decision and turned east. He could hear voices in the Saddlehorn as he passed, but didn't enter the saloon. Crossing Austin Street, he glanced inside the sheriff's office. Tillman was seated at his desk, hands crossed at the back of his head; the swivel chair was tilted back and the sheriff appeared to be half asleep. A tattered half length of cigar was protruding from his lips, and Quist could see blue smoke spiraling thickly from the end.

Quist stepped on the porch and headed through the doorway of the office. At sound of his step Tillman opened his eyes and straightened in his chair. He removed the cigar from his lips and eyed it with some disapproval. Quist chuckled. "Smells like somebody was shoeing a horse in here. Or maybe a combination of smoldering cabbage leaf and old burlap."

"It's this damn cigar." Tillman smiled ruefully. "I'll have to tell the Red Ball to carry a better line."

"Skimpy Degnan carries good cigars in the Saddlehorn."

"Yeah, I suppose he does. This damn weed don't do nothing but smoke like it had been soaked in coal oil." As though reminded of oil, Tillman turned the wick of his lamp a little higher and managed to drop the cigar on his desk as he reached across his scattered papers and reports. Tillman cursed, picked up the cigar, and hurled it in the general direction of the cuspidor near his feet. "That's the way to finish that," Tillman growled.

"It's one way to finish this whole office," Quist said. He stood leaning against the jamb of the open doorway.

"What do you mean?" Tillman swung around in his chair.

"You missed your aim. That cigar bounced under your desk. Leave it there and you might be able to collect some fire insurance."

"T'hell you say!" Tillman struggled up from his seat and shoved back the chair. With considerable puffing and groaning he groped into the kneehole of his desk. Then more cursing and "Strike a match for me, will you, Greg? I can't find that damn weed."

"Your nose should lead you to it. Just pick it up." Quist laughed.

"Pick it up, hell! It's dark under here. You think I'm a cat?"

"I reckon you can't see in the dark at that," Quist said.

He heard the sheriff's quick intake of breath; then, picking up the lamp from the desk, he held it where the light would shine in the kneehole. "Got it," Tillman grunted. With some effort he regained his feet, swore again, and slammed the smoking cigar into his cuspidor.

"Bull's-eye!" Quist laughed.

Tillman dropped like a ton of lead into his chair and mopped his forehead. "Reckon I'm getting too old to go doubling myself into such cramped positions," he said sheepishly. "Hey, take a chair and lift a load from your feet. You drop in for anything special?"

Quist shook his head. "I was just strolling past, looked in, and saw you. Where's Clem, at supper?"

Tillman nodded. "Why, you want to see him?"

Quist said no, adding, "There's nothing he could do for me you couldn't do, Matt. Nope, I'm just killing time."

"Glad to have you visit a spell. Don't suppose you've made much progress yet, have you, on them freight thieves and Reed Haldane's killer?"

"Nothing I'm ready to talk about," Quist said evasively.

Conversation rather dwindled. They spoke of the weather, stock conditions, business in town, and various similar matters. Suddenly Quist said, "That reminds me—" He gestured toward a .44 Winchester rifle standing in one corner.

"Reminds you of what?"

"I just discovered this morning," Quist said

casually, "that I'm out of .44 ca'tridges for my six-shooter. Been intending all day to buy some, but now the stores are all closed—"

"You mean you're carrying an empty gun?"

"No. My cylinder's got its quota, but I like to have plenty of extras. If you've got some extras, or even a full box—?"

"Hell, yes! I never use that rifle. There must be shells around here." The sheriff broke off and commenced rummaging through his desk.

"I never could understand," Quist commented, "why there's so many .45 six-shooters used in the West, when if a man carried a .44 rifle and a .44 six-shooter he just has to have one caliber ca'tridges on hand—"

"Here y'are," Tillman interrupted. He produced a box of .44 cartridges and handed them to Quist.

"Thanks, you've helped a lot, Matt." Quist thrust the box into his coat pocket. "Now if you'll just make me out a bill for these—"

"Bill?" Tillman looked blank.

"Saying how much they cost," Quist explained. "You see—"

"Hell's fire! Take them ca'tridges as a gift from the county."

"Nothing doing." Quist shook his head. "The T. N. & A. S. likes to pay for what it gets—"

"It's not a big enough amount to matter—"

"You're wrong there, Matt. You know and I

know it doesn't please your constituents to have you adding to county expense by giving away what their taxes pay for."

"T'hell with 'em if they don't like it—" Tillman broke off and smiled slyly. "Reckon I shouldn't have said that."

"It's this way, Matt. According to my contract with the T. N. & A. S., I have to give an accounting for every expense I incur. So if you'll just make me out a bill for these loads, I'll send it in to the company and they'll send you a check the first of the month. In that way everything's businesslike. Otherwise I'd have to pay you out of my own pocket, and you apparently wouldn't like that. But surely you've no objection to a powerful road like the T. N. & A. S. paying you for what it buys."

"Sounds like a waste of time to me," Tillman growled, "but if you insist." He pulled over a letterhead bearing the imprint of Sheriff's Office, Mascarada County, and made out a bill to the Texas Northern & Arizona Southern Railroad for one box of fifty .44-caliber cartridges delivered to Gregory Quist, and signed his name, as sheriff, with office at Masquerade City. Then Tillman threw down his pen, replaced the stopper in the ink bottle, and shoved the paper toward Quist, who glanced at it, then folded the bill and placed it in an inner pocket.

"All damn foolishness," Tillman grumbled.

"When a man can't give a few ca'tridges to a friend without all that fooforaw—"

"I know, Matt," Quist said soothingly. "Between you and me, it's a lot of nonsense, but I work for a company that demands such accounting. You know how it is, with your own expense accounts for county business. I regret it was a bother, but you've no idea how much you've helped me. I appreciate it a lot."

He twisted a cigarette, and while he was inhaling the first mouthful of smoke Clem Vincent returned from his supper. Quist chatted with the deputy a few minutes, then with a laughing warning to Tillman not to smoke any more cabbage leaves he left the office.

"Yep," he chuckled inwardly, "a fire could have been set under Matt Tillman even before I left, but I guess it's just as well it's put off for a spell."

FIFTEEN: Rain Clue

Ramon was at the railroad station the following morning when the nine twenty-three Limited deposited Chris Baxter on the depot platform. Chris looked uncomfortable in his "city" clothing, and while his greeting to Serrano wasn't exactly cordial, still there was no trace of animosity in it either.

Chris asked first, "Where's Greg?"

"Waiting for you on the hotel *galería*. He receive' your telegram late last night—Wait, you are not to go to the hotel yet."

"What's the idea?" Chris bristled. "I'm aiming to see Greg. You telling me what I'm to do, Ramon?"

Serrano shook his head. "Long ago I learn' I can tell you nothing, Chris. Me, I only relay the message from Greg. He says you are to go first to our boardinghouse and remove those dress-up clothes before somebody sees you and asks where you have been."

Baxter's face cleared. "Oh, like that, eh?"

"Is like that," Serrano replied. "The fewer people who know you have been out of town, the better. Only yesterday the sheriff mention'

229

he has not seen you. I told him you were around. You know, with the shrug of the shoulder, like careless. Maybe he thought you were at the Rafter-RH—"

"You been out there?" Baxter said quickly.

For a moment Serrano was inclined to bait his companion; then, "*Socorro!* With Greg to keep me busy, I have been no-place from theese town of Masquerade."

Baxter relaxed. "All right. Tell Quist I'll be along *pronto*."

He hurried away, choosing a course that led along the railroad tracks, behind Main Street's buildings, rather than head over to the principal thoroughfare. Serrano turned and started toward the hotel.

Twenty minutes later Baxter joined Quist and Serrano on the hotel veranda. Quist shook hands and asked, "Had breakfast yet?"

Baxter shook his head. "That can wait. I got a good sleep on the train. Didn't wake up until we were nearly here."

"All right. I won't keep you long. What did you learn in Rawnston, Chris?"

"Not much, I'm afraid." Baxter frowned. "Your Redmondton Agency friend, Tom Fitzgerald, met me at the train. I guess you told him by telegram what was needed, didn't you? Anyway, he had a list of stores for me to call on—"

"Tom didn't go with you, did he?"

230

"Not in the stores, no. He waited on the street or in nearby bars. He seemed to know what stores might be interested in buying stolen goods."

"Tom would," Quist said. "Kind of wet walking around in the rain, wasn't it?"

"Rain?" Baxter looked startled.

"Didn't it rain while you were up there?"

"Did it rain! Whew! It was like the whole sky opened up. Mister, did it come down! Didn't clear up, either, until just a few hours before I left. But—but, Greg, how did you know it rained in Rawnston?"

"Sheriff told me. Proving he was up there. That settles one thing anyway. He was in Rawnston."

Serrano pointed out, "Perhaps somebody told him by telegram wire that eet was raining in Rawnston."

Quist looked sharply at Serrano. "Can you think of any reason why anyone should do that— especially in view of the fact Tillman was out of town while it was raining?"

Serrano shook his head. "I can think of no reason for a lot of things what happen," he said humorously.

Quist laughed. "I don't know all the answers either." He was silent while a couple of men passed on the sidewalk just below the veranda; then, "All right, I think we can feel pretty certain that Tillman was in Rawnston, even though I had a wire from Fitzgerald stating no one of Tillman's description had alighted from the train the sheriff was supposed to have been on. Let's call that much settled, even though there's a chance I might be wrong. Now, Chris, what luck did you have offering stolen freight goods to the various shady merchants of Rawnston?"

"In the first place," Chris said, "I didn't tell anyone what I was offering had been stolen, and in the second place none of the merchants were much interested in buying."

Quist looked interested. "Fitzgerald would never have sent you to the wrong places. Did you find out why no one wanted to buy from you?"

Chris nodded. "Every blasted place I went to told me I was too late. They'd already done their contracting for the same goods."

"T'hell you say," Quist exclaimed.

"That's how it was," Baxter insisted. "I offered Samuels & Tempfield six-shooters to gun shops and hardware stores; Sultan crackers to general stores and groceries; Broadway-Style suits to clothing stores; Pepper whisky to bars—Cripes! You know the list as well as I do. And every place refused."

"Give any reason?" Quist asked.

"Practically everybody I approached said at first they were overstocked for the present. After a little questioning they admitted somebody had been ahead of me with the same line of goods. The store where I offered the six-shooters told me my pardner had already been there and that we should get together on our plans." Baxter paused to roll and light a cigarette.

"And then," Quist prompted, "I suppose you asked what pardner."

Baxter snorted out a puff of gray tobacco smoke. "Like hell I did," he stated. "I may be dumb, but not that dumb. I just said I was sorry there'd been a mix-up. From then on, when I talked to merchants I did a mite of questioning. Picked up a little here and a little there, until I commenced to get an idea what this supposed 'pardner' of mine looked like." Again Baxter paused, marshalling his thoughts.

"All right," Quist said, "don't keep Ramon and me in suspense. Give details."

"He isn't anybody I know, so far as I can figure," Chris said. "You've probably got it half in mind, Greg, that he was Sheriff Tillman, but you're wrong."

"I'm still waiting to hear," Quist said patiently.

"This fellow," Baxter commenced, "was a city man. Neatly dressed and pressed in spite of the rain, apparently. I suppose the press disappeared after a time. Big man, looked like he'd just come from the barber's, talcum powder on his face and hair slicked down with bay rum. Derby hat. Black hair and black mustache, curled at the ends. Fancy vest with a heavy gold watch chain across the front. Talked like 'a real gent,' one merchant said, and mentioned how he'd be glad to get back to Chicago when his business was concluded."

"I'll be damned!" Quist exploded. A deep scowl creased his forehead and he looked disappointed.

"So there you are," Baxter concluded. "I did my best, Greg."

"You did noble," Quist said warmly, "even if you have upset a couple of my ideas. You did a fine job, Chris. Thanks."

Baxter flushed with pleasure. "Glad I didn't let you down altogether, Greg, but that's how it is. Tillman may have some connection with the freight thieves, but somehow I can't see him with enough get-up-and-go for stuff like that. At any rate, it looks as though you'll have to start searching someplace else for your man who sells stolen property."

"Blast such luck," Quist said testily. "The rain gave us a clue that said Tillman was in Rawnston, but what good does that do us?"

The other two were silent, crestfallen. "Is ver' bad," Serrano offered, shaking his head.

Quist suddenly laughed. "Cheer up, you two! We're not licked yet. I've just got to set my wits to work and figure out this business. Maybe Tillman did go up there to visit his mother after all. But if that's the case, why didn't Tom Fitzgerald see him get off the train?"

"Maybee theese Fitzgerald make the slip," Ramon said.

"You wouldn't say that if you had ever met him," Baxter said quickly. "Fitzgerald is a right cagey customer, I'd say. How about it, Greg?"

Quist said, "Correct. They don't come much smarter than Tom. If anyone answering Tillman's description had alighted from that train, Tom Fitzgerald wouldn't have missed him, you can bet your bottom dollar."

"Could Tillman have alighted at some other station and hired a horse to get to Rawnston?" Baxter speculated.

"I can't think of any reason why he should—" Quist broke off. "Maybe you've given me an idea at that, Chris." His eyes narrowed. "Maybe you have," he repeated slowly. He sat lost in thought for several minutes while the other two waited. Finally Quist roused himself. "No, I don't think Tillman arrived in Rawnston on a horse, but what you said, Chris, started a train of thought in my noodle—"

"In what way?" Baxter asked.

"I'm not yet ready to say. Haven't got it all straightened out in my mind yet. You better go get your breakfast, Chris. Ramon, you clear out of here too. I've got to be alone for a spell and work out something in my think tank."

The two disappeared. Quist rolled a cigarette, lighted it, and with his sombrero pulled low on his forehead he slumped down in his chair, feet on the veranda railing, and concentrated on his

235

problem. On various problems, in fact. Once he muttered, "If Haldane and Tillman weren't on friendly terms exactly, as Skimpy said—" Then he broke off, swearing softly in perplexity. And later, with some conviction, "It's got to be that way. It's simply got to be. Now if I can only get proof."

Five minutes later he rose from his chair and sauntered across the street, then turned toward the sheriff's office. As he crossed Austin Street he saw Matt Tillman in close conversation with Pitt Shattuck on the sidewalk before the Red Ball Saloon. The sheriff and Shattuck didn't see Quist, so deeply engrossed in their conversation were they. Quist turned in at the office when he saw Clem Vincent at the desk.

Vincent said, "Mawnin', Greg. What's on your mind?"

"Not a thing." Quist stood lazily in the doorway, leaning against the jamb. "Just sort of sashaying around." He gestured across the street. "Matt got on the job earlier than usual this morning, didn't he?"

Vincent nodded. "I'm as surprised as you are, though it happens once in a while. Matt said it was just too hot to sleep in his room."

"You'd think anybody been here as long as he has would pick out a cool location," Quist commented idly.

"I'd say he had a good location. Know where

236

he lives?" Quist shook his head. Vincent went on, "That two-story white frame house at the corner of Yucca, over on the next street. It's a big house and there're some huge cottonwoods towering over it. It shouldn't get too warm there—particularly as Matt's room at the boardinghouse is situated on the rear southwest corner, on the second floor. Takes a while for the sun's heat to penetrate those cottonwoods at that point."

"I reckon," Quist said casually. "Well, I guess I'd better be pushing on. 'Bout time for my morning beer."

He left the office and was in time to see Tillman entering the Red Ball Saloon. Pitt Shattuck was at the hitch rack by this time, just mounting his horse. Turning the pony, Shattuck headed west along Main Street. Quist stood on the sidewalk, looking after him, and saw Shattuck turn north at Apache Street.

"Heading back to the Triangle-S," Quist mused. "Now I wonder why he's going home this early in the day." He pursed his lips, scowling. "Maybe that gives me an idea too," he muttered at last. "Things are commencing to jell into shape. I reckon I'd better get moving."

Five minutes later he was approaching Matt Tillman's boardinghouse. It was a large structure, the sort capable of accommodating a number of boarders. Quist glanced at his watch. It was approaching dinnertime. Doubtless the landlady and her servant would be busy in the kitchen at this hour. Quist slowed step a trifle. "Half the time one boarder doesn't know another, in case somebody sees me," he mused. "At least there's a chance I'd be considered some new roomer. It's worth a try, anyway."

Going boldly up the path to the entrance, he tried the front door and found it unlocked, as he had expected. A moment later he was in the house, the door closed silently behind him. Here he paused a moment, listening. He was in a long hall that stretched to the rear of the building, from whence came the sounds of clattering pans and dishes. On either side were closed doors, and directly ahead a flight of stairs led to the second floor.

Catlike, Quist moved up the stairway and found himself in an upper hall with three closed doors on either side and a window at the end, through which Quist could see the leafy boughs of tall cottonwood trees. Here Quist paused to listen a moment. The sounds he had heard from the lower part of the house came more faintly now. Quist nodded with satisfaction. Now if he could only gain an entrance to Tillman's room without too much trouble . . . There wasn't any doubt in Quist's mind as to its location: Vincent had stated it was the room on the southwest corner of the second floor.

Quist moved silently to the door and tried the

knob. The door was locked. He frowned and produced a bunch of keys from a hip pocket. The first key he inserted failed to work, and the second and the third as well. The fourth stuck in the mechanism, and it was with some difficulty Quist managed to free it. Again he paused, listening.

There came from below a slight noise. Someone was starting up the stairs. Quist froze to immobility, rapidly running over in his mind his various excuses for being found on the second floor. A long sigh escaped his lips as the steps halted, then turned back to the lower hall. It had sounded like a woman's step.

"Whoever it was," Quist told himself, "may return any minute. Lord, I'd better get busy *pronto*."

He studied the key that had been stuck in the lock, noting certain fresh scratches on the metal surface, then chose a long slim key from the bunch in his hand and inserted it in the keyhole. This time the lock turned easily. Quist withdrew the key, thrust the bunch into his pocket, and seized the knob. The door opened instantly under his hand, and Quist entered Tillman's room, softly closing the door at his rear.

His gaze swiftly took in Tillman's sleeping quarters. The floor was covered with faded carpet. To Quist's right a bed stood against the wall. The two outer walls showed open windows;

next to one was a dresser. Quist started to turn, his eyes in search of a closet of some sort, then he stiffened at a slight sound of breathing from his rear. The realization struck him with considerable force there had been someone else in the room before him; whoever it was had hidden behind the door when Quist entered.

Then a cold, vicious voice reached Quist's ears. "Don't move, you bustard! You're due to catch a chunk of lead."

It was Mustang Neale's voice.

SIXTEEN: Cornered

Quist didn't need any orders, he knew he was cornered as he raised his arms in the air and clasped his hands on top of his sombrero. He said quietly, "This is quite a surprise, Mustang."

A harsh laugh behind him; then, "Hah! You know it's me, eh?"

"I'd recognize your melodious voice anywhere," Quist answered.

Neale swore. "Don't give me any of your joshing. It don't go down. And you don't catch me off guard. One bad move from you and you get it, see, pal? I ain't fooling."

"I see—pal," Quist returned. He could almost feel the flat opaque eyes boring into his back. He could hear Neale's heavy breathing and sense the menace of the .45 muzzle bearing on his spine.

Again that cruel laugh of Neale's. "This is better than I expected. This'll teach you a lesson, Quist, not to push Mustang Neale around. A lot of hombres have tried to get you, ain't they? But it takes Mustang to put the quietus on the great detective. I reckon you've pushed your luck too far, Quist. You got snoopy once too often. What you want in Tillman's room, eh?"

"I might ask the same of you," Quist countered. "Go on and ask, pal."

"I'm asking. What brought you here?"

"Figured maybe I could make a deal with you, Quist, but now that's off. A certain double-crosser needs his comeuppance, but I'll get him some other time. This is a heap better. Did you know there's money—good money—offered to me when I get you?"

"I'm not surprised," Quist said calmly. "But about this deal you mentioned—?"

"Nothing doing, pal. You ain't got a chance in the world of making a deal with me now. You're due to take a long trip, Quist. Where you want it, through the back or in the head?"

"You'd better think twice, Neale. How would you explain things if you rubbed me out here? The sheriff would ask questions—"

"I reckon Matt wouldn't be bothered much when I told how I trailed you up here."

Quist laughed suddenly. "Maybe we can split the money."

"Huh! What you giving me, pal? What money?"

"Didn't you come after that roll of bills Tillman always keeps cached in that box under his bed?"

The floor creaked slightly under Neale's weight, and Quist knew his bluff had worked: for just an instant Neale had taken his gaze from Quist's back to glance toward the under part of the bed. And in that moment Quist moved.

Like a flash his hands came down from his head, and he whirled, springing to one side as his right hand darted to holster. The two explosions came almost together. Quist heard the thud as Neale's bullet struck the plastered wall. The impact of Quist's slug slammed Neale back and he went to the floor, his gun clattering from his hand. As he crashed down there came the sound of broken glass. A bottle he had been holding in his left hand was broken to fragments, and its contents, something like very black ink, were soaking into the carpet.

"Damn and blast the luck!" Quist rasped. "Now I am in for it."

Smoke swirled through the room while he stood listening. From below had come a sudden silence, then the noise of excited voices. Quist moved across the floor. There was a bolt on the inner side of the door, and he shot it into place. Then he stooped by Neale's side. The man was already dead, his eyes wide open, staring. A dark stain had seeped into his shirt front.

"If these would-be killers would only shoot and not let themselves be dragged into a conversation," Quist muttered, "they might accomplish something." He reholstered his gun after quickly reloading.

He straightened up and saw an open closet door in the right-hand wall. The voices from below sounded nearer now. Quist rapidly scanned the contents of the closet: shirts waiting to be laundered, a suit of pepper-and-salt clothing with a black stain on one coat lapel and collar. A pair of lace shoes were tumbled in a corner of the closet. A closed satchel stood in another corner.

There were voices in the outer hall by this time, women's voices. Doors were being knocked on. A woman called, "Are you in your room, Sheriff Tillman?"

Then a second woman's voice: "See, Minnie, he doesn't answer. There's no one there." A hand tried the knob. "The door's locked."

"But I tell you I heard shots from up here, Clara."

"Maybe you heard shots, Minnie, but they probably came from outside."

"I don't believe it. I'm going to get into that room, anyway. Oh, fiddlesticks! My keys are downstairs. I'll run down and get them."

"I'll go with you, Minnie. If anything is wrong, I'm not going to be left here alone. Let's wait. The men will be coming for dinner soon."

"Why can't we call Charlie? He's out in the woodshed—"

"Pile of good that would do. Charlie was drunk right after breakfast. Likely asleep now. However do you stand that shiftless brother?"

The voices faded as the two women descended the stairs. Quist swore softly. "If I don't get

244

out of here right soon, there'll be explaining to do—and I'm not yet ready to explain anything."

He glanced from the open window in the rear wall and found himself looking down into a yard fenced along the alleyway. A shed was built against the fence. Directly before him Quist saw a tall cottonwood with one thick bough reaching almost to the house. A moment later he had crawled through the window, grasped the edge of the overhanging roof, and hauled himself to a standing position on the ledge. Now the big cottonwood limb was but a couple of yards distant. Quist gathered his muscular form and leaped through the air. The next instant his arms had wrapped themselves about the thick bough; from there it was a simple matter to work his way toward the trunk until his feet found a resting place on another limb. Here, hidden among leafy green, he was momentarily safe.

Drawing a deep breath, he prepared to descend from the tree, when a woman's voice called loudly for Charlie. A minute later a slouchy, bleary-eyed man shuffled from the shed and into the house. Followed several minutes' silence. In his imagination Quist could visualize Charlie and the women ascending the stairway. Dimly to his ears came excited voices. There sounded a sudden dull thump, followed by a second heavy blow.

"Charlie's breaking down the door," Quist told

himself. "Probably by this time some of that burned-powder smell has seeped under the door. I'd better get out of here."

He glanced down through the leafy branches. The yard was below him, and there was no fence separating it from Yucca Street. No one was, at the moment, in sight on the street, either. "Now's the time," Quist muttered, "while they're concentrating on the door."

He worked his way down the big tree trunk and stepped to the earth. A few more steps carried him to Yucca Street, where there was a worn path but no sidewalk. As he started away he heard faintly the sound of a scream.

"Sounds to me," Quist mused, "as though Charlie had gained entrance."

As he neared the hotel on the corner of Yucca and Main, Quist heard a voice hail him. He glanced toward the veranda and saw Ramon and Chris seated there, then mounted the steps and sank into a chair at their side.

"We looked into the hotel dining room, but as you weren't there, we figured you'd be along right soon," Chris was saying. "Feel like an appetizer?" He motioned to three opened bottles of beer on the floor near Quist's chair.

"We theenk maybe you be thirsty on so hot of a day." Serrano smiled.

"This is the finest idea yet." Quist chuckled. "I've been here quite a while, haven't I?"

The other two looked puzzled. "You have jus' arrive—no?" Serrano asked.

Quist shook his head. "I insist I've been here around three quarters of an hour, anyway—you've been waiting about that long, haven't you?"

"We-ell," Baxter said uncertainly, "if you insist. But what's the idea of the cottonwood leaf stuck on top of your sombrero?"

Quist removed his hat, and a leaf floated to the veranda floor. "I'm glad you mentioned that," he said, and kicked the leaf through the railing to the sidewalk, where it fell into a crack between boards.

"You might say I was 'leafing' in a hurry from someplace," he went on. Baxter and Serrano looked reproachfully at him.

Baxter said, "Something's going on I don't understand."

"There's a heap you don't understand," Quist answered. "For instance, you won't understand why you're going to see a feller hellbent for the sheriff's office before many more minutes pass— No, wait, it'll not be that long."

Quist had just caught the sound of pounding footsteps, and a moment later the man known as Charlie rounded the corner of Main at a gallop. His face was white, his mouth open, as he went tearing diagonally across the street in the direction of Tillman's office.

Baxter and Serrano stared at Quist. Serrano said, "You certainly call' the turn on that one, Greg. What is up?"

"Someday," Quist said, "you hombres will learn you can get answers without asking questions all the time—"

"That feller," Baxter said, "is Charlie Jaeger. Works at the sheriff's boardinghouse—"

Serrano cut in, "Look, is coming down the street the sheriff and Deputy Vincent. And Charlie. *Diantre*! I do not remember when I have seen Matt Tillman move so fast. I deed not theenk it was possible."

Tillman and his two companions were approaching rapidly along Main Street, the sheriff's face clouded up like a thunderstorm. As they were passing the hotel, the sheriff glanced up and spotted Quist on the veranda. He skidded to a fast stop.

Quist asked quietly, "Something gone wrong, Matt? You three look sort of serious."

"Plenty's gone wrong," Tillman snapped. "How long have you been sitting there, Greg?"

Quist shrugged his shoulders. "I don't know exactly. It was hot and it's peaceful to sit here drinking beer." He held up his bottle, which was practically empty, then turned to his companions. "How long would you say we've been here?"

Baxter said, "I don't know. Maybe three quarters of an hour."

"At leas' the half hour." Serrano nodded.

Quist said, "What's wrong, Matt?"

"Charlie, here"—gesturing with one thumb toward the bringer of bad news—"tells me somebody shot Mustang Neale in my room—"

"When was this?" Quist sat straighter in his chair.

The sheriff looked at Charlie. Charlie said, "Must have been within the last ten minutes or so—'cording to Minnie and Clara. They said they heard the shots. I was choppin' wood in the shed—"

"More likely you were sleeping off a drunk, as usual," Tillman said angrily.

"Could be," Charlie said placidly. "I hit my jug right hard after breakfast. Come to think of it, I was sort of dozing—"

Tillman ripped out an oath. "Did you hear any shots, Greg?"

Quist turned to his companions. "Did we hear any shots?"

Serrano and Baxter said they hadn't heard anything. Tillman frowned. "At this distance, I don't reckon it's likely you would. There's plenty noise along Main Street—" He broke off and said to Vincent and Charlie, "C'mon, we're just wasting time here."

Quist said, "I'll be glad to go along with you, Matt."

The sheriff shook his head. "This comes under

my jurisdiction, Greg. I wouldn't want folks to get an idea I had to have Greg Quist help me out when a killing is done. Later, maybe, you can lend a hand. I might need some advice from you. But not now."

"Just as you say, Matt." Quist relaxed back in his chair, looking as though his feelings had been hurt. Tillman and his two companions hurried off down Yucca Street. Quist gazed after them, smiling grimly.

There was a minute's silence on the hotel veranda after the sheriff disappeared. Baxter said softly, "I just happened to remember, Greg, those big cottonwoods around Tillman's boarding-house. Now how do you suppose that leaf got on your sombrero?"

Quist said tersely, "Ask me no questions and I'll tell you no lies. Look here, why don't you and Ramon go get your dinner? I've got some thinking to do. Later, if I can get a couple of ideas straight in my mind, I'll probably have a job for you."

"Aren't you going to eat now?" Baxter asked.

"Circumstances have sort of taken away my appetite," Quist said harshly. "And if that answers any questions you have in mind, just forget that you've heard the answer."

The two stared silently at him a moment, then withdrew to the hotel dining room. Quist sat gazing moodily out toward the street. A few men

250

passed on the sidewalk; one or two nodded to him. Quist scarcely acknowledged the greetings. He was watching a woman on the far side of the street, without actually seeing her, as she tripped along with a sun parasol and a small dog at her heels.

"Dammit," he muttered half to himself, "it simply has to work out like that, unless I've slipped someplace in my figuring. Neale wanted to get even—" He broke off, scowling, then added, "But he wanted more to show he could beat me to the draw, the poor bustard. He must have fallen down a manhole at the time brains were being passed out."

He shifted his booted feet irritably from the veranda railing to floor and back again, scowling at the roadway before him. After a time he saw the sheriff and Deputy Vincent coming along Yucca Street. They crossed over and mounted to the hotel porch. The sheriff appeared in an ugly mood. Leaning against one of the uprights supporting the veranda roof, Tillman said, "You're right sure you didn't hear any shots, Greg?"

"I already answered that one," Quist said quietly. "You heard what Baxter and Serrano said."

"Where are those two?" Tillman demanded.

"In the hotel dining room, in case you want to talk to them some more. You found Neale dead, eh?"

"As a frozen mackerel," Tillman replied.

"It's not surprising shots weren't heard at this distance," Quist pointed out. "Baxter says your boardinghouse is a block from here. There's noise along Main Street. I suppose your windows were closed to keep out the heat—"

Clem Vincent cut in, "Both windows of Matt's room were open."

Tillman nodded. He said heavily, "Whoever killed Neale must have left by a window. Charlie Jaeger swears the door was bolted on the inside and he had to bust it down."

"Maybe there were two killers," Quist said dryly. "Two windows were open, you say."

"If you're trying to be funny—" Tillman commenced.

"I'm sorry, Matt," Quist said, "but that's a possibility, you know. If I was in your place—so long as you refused my help—I'd examine the earth beneath the windows, to see if any boot prints were to be seen."

"I already thought of that," Tillman growled. "There weren't any."

Vincent said, "For that matter, maybe the door wasn't even bolted. It had been torn loose from the door when Charlie busted in."

"I'd say it had been bolted," Quist offered. "Otherwise it wouldn't have been torn loose. How many times had Neale been shot, Matt?"

"Just once—"

"You mentioned 'shots,'" Quist reminded.

"I reckon Neale shook one load outten his barrel. We found where it had hit the wall. B'Gawd, I didn't think there was a man around here could beat Mustang Neale to the shot, unless"—he looked meaningly at Quist—"it was you. From what I hear of your rep with a hawg-laig—"

"You making any accusations, Sheriff?" Quist's voice had suddenly turned frigid.

"You're the only one that has had trouble with Neale," the sheriff said doggedly.

A scornful laugh left Quist's lips, but there was nothing of humor in his topaz eyes. "And so I got Neale to your room and shot it out with him. Can you think of any reason for that? Why I should pick your room for my scrapping?"

Tillman's eyes dropped. He cursed savagely. "I'm damned if I can figure what Neale was doing in my room. Or how he got in—"

"Did you forget, Matt," Vincent interrupted, "that we found a skeleton key in his pocket?"

"That's right. I had forgot," Tillman grunted. "But what did he go there for in the first place? He—it was him or his killer—had spilled my boot polish all over the floor—broke the bottle. Does that make sense to you, Greg?"

Quist glanced down at Tillman's scuffed and dirty boots with their run-over heels. "That you had boot polish?" he asked dryly. "I'd never have believed it, Matt."

The sheriff glanced down at his boots. Color seeped into his cheeks. "Damn it, you know what I mean."

"It still don't make sense," Quist conceded. "Was Neale still breathing when you got there? Couldn't he say anything, tell you—?"

"I already told you he was stone dead," Tillman interrupted wrathfully. "I sent for Doc Woodward as soon as Charlie brought the news. Woodward was there nigh as fast as I was. He stated that Neale had died instantly. Hell, the body wasn't yet cold when we got there."

"Anything stolen from your room?" Quist wanted to know.

"I didn't see anything gone. You're sure you ain't got any ideas on the subject, Greg?"

"Look," Quist said huffily, "I offered to go with you the first time you came by here. Apparently you didn't need any help from me. So that's how it stands."

"Aw, you needn't get sore," Tillman said. "If I spoke hasty, I'm sorry. But if you know anything, Doc Woodward is calling his jury for a coroner's inquest this afternoon. I'd like any help you could give."

"My personal feelings have nothing to do with it," Quist said coldly. "Do you actually think that if I knew something to your advantage I'd withhold information and obstruct justice?"

Tillman gulped. "I reckon you wouldn't, Greg,"

he said, removing his sombrero and mopping at his moist forehead with a soiled bandanna.

Quist asked, "How did Neale stand with the Triangle-S crew? Maybe he'd had some sort of fuss with one of Shattuck's hands."

"Could be," Tillman said dubiously, "but I doubt it. Even if that were true, why should they pick my bedroom to settle their differences?"

"You tell me and I'll tell you," Quist said laconically.

"Wish t'gawd I could," Tillman said heavily. "What in the devil was Neale trying to do there in the first place? That's the problem. I could understand the killer following Neale to my room, but I can't figure a reason in the world why Neale should go there."

"Maybe," Quist said, "he was just aiming to borrow your boot polish—"

Tillman swore. "That ain't funny, Greg." He gave a hitch to his trousers, which were slipping down over one hip, and tucked in his dingy-looking shirt. "Maybe the inquest will produce something I can put a finger on. Will you be there, Greg?"

"Don't know why I should. I might drop in if I have nothing better to do, but can you think of any evidence I might give?"

"Offhand I can't," Tillman said frankly, "aside from the fact you and Neale weren't what's called close friends."

255

"How many close friends did Neale have around here?" Quist asked.

Tillman looked angrily at Quist, then without another word descended the hotel steps. Deputy Vincent winked at Quist and followed his chief. Quist settled back in his chair, chuckling inwardly as his gaze followed Tillman's furious strides along the street.

"Now, you bustard," Quist mused, "you've really got something to bother you." He sobered suddenly. "I have too, I reckon. Wait until Doc Woodward probes the lead slug out of Neale's body and you discover it's a .44 caliber. You'll descend on me like a swarm of mad hornets, and I'll have to do some fast talking."

SEVENTEEN: The Net Closes

Baxter and Serrano emerged from the dining room a short time later. Baxter said, "Anything new regarding Neale's killing?"

"Not so far as I know," Quist replied. "Tillman stopped here on his way back from seeing Neale. He's pretty much in a huff. I think he has an idea I know more than I've said."

"And do you, Greg?" Serrano asked, smiling.

"I'd be a fool to tell everything I know, wouldn't I?"

"I'm think so—yes."

"That's settled then," Quist grunted.

"I could wish a few other things were settled too," Baxter said. "It just doesn't seem like we're making headway, Greg."

"If you knew what I know," Quist said shortly, "you'd think we've made plenty headway. The net's closer to closing than you think, unless I'm shooting far wide of the mark. Things are clearing in my mind a heap—"

"You mean," Serrano asked eagerly, "you know who killed Reed?"

"I'm right sure of it—Now, wait"—as questions poured on him—"I'm not doing any talking yet."

257

He changed the subject. "I saw Pitt Shattuck in town earlier today. He didn't stay long. He was talking to Tillman, then got on his horse and rode off. I didn't see Todd Shattuck or any other of the Triangle-S hands around town, though."

"Does that mean anything in particular, Greg?" Baxter asked.

"To me it does. As I understand it, that Triangle-S crew spends about as much time in Masquerade City as it does working—at least at the ranch."

"Is true." Ramon nodded.

Quist asked, "How good are you two at trailing?"

Ramon and Chris exchanged glances. "We do all right when it's necessary," Chris said. "Reed Haldane saw we were well taught. Whose trail you want us to pick up?"

"The Triangle-S. It shouldn't be hard. No close business of reading hoofprints or anything like that. At the same time, I don't want either of you to get careless."

"What do you want us to do?" Chris asked.

"Get out of town. There's an inquest on Neale coming up this afternoon. I don't want either of you called to swear how long I was with you on this porch at the time Neale was shot."

"But where do we go—the Rafter-RH?" Ramon asked.

Quist shook his head. "Get your horses and

pick up a sackful of chow on your way out of town. You may be gone a couple of days. I want you to ride out and spy on the Triangle-S. I've got a hunch there's a move afoot in that direction right soon. Dammit, there has to be!"

"You are certain?" Ramon said.

"Yes—the way I've got things figured in my mind. Otherwise, I just don't know. But you two get out there. Pick a spot where you won't be seen. If anything unusual takes place, I want to know about it. Is this clear?"

"Could you give us a hint on what to watch for?" Chris asked.

"I'm expecting the Triangle-S to leave in a body for—someplace. I want to know where they go. That's where the trailing comes in. And for cripe's sake don't get caught. I don't want any more on my conscience than I have now. All right, get going."

He shook hands with them and watched them leave for the livery stable. Half an hour later he too got his horse and rode out of town. It had occurred to him it might be rather pleasant to spend the afternoon with Francisca Haldane, and incidentally not be available if called as a witness for the coroner's jury at the Neale inquest.

It was close to ten that night before Quist got back and after returning his horse dropped into the Saddlehorn Saloon. There were a few customers at the bar, and Quist sought a place by himself at the far end. Skimpy Degnan took his order, then set out a bottle and glass on the bar. He said, "You've been out of town."

"I hope that hasn't inconvenienced anybody."

"Sheriff Tillman," Skimpy said.

Quist looked unconcerned. "What about him?"

"He's been in here a dozen times. Left word you was to come to his office when you got back. Looked for you all over, he claimed. I asked if he'd tried the hotel. He had. Been there a dozen times too. Maybe you should leave word when you go away, Mr. Quist." The barkeep's eyes twinkled.

"I'll try to remember hereafter." Quist nodded. "What was all the fuss about?"

"Tillman planned to have you at the inquest, I guess."

"Oh yeah. Neale. What came of that?"

"Just about what you could expect. The jury brought in a verdict of homicide. Killer unknown. Tillman was directed to take immediate steps to apprehend the murderer. Reason for the murder unknown too. That's all, I guess. Then the jury scattered to come here and discuss what really happened to Mustang Neale and why. Nobody came up with any sensible answers. I didn't hear any regrets voiced over his death, either. Neale wasn't popular."

"I don't suppose I'll be popular with Tillman either."

The swinging doors parted and the sheriff stuck his head in and glanced around. Then, seeing Quist at the bar, he came all the way. Quist had just put down his glass—having already spotted Tillman, without turning around, in the bar mirror—when the sheriff barged up to him, saying harshly, without any preliminaries, "Where in hell have you been, Quist?"

Coolly Quist looked over the sheriff. "Since when," he asked quietly, "do I have to account to you for my actions?"

Color flooded the sheriff's face. "B'Gawd! Maybe I can make you. After all, I'm sheriff in this county—"

"This county," Quist said crisply, "does not control the T. N. & A. S. Railroad, and I'm responsible only to the company."

"B'Gawd, we'll see about this—" Tillman started huffily.

Quist suddenly laughed. "Look here, old-timer, what bee got into your bonnet? A few more words and we'd be at each other's throats. This is no way for us to act."

The sheriff calmed down. "Maybe it ain't at that," he grumbled. "Just the same, I'd like an explanation why you wasn't at the inquest today."

"What inquest?" Quist frowned.

"Blast your eyes! Have you forgot? The inquest Doc Woodward held on Mustang Neale."

"Sure enough." Quist looked surprised. "Why should I come to the inquest? I didn't know you wanted me."

"I asked you today at the hotel," Tillman reminded, "if you'd be there. You said if you had nothing better to do, maybe you would."

"I had something better to do." Then to check the rise of color in Tillman's face, Quist continued, "What did you expect I could tell the coroner's jury, Matt?"

"That's what we wanted to find out. I was all for having Doc subpoena you, but he didn't think it necessary after I told him where you were when the shots were fired."

"Doc was smart. I wouldn't have been here for his subpoena if he had issued one—"

"But that was before," Tillman said.

"Before what?"

"Before Doc had probed the slug out of Neale's carcass. That made things different."

"How different?"

Tillman said dramatically, "It was a .44-caliber bullet."

"That's surprising," Quist said easily. "You don't find too many people toting .44's. I've often wondered why—"

"That's just the point I'm making"—triumphantly—"because you carry a .44 six-shooter."

262

Quist stared at the sheriff. "You don't mean I'm a suspect?"

"Why not?" Tillman said doggedly. "You use a .44. You're the only man that's had trouble with Neale lately—"

Quist's scornful laugh cut short the words. "Now use your head, Matt. Sure I carry a .44. That's no sign I killed Neale. There are other guns for that caliber around, if you'll only look. Now stop a minute and think. Where did I get my last .44 ca'tridges? From Sheriff Matt Tillman. He owns a .44 rifle. Just what trouble have *you* had with Neale lately, Sheriff? Remember something else, it was *your* room he was shot in—not my room."

"Now you're talking foolish, Greg," Tillman protested. "It was a six-shooter that killed Neale—"

"Can you prove it by the slug?" Quist demanded swiftly.

Tillman hesitated. "No, b'Gawd," he burst out angrily, "you know damn well I can't. That size slug can be used in either gun—"

"Now, that's just the point *I'm* making." Quist smiled coldly. "What dealings have you had with Neale, Tillman? I talked to him one day, and he called you a damn double-crosser. Maybe it might be a good idea to run down that angle and see where it brings us—"

"When was this?" The sheriff looked startled.

"I'll tell that—under oath—any time you get any more of your subpoena ideas in mind, Matt. Now, it's up to you. Where do we go from here?"

"You're talking damn foolishness, Quist," Tillman grumbled. "Anybody knows I wouldn't kill Neale—"

"I don't. You could have done it. For what reason, I don't know for sure—yet. But if you want to get down to brass tacks on this business, I'll make it my business to find out. I'd welcome the chance. Right now I've got my hands full with other matters, but if you think you can get tough with me, Tillman, you've got another think coming. You won't know what tough means until I get through with you."

"Now, now, Greg—" Tillman commenced placatingly. He seemed somewhat taken aback and glanced uneasily around the barroom. Two or three of the other customers had caught snatches of the heated conversation and were looking inquiringly at Quist and the sheriff.

"Don't 'now, now' me," Quist snarled. "Your whole trouble is that you're too fat and lazy for your job. Rather than get out and dig like a good law officer, you figured it was easy to accuse me just because I use a .44 six-shooter. I'm getting pretty damn sick of your easygoing, slack methods."

Tillman swallowed hard. "Now don't get excited," he protested. "I ain't meaning to stir up trouble. But look at things from my standpoint. You use the right caliber gun for the job that finished Neale, and you'd had trouble with him—"

"Oh lord," Quist said wearily, "don't start repeating all that again. A good law officer gets more proof than that. Regardless what gun I shoot or who I had trouble with, you know pretty closely what time Neale was killed. Also, you heard Baxter and Serrano state how long I'd been with them on that hotel porch. If that doesn't alibi me, what does?"

"That's something else," the sheriff burst out. "Where are them two *hombres*? Looked all over town for 'em—wanted them at the inquest. Where did they go?"

"I couldn't say exactly where they are at present," Quist said shortly. "But if you need 'em for my alibi, I'll dig 'em up when necessary. They told you I'd been with them—"

"They're friends of yours," Tillman cut in. "They'd swear to anything for you. I'm not sure their alibi is acceptable—"

"It should be as acceptable as Pitt Shattuck's was for his brother Todd when Haldane was killed. I never heard you object to that, Tillman. Now you tell me where one alibi is any different than the other."

"You hinting that I overlooked something where the Shattucks are concerned?" Tillman looked uneasy.

"I'll tell you better," Quist snapped, "when I've dug into the business deeper. And don't think I'm not digging, Sheriff."

"I don't like your tone, Quist," Tillman said bellicosely. "I've got a good notion to place you under arrest—"

Quist threw back his head and uttered a loud scornful laugh. "Don't talk like a damn fool. You know you haven't any such notion. That's sheer bluff—and your day of bluffing this town is just about past. Go ahead, try to arrest me. You'd have the whole T. N. & A. S. law department climbing your frame. On second thought, though, I believe I'd welcome the chance to resist arrest. And what do you think of that, Tillman? Go ahead. Try to arrest me."

Tillman was shaking with anger, but something cautioned him not to press Quist too far. He got his feelings under control, saying weakly, "You can't deny the fact of that .44 bullet—"

"How do you know it's a .44? Might be a .45."

Tillman shook his head, on firm ground now, he felt. "Jesis! Don't you think I know a .44 when I see one, Quist?"

Quist considered, then said more quietly and with apparent concern, "Ye-es, Matt, I reckon you do. A man in your position has to know his ca'tridges, guns, and so on. I won't attempt to deny that. Maybe you've scored a point— from your standpoint. Just where did the slug hit Neale? Could Doc Woodward determine that with any accuracy? I mean, the course the slug took, where it entered—that sort of thing."

Overconfidence at Quist's apparent surrender led Tillman into a trap. "The slug scored a bull's-eye through Neale's heart, struck a back rib, and glanced off to plow into the spine, according to Doc Woodward. Death was instantaneous."

Quist whistled softly. "Doc's word is good with me. Cripes! That slug really traveled. It must have got battered a little, striking all that bone."

"A little?" Tillman scoffed. "It got battered plenty."

"In that case"—Quist struck swiftly—"you're going to have a tough time proving it was a .44 bullet. A .45 weighs about two hundred fifty grams against the .44's two hundred. Now a gram is a very tiny unit of weight. Battering often knocks off small bits of lead from a slug. It wouldn't take the loss of many such bits to reduce a .45 to the weight of a .44. So now maybe you've got something else to prove, Tillman."

"Now look here"—Tillman was suddenly furious—"that bullet wasn't battered that bad—"

"Too late." Quist smiled contemptuously. He waved a hand around the bar. "Quite a few men have heard you say that slug was battered plenty. That was your word. *Plenty.* All right, Sheriff, take this case into court and me with it, and see how much chance you have of proving me guilty.

I'll just make a fool of you—an even bigger fool than you are now."

And without giving the fuming Tillman an opportunity to reply, Quist brushed past him, nodded good night to Skimpy Degnan, and stepped out to the street, hearing behind him, as he departed, a number of snickers at the sheriff's expense.

As he stepped to the sidewalk outside the Saddlehorn, Quist glanced across Austin Street and saw Dr. Woodward just emerging from the sheriff's office, where a lighted oil lamp shone its light through the window. Quist hailed him, and the doctor crossed the street, saying, "So you're back. Your absence had Matt Tillman bothered crazy."

"So I understand." Quist laughed. "I was just talking to him in the bar."

"I was wondering where he was," Woodward said.

"Were you looking for him?"

Woodward nodded. "I wanted to turn over to him, for evidence if needed, the bullet that killed Mustang. Also my written report of the inquest. You know, Greg, I expected you'd be present."

"Didn't know of any evidence I'd give your jury."

The doctor hesitated. "Did Matt mention it was a .44 slug that killed Neale?" Quist said he had. Woodward continued, "Matt was all for having you called to testify as to anything you might know. Then when he tried to find you, you weren't around town—"

"Look here, Doc," Quist interrupted, "you don't think I had anything to do with that killing, do you?"

"Don't talk foolishness, Greg." Woodward laughed. "Still, if you had been at the inquest you might have given us the benefit of your experience, might have given us some ideas. That was my only thought in the matter. As a matter of fact, it was Clem Vincent that pointed out to Tillman that you weren't the only man to use a .44, and he reminded the sheriff that there was a .44 rifle in the sheriff's office. You know"—the doctor frowned—"while I don't say Tillman had anything to do with the shooting, I do say it was mighty queer the killing was done in his room. Of course Tillman was in his office at the time I figured Neale died, so there you are."

"And I reckon Matt told you of the conversation he had with Baxter, Serrano, and me right after he was called to go to his boardinghouse?" The doctor said he knew of Quist's alibi, so that put him in the clear. Quist went on, "Right now Matt isn't even sure it was a .44 slug. No, don't ask me to explain. Go on in the bar and talk to him. I'm going to get to bed."

Woodward said good night and entered the Saddlehorn. Quist started toward his hotel.

"Lord," he mused wearily, "why did I ever take this sort of job for my life's work? If I had any sense I'd marry a nice girl like Francisca—if she'd have me—and settle down to raise beef. There sure isn't much profit in being shot at and shooting crooks. But, by Jehovah! There is a lot of satisfaction in trapping such bustards. Things are coming to a head, and if I don't close the trap right soon, I'll be almighty surprised."

EIGHTEEN: Saddle Pounders

The following day passed uneventfully. By the time evening came, Quist was as irritable as a she-wolf in fly time. He ordered a big dinner, then found he had little appetite for it. His mind was too crammed with thoughts of the various things that had happened—and that were due to happen if all his deductions dovetailed—for concentration on food. Mostly he was bothered by thoughts of Chris and Ramon. By this time he thought he'd surely have heard from them. Suppose they had been captured by the Triangle-S and were being held—or even worse. If anything happened to that pair, he'd have a difficult time facing Francisca, regardless of how his other plans worked out.

Leaving his dinner practically untouched, Quist donned his sombrero, went out, and restlessly walked about town. He dropped into various bars, but nothing held his interest long. At nine o'clock he stopped at the sheriff's office and found Clem Vincent there, smoking idly. From Clem he learned that Matt Tillman had already left for his boardinghouse and bed.

"I think I'll follow Matt's example." Quist

yawned. "Been pretty much on the go. Doesn't look as though there'd be any excitement around town tonight."

"Things are pretty quiet," Vincent agreed. "I picked up a drunk earlier in the evening and saw that he got home safe. That's the nearest to any excitement I've had. Now if any of the Triangle-S crowd had been in town things might be different. Don't know what's happened to that crew the past couple of days. They must have gone on the wagon."

"That I find hard to believe." Quist laughed. "Well, I'm going to my room and catch some shut-eye. See you *mañana*, Clem."

The deputy said good night and Quist went to his room, undressed, and went to bed. Instantly he was sound asleep.

It was going on to eleven o'clock when there came a soft rap at his door. Quist was instantly awake and at the door, his gun in hand. "Who is it?" he called.

"Chris—Chris Baxter."

Quist relaxed and unlocked the door. Baxter entered. There were weary lines about his eyes. His clothing was dust-covered. But he carried news. All this Quist saw as he lighted the oil lamp on his dresser, then relocked the door. "Lord, am I glad to see you back. Is Ramon all right?"

"Was when I left him."

"Where'd you leave him?" Quist snapped.

"Talk, Chris." Even while he spoke Quist was getting into his clothing and rolling a cigarette.

Baxter replied, "He's keeping a watch at the edge of the Masquerades. There's a pretty heavy clump of mesquite trees at one point—"

"Never mind the trees. I'm not interested. Or maybe I am. Go on, I'll not interrupt again."

Chris continued, "Ramon and I went out to the Triangle-S to spy, as you told us. Nothing happened until early this morning. Then we saw the Triangle-S crew pull away and head west. We were hidden some distance off, flat on our bellies, near the crest of a low hill. Both Pitt and Todd Shattuck were with the crew. We couldn't follow too close behind, you understand, so we waited a while before lighting out after them. They weren't riding too hard, luckily, so we could keep 'em in sight."

Baxter paused to marshal his thoughts and continued, "Finally we got into the foothills of the Masquerades. After that Ramon and I made better time—it wasn't so easy for them to spot us. Then, when we were right well into the lower slopes of the mountains, we topped a rise of land, taking it easy as we'd done right along, when we struck the high points. You can imagine how surprised we were to see that the men we'd been following had plumb disappeared."

"Maybe you were surprised," Quist put in. "I thought something like that might happen."

"We didn't," Baxter said. "It sure had us puzzled. There wasn't a sign of a pass through the mountains as far as we could see. Then Ramon spotted this thick stand of mesquite trees—it was a regular forest of mesquite trees—"

"Where mesquite grows extra tall and thick, there must be water."

"That's the way this was. There's all kinds of mesquite over in that country, but this one wide clump grew higher than the rest. And, like you suggest, Greg, there was water. Ramon and I pushed on, right cautious, too, and reached the tall mesquite. Here we saw prints. We followed the sign through the trees and noticed the earth was sort of damp. Eventually the dampness changed to a narrow stream—Cripes! You could jump across it easy. We followed up the stream and found where it emerged from a pass in the rock between high bluffs. It goes in at a sharp angle and narrows considerably higher up, which was the reason we hadn't spotted it at first. Unless a person just set out to look for something of the sort, he'd never discover or dream there was a pass there. If you could call it a pass. It's just about wide enough to let a wagon through—"

"All right, where did it lead to?" Quist asked impatiently.

"I don't know. We decided one of us should come back and bring you the information. We tossed a coin for it. Ramon stayed. He'll wait

274

there to see if anything happens and keep an eye on activities. Could be that pass cuts clear through the Masquerades. But where do you suppose all those Triangle-S riders were headed—and why?"

"Freight thieves," Quist said shortly. "Heading to pick up the stuff they stole and deliver it to Rawnston."

Baxter said excitedly, "Do you know that for a fact?"

Quist shook his head. "I'm guessing at it, staking my reputation that I'm right. The thieves have to have someplace to cache the goods until they get orders to deliver. The two most likely towns to buy such goods are Masquerade City and Rawnston, because they're the largest towns around here. It's known I'm here, so Rawnston is the likeliest place." He was slipping into his gun harness now. "All right, we've got to move fast." He paused. "How many Triangle-S riders were there?"

"We counted twenty-one."

Quist groaned. "Where in the devil can I raise a gang of riders to oppose 'em? We haven't time to canvass the ranches around here. There's you and me. Ramon, when we catch up to him. How many hands will the Rafter-RH furnish? Got any idea? Men with guts. It's going to be rough."

Baxter said promptly, "Ten." His eyes twinkled.

"How do you know?" Quist snapped.

"I stopped there on my way back."

Quist stared at him. "You took time to drop off and see Francisca—?" he began slowly. "Chris, at a time like this—"

Baxter's cheeks reddened. "I didn't even see Francisca. I didn't know but what you might need riders. The ranch was practically on my way back. Thought it might save time. I didn't mention to Brose Tucker or the others what was up, because I didn't know. I just asked how many would be ready to side us if you needed riders. They'll be ready and waiting when we get there, Greg—"

"I'm sorry, Chris. I'm such a bustard at times. You've done wonderfully. Let's get going." They left the room. The dozing clerk in the hotel office looked somewhat surprised as they passed. On the street Quist said, "Get my horse saddled. Maybe you'd better get another mount for yourself, too, and have the liveryman saddle Clem Vincent's horse—"

"The deputy going?" Baxter asked in surprise.

"Yeah—though he doesn't know it yet. I figure him for a square shooter."

The two men parted. Main Street was almost dark. A light shone here and there. Baxter cut across the street to the Lone Star Livery. Quist crossed diagonally farther on and entered the sheriff's office. Vincent looked up from the seat at his desk. "Thought you were going to bed. I was just about to turn in myself."

"I was in bed. Changed my mind. Or had it changed for me. I want to borrow that .44 Winchester"—gesturing toward the gun in the corner—"for a while—"

"Sure, Greg. What's up?"

"And another rifle and you with it."

Vincent's jaw dropped. "You on the trail of something?"

"Freight thieves. In your county. Can I depend on you?"

"Hell's bells, yes!" The deputy was already out of his chair, shrugging his shoulders into his coat. "But I can't leave the office without telling Matt—"

"Forget him. This is damn important, and we've got to work fast. If we take time to rouse him—Oh, cripes! You know how long it would take him. Lock up your office and come on. I'm having your pony saddled at the livery."

Vincent grinned. "Right sure of me, weren't you?"

Quist nodded. "I've been sizing you up for several days. C'mon. I'll give you the story as we go along."

Five minutes later the three men were pounding out of town, riding in the direction of the Rafter-RH as fast as they could travel.

In something under two hours the three guided their weary, foam-flecked mounts into the

Rafter-RH. Lights shone from the bunkhouse. There was also a light in the ranch house. A group of saddled ponies were tethered near one corral. A few clouds drifted overhead, and the moon now and then shone down, to filter through the branches of the big oaks clustered about the buildings.

Brose Tucker and the other cowhands greeted Quist and his companions when they swept in. There were but few preliminary greetings. "We're ready for whatever you've got in mind," Tucker said. "Chris couldn't tell us much, but any man that's working to find Reed's killer has our backing. You can count on every man of us, Quist. There'll be ten backing you up. Only Cookie will stay here. I figured some man should stay 'count of Francisca."

Quist said tersely, "Thanks. I'm not sure what I'm letting you in for. I'm after freight thieves, and I'm right sure now that means the Triangle-S gang." He raised one hand to silence the exclamations of surprise. "It's not going to be easy. We'll be outnumbered. They'll have at least twenty-one men, I think. By the time we pick up Ramon we'll be only fourteen. The odds are against us, unless we can take 'em by surprise— that means getting to them by sunup, if possible. We'll be riding like hell—"

"Likely you three better get fresh mounts," Tucker put in. He spoke to a couple of the

278

cowhands, and they rushed to saddle fresh horses.

"That was a good idea." Quist nodded. "We sure pounded hell out of our saddles to get here. Now, catching freight thieves isn't your game, maybe, so if anybody wants to back out, now's the time to say the word." He waited. No one spoke. "All right, now I'll tell you that I believe Haldane's murder is tied in with this freight-thieving business, so when you ride with me, you'll also be helping Haldane. Let's get started."

"Francisca wanted to see you and Chris before you left," Tucker said. "She's sort of bothered as to what's up."

Quist and Chris exchanged quick glances. Quist hesitated. Then he said gruffly, "Chris, you dash up to the house and see her. Tell Francisca I'll talk to her on the way back." He yanked out his watch and looked at it in the light from the moon. "I'm giving you just two minutes. Hurry!"

Baxter sprinted toward the ranch house. Brose Tucker said, "After that scary talk you give us about fighting against odds, you sound like you're certain you'll be back."

Quist said harshly, "I'm not, and I'm not sure Chris will be back either, but there's no use letting Francisca know that. If it wasn't for Ramon waiting for us, and if I didn't need Chris to lead the way, once we're started, I'd leave Chris behind with Cookie. C'mon, let's get into saddles. And any man that owns a rifle had best bring it along too."

Quist strode over to the waiting horses and sized up the fresh mount that had been given him. It was a big rangy black that looked as though it could cover ground. He made a slight adjustment of stirrup leathers and climbed up. Chris came running back from the house and mounted at Quist's side. Quist looked at him a moment. "You got stars in your eyes, Chris," at the same time thinking, And what will happen when she next sees Ramon?

Chris grinned happily. "That ranch house just floats in stardust, Greg, seems like. Francisca sent—she sent you her love and said to hurry back."

"It's a different kind of love then," Quist grunted. He twisted in the saddle. "Your men ready, Brose?"

"We're waitin' for you to give the word," Tucker said.

"You've got it," Quist said, and put spurs to the rangy black horse. The small cavalcade swept into instant motion, the ponies kicking up dust as they got under way, those in the rear being reined wide to avoid the dust of the leaders. Quist, with Chris Baxter riding close to his side, led the way.

Quist called to Baxter through the rush of wind. "It's up to you, Chris, to lead us to that stand of mesquite the shortest route possible. Every minute counts."

"I'll take you straight there," Chris called back, indicating a northwesterly direction.

The moon was sailing directly overhead now, picking out from time to time sharply highlighted peaks of the Masquerade Mountains that seemed now to hover almost above them, though Quist knew it would be some time before they reached the foothills.

For an hour and a half the men pushed steadily on, mesquite, grass, and cactus forming a smoothly flowing panorama on either side. The moon swung in a great arc across the heavens; now and then passing clouds obscured the light, and Quist hoped fervently that none of the horses would step into a gopher hole in the darkness and throw its rider or break a leg. Wind whipped into faces as the riders plunged on through the night.

Finally Quist called a halt to breathe the horses. Men slipped down from saddles and fumbled for papers and tobacco. Quist passed the word around, "Stay close to the ground and shield the flame when any of you strike matches. For all we know, those bustards may have a guard on watch. Chris says it's not much farther from here. If there was a guard out, Ramon wouldn't have any way of warning us."

Quist removed his saddle, rubbed the big

281

black's back with the saddle blanket, and a few moments later was retightening his cinch. Some of the other men followed his example. Cigarettes were snuffed out and the riders once more mounted and kicked spurs into their ponies' ribs. Another hour's travel took them into rising ground, and before they realized it they were moving through the foothills. Now the mountains seemed to rise sheer above them. Time passed swiftly. By this time the moon had passed to the far side of the Masquerades, and only a faint aura of light showed beyond the peaks. A gradual darkness settled over the range, and directly overhead the stars looked brighter now, though there was a faint tinge of light showing along the eastern horizon.

"Blast it," Quist muttered to himself. "Dawn's going to be on us before we know it. One good thing, those high mountain peaks will hold back the light from what's beyond the pass Chris mentioned for quite a spell after the country on this side of the peaks will be full-lighted." He raised his voice and spoke through the wind whipping into his face. "How much farther, Chris?"

"Can't be many more miles," Chris returned. "We're drawing near . . ." Whatever else he might have said was lost in the steadily drumming sound of ponies' hoofs.

"We've got to do better than this," Quist

growled. He spoke a few words to Chris, then called orders back to Brose Tucker. The riders increased speed. The eastern horizon was far lighter now.

NINETEEN: Battle!

Quist wasn't sure how much longer they continued on. Maybe it was only fifteen minutes; to Quist it seemed forever. Abruptly Chris voiced an exclamation. Quist squinted through the gloom and glimpsed a tiny pin point of light. It was extinguished, and immediately a second match showed a momentary flash. Chris said, "There's Ramon! That's the signal we agreed on. Likely he could hear us coming."

Five minutes later the riders had pulled to a halt in a thick grove of mesquite trees, and questions and answers were flying between Quist and Ramon after Quist's first relieved handshake. "What's the setup, Ramon?" Quist asked tersely.

"Once through these trees," Ramon said, "we enter the pass. Ver-ee narrow at first, but then it widen'. Steep canyon wall on each side, an' the small stream floweeng through, of only about the inch deep. Ver-ee shallow." Quist asked how far Ramon had penetrated the canyon. Ramon laughed softly. "Time was heavy on the hand last night, so I'm go all the way on foot. Is only about a mile, then you see the big valley surround by tree' on all side."

"Good lord," Quist said. "You went all the way in? Quick, what did you see? How many men? Give it to me, Ramon."

"Twenty-two man, includeeng the cook. We are fourteen. I think that not so bad of odds. One man I theenk they keep there all the time, to look after the horses—have many horses and wagons. A good water hole where rises the stream that flow' through the pass. Shelters have been built, but what is beneath I do not know, as they are covered with tarpaulin."

"Stolen freight goods," Quist said grimly.

"I entered on foot and worked my way through the tree'. No, they did not set out the guard. They feel they are very safe, I'm theenk. We shall take them by surprise—no?"

"Yes," Quist said sternly. "I aim to show that Triangle-S crowd that the time has come when thieves masquerading as honest men are due to be unmasked—and with resultant penalties. Lead the way, Ramon, we'll be right with you."

"One minute, until I get my *caballo*."

The horse was tethered to a mesquite limb a few yards away. Five minutes later the riders had passed through the trees and were entering the narrow slash in the rock. For the first hundred yards there was but little space for more than two horses to travel abreast. On either side precipitous cliffs rose straight toward the sky, seen but dimly overhead at present as a thin strip of deep gray, only a shade lighter than the blackness of the rock on either side.

Footing for the horses was uncertain, and hoofs slipped from wet rocks in the shallow stream, the noise resounding loudly from the walls on either side. "Dammit! Those bustards will hear us before we get there," Quist swore.

But a short distance on the way widened. There was firm earth on either side of the stream, and the riders were enabled to make better time with less noise while the canyon pass twisted and curved every fifty yards or so. Quite suddenly the pass widened and the men found them-selves in another thick growth of mesquite. It was lighter by this time and, gazing through the leafy branches, Quist could see the saucer-shaped valley surrounded by trees as Ramon had described it. A fire was burning at one side not far from some corrals, and Quist saw the silhouetted figure of a man moving near the fire from time to time. "Probably the cook," he speculated. It looked as though the other men were still asleep. Quist considered the situation a minute, then gave orders:

"We'll split into two groups. Chris, you go with Brose Tucker and half his men. Work your way through the trees as quietly as possible, until you're on the slope above the campfire. Ramon and the rest of the men will come with me. Chris, you and Brose hold your fire until we've opened the attack. Then while the Triangle-S is occupied with us, you hit 'em on the flank. I'm hoping in the confusion they'll not realize we're outnumbered. All clear? All right, get going. I'll give you fellows fifteen minutes to reach your places."

Tucker, Chris, and the others moved off. Quist settled down to wait with his men. By this time gray light had flooded the valley, and Quist could see men stirring from their blankets on the ground. Two or three of them headed for the water hole a hundred feet from the campfire. Here and there a match flamed as cigarettes were lighted. Far up the slope to Quist's ears came the voice of one of the men telling the cook to "hurry up with that coffee." The minutes ticked away in silence. Finally Quist spoke to his little force. "Let's go!"

They worked the horses carefully through the trees until they'd reached the grassy clearing at the edge of the valley. Here Quist put spurs to the big black and reached to the rifle in his saddle boot. The horses charged down the slope toward the campfire. Quist heard a wild yell and saw startled faces turned in his direction. A moment later there were more yells and guns commenced to crack.

Quist lifted the rifle to his shoulder. He was riding too fast for accurate shooting, but he saw one man stagger back and then rise again, jets of fire spurting from his hand. Two or three of the Triangle-S men seized saddles and started for the corral, shooting as they moved. There were more wild yells and orders from Pitt Shattuck. Quist had spotted both the Shattucks by this time. The Triangle-S swung around and started concentrating their fire on Quist and his men. Then at the opportune moment Tucker, Chris, and the other Rafter-RH punchers cut loose with their guns and came plunging from the trees.

Wild yells of dismay lifted from the Triangle-S hands as they swung about to face this new threat. Guns were sounding like mad by this time. Quist emptied his rifle and shoved it back into the boot as he reached for his .44. Two of the Triangle-S punchers had mounted by this time and came charging toward Quist and his men.

Powdersmoke drifted across the valley. Dust rose in thick clouds. Here and there a man was seen rolling on the earth. Rifles and six-shooters cracked and thundered as the warring factions closed. A man leaped for Quist's bridle rein, trying to pull him down. The .44 exploded in Quist's hand and the man vanished from view in the rising dust. A horse screamed and went down, hoofs thrashing. Its rider, loosening feet from stirrups, rolled catlike to his feet and came up with his gun blazing.

The firing rose to a sharp crescendo, then suddenly slackened. Yells of surrender were heard from Triangle-S throats here and there. In no time at all the din had ceased as suddenly as it started. Half of the Triangle-S men had thrown away their guns and were standing with upraised arms, sullenly awaiting capture. The rest of the Triangle-S were sprawled on the earth, silent, in most cases, though an occasional groan was heard.

The Rafter-RH men gathered about Quist as soon as captives were bound. Brose Tucker came up to Quist. "We got both the Shattucks. No, neither wounded. They were trying to sneak off through the trees."

"How about our men—any bad hurt?" Quist asked.

"We were pretty lucky. The surprise of our attack saved lives for us. Hub caught a broken arm. Slim Brooks took a slug through the fleshy part of his right thigh. There's some odd scratches. That's all." Tucker's voice turned grim. "Half the Triangle-S men are dead."

Chris Baxter approached Quist, his face sweaty and powder-grimed. Quist asked a question. "Yeah, I'm all right," Chris replied. "Ramon got hit. He's over near the fire. Hey, don't get excited. It's only a scratch." Quist looked relieved but nevertheless started for the fire. On his way he stopped at the various shelters that had been erected and checked into the tarpaulin-covered contents beneath. He smiled as he noted the objects he looked at were goods from the wrecked freight. Then he went on to the campfire.

Ramon was seated on a log, talking to an old grizzled Mexican. He greeted Quist with a smile and in answer to Quist's query laughed and said, "A bullet cut through my shirt. I'm think it took some flesh from the thick part of the shoulder. It is nozzing." He gestured toward the old Mexican. "You remembair I speak of a Mexican who had disappear? Is here. Diego Santandar." Quist nodded to the Mexican, who bowed gravely. Ramon went on, "He was kidnap' by Pitt Shattuck, who needs one who can cook. Diego went with Pitt to the Triangle-S for the job, but they refuse' to let him send back word to his relation'. Nor do they let him leave. The regular cook is have an accident and cannot ride. A cook is need' for the outfit in theese valley. So by force they make Diego come here. Is unlucky for him the day he see Shattuck in the saloon and tell how he can cook."

"That's something explained, anyway. I'd hate to think what would have happened to Santandar when Shattuck was through with him. Ramon, strip off your shirt and let's have a look at that wound." Ramon protested it was nothing, but Quist insisted. Reluctantly Ramon removed his shirt, then the undershirt. Quist found a shallow wound where a bullet had plowed across the fleshy part of the shoulder. There was water nearby and he cleansed the spot and bandaged it with bandannas as well as possible. "There, Ramon Serrano is as good as new." Quist smiled.

Diego Santandar had been studying Ramon, a thoughtful frown on his face. Chris came striding up. "Brose has the two Shattucks over there, but they refuse to talk. They act like they still think they could get out of this. How's the shoulder, Ramon?"

Ramon said, "All right."

Santandar said suddenly, "I once knew a family named Serrano." He spoke in Spanish. No one paid much attention to him.

Chris was still talking. He said to Quist, "Now if you can only find Reed Haldane's killer, the score will be wiped clean." Santandar asked a question. Chris said, "Yes, I said Haldane. What about it?"

"I also once knew a person of that name," Santandar said.

"That's fine," Chris rushed on. "Probably not the same one—"

"Wait a minute, Chris," Quist interrupted. He turned to Santandar, speaking rapidly in Spanish. "And what of this Haldane you knew?"

"It was a woman of Spanish blood, named Magdalena Ruiz Haldane. The husband— Haldane—I never saw—"

"Judas priest on a tomcat," Quist exploded. "That was the name of Reed Haldane's wife."

Then to Ramon and Chris: "You know the story of Francisca's mother?"

"Francisca told us not so long ago." Chris nodded. "Reed never knew she told us."

Quist turned back to Santandar. "Where did you know the Señora Haldane? And when and how?"

Santandar replied slowly, "It is now over twenty years past. At that time I had a wife and a small farm. She arrived at our door one night, sick and weary. We took her in when she told us she was riding to Mexico City—a very long way—from a *rancho* near a town named Rosario Wells—also many miles distant. For some days she was ill and we tended her until she was strong. Then my wife and I, we catch a smallpox disease, and this Magdalena Haldane stay and nurse us to health. No, she does not contract the smallpox, but she say she has found peace with us and requests to stay. It was not long before we see the reason for her remaining. A little she told us of her life, of some trouble with her husband named Reed—"

"Jeepers!" Chris burst out. "Francisca's mother. What became of her, Santandar?"—phrasing the last words in Spanish.

"She is dead," Santandar replied. "Seven months after she came to us she gave birth to a small *niño*—a baby boy—but she is not strong and she die in the birth-giving. It was her wish the boy be named Ramon—"

"Just like mine," Serrano said dumbly. He

looked uncertainly at the others—uncertain of the thoughts coursing his mind.

"Ramon Haldane he was to be called," Santandar went on. "It was her wish and we had him christened as such. For two years we bring this Ramon up as our own, then my wife died and I am forced to go away for a time. I left Ramon with a family named Serrano, who promise to take the best care of him. By the time I return from my trip, the Serrano family have moved someplace—I never learn where." He directed his next words to Ramon. "You are Ramon Haldane. I know of a certainty. There remain still familiar lines of the face. What is more, I noted when you removed your shirt, you have a white triangular scar over your left ribs. Is it not true?"

Ramon looked very white. "It is true. I do not know how I came by it—"

"I, Diego Santandar, can inform you of that. When you were one year old, toddling about with a sharp piece of steel in your hand, with which you played, you experienced a sudden fall and the steel tore a deep gash over the ribs—"

"*Socorro*! What next will I hear?" Ramon exclaimed. "As to the Serrano family, I thought I was related to them in some way. I grew up with their name. They never told me different. They worked me ragged and beat me. One day I ran away. In time I came to Masquerade City. Reed Haldane picked me up—"

"Good lord!" Quist burst out. "Ramon! You're Francisca's brother! Do you realize that?" There were similar exclamations from Baxter. Ramon looked stunned at the news. He tried to speak, but words failed him. Quist shook his head in amazement, thinking, *No wonder Francisca thought she was in love with him, felt such an attraction for him. The call of the blood was there all the time, working on both Ramon and the girl, even when she felt drawn to Chris.* Quist continued, "Things are clearing up fast. We know now what became of Haldane's wife—Francisca's and Ramon's mother. This is—"

"Greg!" Chris cut in. "Why can't Ramon and I cut away from here now? We've got to tell Francisca—"

"Yes, we must both ride to her, Greg." Ramon had finally found his voice. "There is so much to tell her of us and our mother."

"The three of us will ride," Quist said. "Bring up our horses while I go talk to Brose." He turned to Santandar. Chris and Ramon were pumping the old Mexican's hand. Quist, too, took his hand, saying, "We owe more than can be put into words to you, Señor Santandar." Then he strode off toward Tucker and his men, who were standing guard over the captive Triangle-S men.

Pitt and Todd Shattuck eyed Quist sullenly as he came up. Quist said, "Your game's finished, Pitt. They tell me you won't talk. Bear in mind,

295

the faster you own up, the easier I'm going to make it for you."

"Aw, don't pay no attention to the bustard, Pitt," Todd snarled. "If our hands wa'n't bound behind us, he'd not shoot off his mouth—"

Quist looked narrowly at Todd. "I'll untie you if you think you can back up those words, *hombre*." Todd dropped his eyes and didn't reply. Quist went on, "Pitt, you're only making it harder on yourself by keeping your mouth shut. Take my advice and talk. No one's going to be able to save your skin at this late date. I can make it easier on you, maybe. Now use your head. Never mind your brother. You'd better think of saving your own skin."

"I'll talk," Pitt said suddenly. "What you want to know?"

For several minutes questions and answers flowed between the two men, while the Rafter-RH men listened in shocked astonishment. "All right," Quist said finally, "you and Todd are coming to town with me. . . . Brose, bring up their horses, will you, and see that they're tied tight in saddles? . . . No, I don't want their guns."

Five minutes later Quist, Chris, and Ramon were herding the two Shattuck brothers toward the pass on their way to Masquerade City. The sun was just edging over the tops of the mountains.

TWENTY: Evidence

It was nearing eleven that morning when they approached the town. The two Shattuck brothers rode in advance, with Chris and Ramon riding close behind as guards. Behind them came Quist and Francisca. The girl was saying, ". . . and I just can't believe that Ramon's my brother. It's true, of course, but such a surprise."

"Now that I know it for a fact"—Quist laughed—"I can see the family resemblance between you—same coloring, same nose and chin and eyes. It's a wonder I didn't suspect something like this before. Anyway, it settles your problem, Francisca. Chris—"

"You're quite sure you're not a candidate, Greg?" The girl laughed. "For a while there I had an idea that—"

"Nonsense," Quist growled uncomfortably. "Don't try to kid me, Francisca. You know I haven't a chance against Chris." He drew a deep sigh. "From now on my heart's broken into quivering fragments."

"Nonsense yourself." Francisca giggled. "Don't try to flatter me, Greg."

Quist grinned. "Sometimes you women are just

297

too smart." He changed the subject. "I still don't feel right about you coming to town with us. We should never have stopped at the Rafter-RH—though I guess I couldn't have prevented Ramon and Chris from stopping."

"I can't see why you should feel that way," the girl stated earnestly. "You say you know who killed my father. It's natural for me to want to be on hand when you reveal the name of the person. Don't blame yourself, Greg. I insisted on coming, as you well know. If you'd tried to forbid me coming, I'd have followed you to town anyway."

"That I expected. Just the same, it may not be pleasant for you."

"My grief!" Francisca exclaimed. "I'm no shrinking violet who wilts at hearing unpleasant things."

By this time they had entered the town and were passing the hotel. Various pedestrians on the street had noted the Shattuck brothers were tied in saddles. Vague rumors spread swiftly; a number of people had gathered by the time Quist signaled a halt before the sheriff's office.

Matt Tillman came barging out of the building. "What's this all about?" he demanded, nodding to the group. "Quist, have you seen Clem Vincent—?" He broke off, having just noticed the bound hands and empty holsters of the Shattuck brothers. A shocked oath parted Tillman's lips. His eye caught the girl's gaze, and he made a quick apology to Francisca, then again directed his attention to Quist. "What's the idea of Pitt and Todd being tied—?"

"Freight thieves, Matt," Quist drawled. "We cornered 'em over in the Masquerades. Nice little setup they had there too. Clem? Oh yes. Your deputy will be along later. He's bringing in more prisoners. And Brose Tucker is loading wagons with stolen goods to be brought here too. The Triangle-S's beef raising was just a cover for its freight-thieving activities—"

"B'Gawd! I can't believe it," Tillman sputtered. He kept looking at the two Shattucks. "There must be some mistake—"

"A heap of people hereabouts have made mistakes," Quist said coldly, "but I'm not one of them. There's no mistake. Todd has confessed to quite a number of jobs against railroads running through this part of the country—"

"Why wasn't I told of all this, Quist? I'm the legal law authority here. I don't take it kindly—" He broke off at Quist's scornful laugh, wiped a dribble of tobacco juice from his chin, and said somewhat lamely, "All right, what's done is done. I'll get these Shattucks in cells right *pronto*, where I can question 'em myself—"

"I've got some more questioning to do first," Quist interrupted. He turned to Chris and Ramon. "All right, unleash those two *hombres* and take 'em into the sheriff's office. Watch 'em close."

He stepped down from his saddle and went around to give Francisca a helping hand. By this time there was quite a crowd gathered before the sheriff's office and much excited talking. Tillman, the two Shattucks, Chris, and Ramon had already entered the office. Quist was guiding Francisca around the end of the hitch rack when Dr. Woodward pushed through the thickly clustered group of people gathered in the roadway.

"What's wrong here, what's wrong?" Woodward demanded. Then he spied Quist and the girl and hurried toward them. "I thought there'd been an accident of some sort when I saw all the people."

"It was no accident." Quist smiled. "We just brought in some freight thieves—"

"No!" Woodward exclaimed. His jaw dropped. "Who—?"

"And oh, Dr. Woodward," Francisca said, "we've just learned something more important. Ramon is my brother!"

"Ramon? Your brother? What are you trying to say, Francisca?" He and the girl started talking at once. Quist cut in:

"It's true, Doc. You can get all the details later, but here's what happened . . ." Speaking swiftly, he told Woodward the story he had heard from Diego Santandar.

When Quist had finished, the doctor shook his

head unbelievingly. "Bless my eyes! I've never heard anything to match it."

"The story's not finished yet, either, Doc," Quist said. "Come on in the sheriff's office. I may have another surprise for you."

They entered the office. The Shattucks were standing against the back wall, looking sullenly at Tillman, who was hurling questions at them. Chris and Ramon were listening in some amusement to the sheriff's tirade, which the Shattucks received in silence. "And by the Almighty," Tillman was thundering, "I'm aiming to make an example of you two if Quist can prove what he says. I still find it hard to believe that friends of mine—men I've shaken by the hand—are guilty of such skulduggery—"

"Save your breath, Matt," Quist cut in. He shut the door behind him. "I've a lot to say, so why shouldn't we sit down?" To set the example, he dropped into the chair at Tillman's desk. Glancing through the window at his left, he saw that the crowd in front of the building was starting to break up. There were several straight-backed chairs in the office, and the rest were finally seated. At the left-hand wall Francisca took the chair nearest the door. Next to her was Dr. Woodward. Against the back wall sat the sullen-faced Shattucks, flanked on either side by Chris and Ramon. Tillman looked around. All the chairs were taken. "Quist," he said pompously,

301

"you've got my chair. I should be at the desk—"

"Yeah, I have, haven't I?" Quist said lazily. "Maybe you should stand in a corner, Tillman. That's the general location for dunces."

Tillman reddened. "I don't take that kindly—" he commenced.

"You'll take it and like it," Quist snapped. "Now stand against that wall." Then to Ramon, "Take his gun."

Ramon reached across and slipped the six-shooter from Tillman's holster. He stuck it in the waistband of his overalls and smiled at Quist. "Is done, Greg."

"Wha—wha—what the devil's the meaning of this?" the sheriff asked indignantly. "Serrano, I demand the return of my gun—at once."

"Let him have it, Ramon," Quist said, "across his head, hard, if he makes any false moves. Now you stand there against that wall, Tillman, and listen to me for a spell."

Tillman shook his head bewilderedly. "I—I just don't understand all this."

"Lying won't help you any," Quist said sternly. "Pitt Shattuck has given me the story. There're some things he doesn't know, but of one thing he's certain, Tillman, and that is that you're the leader of the train wreckers and freight thieves who've been operating in this section for the past few years. The Triangle-S simply followed your orders—"

"It's a blasted lie!" Tillman thundered. He swung toward Pitt Shattuck. "What the devil do you mean by saying I—?"

"Don't jump me, Matt," Pitt said in a tired voice. "Quist has got us dead to rights. You might as well own up. He knows things—"

"I never heard anything so ridiculous in my life," Tillman protested. "I'm being framed. As sheriff of Mascarada County my reputation has been stainless. It's only Shattuck's word against mine. I stand ready to prove my integrity—"

"No political speeches, Tillman," Quist said contemptuously. "You're through running for office. Pitt Shattuck simply confirmed certain suspicions I had in mind. You've been putting on an act right along, but I'm afraid you've over-acted, forgot some of your lines when they were needed, or got balled up in 'em. For instance, you have the rep of being lazy, and yet the night of the wreck you mounted your horse and rode out there—so you claimed. You were never near the wreck, according to the T. N. & A. S. wrecking boss, Carstairs. I've had a wire from him to that effect."

"There was no reason for me to talk to your wrecking boss," Tillman blustered. "I saw that—"

"The pompous type you've been acting," Quist pointed out, "would have gone to Carstairs first. Next, a good sheriff would have stayed around until daylight to see if he could find sign. What you actually did was ride out of town a way until one of the Triangle-S hands could bring you something from the wreck. You needed some sort of evidence from that wreck. Pitt Shattuck doesn't know for sure why you wanted it, but I'll get to that later. The evidence that was brought you was one of those Samuels & Tempfield six-shooters. Then you headed back to town. You told Vincent that you didn't arrive until after the sun was up, but you were seen, by a Mexican named Mendoza, riding into town while it was still dark—"

"Poppycock, all poppycock," Tillman raged. "I insist I was at that wreck. Don't you remember, Quist, you and I were talking about that big pool of machine oil that was spilled by the vandals?"

Quist smiled. "I remember bringing it to your attention, but you overlooked the fact that machine oil would sink into sand. And yet you claimed to have seen the reflections of flames in the oil. What eyes you must have. Y'know, Tillman, there wasn't any machine oil carried on that train. That was a trap I set for you, and you fell into it, head over heels." Quist paused, waiting for Tillman to deny it, but Tillman had gone white and was staring at Quist as though hypnotized, without speaking. The Shattuck brothers looked whipped, though it was plain to be seen they appreciated the position in which

Tillman found himself. At any rate, they'd have company in prison.

Quist went on, "Then Porky Gerard furnished more evidence for me when he came to town with a box of Sultan crackers. That brand wasn't carried in town, but it was listed on the waybill of the freight you arranged to have wrecked. Poor Porky, he was a victim of his own appetite. The Triangle-S hurried him out of town with some story of his spilling catsup in the K. C. Chop House. I proved that a lie. To square himself, Porky tried to rub me out. You know how that business ended. Your gang realized, Tillman, that the minute I saw those crackers I might get suspicious of its activities—and I did."

Tillman forced a laugh. "This story gets funnier all the time, Quist. It's quite entertaining—but you can't prove anything."

"I'm glad you're enjoying it, Tillman. You put on a fairly good act yourself. Especially in Rawnston."

"What about Rawnston?" Tillman demanded.

"It was necessary for you to go to Rawnston in order to dispose of the stolen freight to various shady dealers. So you cooked up the story about going to see your dear old mother. I'll admit you had me puzzled there for a time. Here in town you're a fat, sloppy, lazy blow-hard. It's an act that fools a lot of people, Tillman. My operative in Rawnston saw no one of such a description get off the train. And Chris ran down the fact that the man who went around taking orders from dealers in Rawnston was quite the gentleman—derby hat, shaved and talcumed face, black hair, and curled mustaches—very neat, in short. That didn't sound like you, naturally. Then I remembered that, going by train to Rawnston, there's nearly a two-hour wait-over in Packenham, so I decided you took advantage of that two hours to go to a hotel and change into your gentleman 'role.' It's possible, you know."

Tillman laughed scornfully. "I'd like to see you explain the black hair and curled mustaches."

"I decided you used dye." Quist smiled thinly. "A dye that could be easily washed out. As a matter of fact, it washed out so easily that when it rained in Rawnston, some of it washed down on your coat collar and lapel. Oh yes, I found those things in your room, Tillman—derby hat, suit of clothing, lace shoes—"

"By Gawd!" Tillman blurted. "It was you that killed Neale."

"I killed Neale," Quist admitted. "I went to your room looking for evidence, and Neale almost got me. He was after evidence too. He knew about your hair dye and had the bottle in his hand when I came into your room. I'm not sure what he had in mind, but he said something about making a deal with me, and he had that hair dye to prove his story. Then when he thought he had a chance to knock me off, he couldn't resist the thought of the prestige that would bring him—particularly when he had a gun at my back, with no risk to himself—as he thought."

Dr. Woodward put in, "But what sort of deal did Neale want to make—and why?"

"He was sore at Tillman," Quist explained. "The first time I ever saw those two, Neale tried to get tough with me. Tillman didn't object, so I guessed there was something between them. Later, when Tillman wanted to get rid of me, he tried to scare me out of town by sending me a note of warning, using the word 'pal,' a word Neale was inclined to overwork. Tillman figured I'd suspect Neale and we'd shoot it out. If Neale killed me, fine; if I killed Neale—well, maybe Neale knew too much about the sheriff. I showed the note to Neale, and he blurted out something about Tillman being a double-crosser—"

"You can't prove I ever wrote that warning note," Tillman bellowed.

Quist smiled thinly. "Oh, but I can. You got worried about that note after you'd written it, for fear I might trace it to you, tried to keep it when I showed it to you. There was no similar paper to be had in town, so I figured it had come from outside town. My next thought was that stationery for the sheriff's office was likely sent from the capital. So I bought some .44 ca'tridges from you, Tillman, and persuaded you to write

307

out a bill for them. You slipped there." Tillman made an enraged strangling sound. Quist went on, "That gave me a sample of paper, ink, and handwriting. The handwriting was disguised, of course, but not well enough disguised in the warning note. You should have remembered to form letters differently and not use certain little quirks that are customary in your writing. You wrote both papers, of course—"

"You're crazy," Tillman blustered. "Why should I want you run out of town or killed by Neale?"

"You wanted me out of town because you feared I'd discover who killed Reed Haldane—and I have."

"You can't pin that on me," Tillman half yelled.

Dr. Woodward put in quickly, "Oh no, Greg. Surely Matt Tillman wouldn't do a thing of that sort." He looked aghast. "I don't think I can stand hearing more of this. Besides, I have patients awaiting my calls—"

"Stick around, Doc," Quist said. "This won't take much longer."

"But why should I, if I don't care to—?"

"Because, Doc," Quist replied grimly, "you were the man Haldane opened his door to the night he was killed. Don't deny it."

TWENTY-ONE: Conclusion

A stunned silence settled abruptly on the office. All heads were turned toward Yost Woodward now. All except Francisca's. The girl had sunk back in her chair, white and unbelieving. Quist said, "You'd better leave, Francisca. It won't be easier from here on."

The girl's chin came up. "I'm staying," she stated.

Quist gave her a short encouraging nod and turned back to Woodward, whose face was the color of wet ashes. "No, no," he gasped. "Greg, you don't know what you're saying—"

"Don't try to lie out of it, Doc," Quist said coldly. "You're the man responsible for Haldane's death. You, his best friend—he thought. It was that that gave me the clue that started me thinking. Haldane hadn't any close friends I could learn of, except you and Chris and Ramon, and those two—well, they were like sons. One of them was, in fact. So when I learned that Haldane had said he'd never open his door at night except to a friend, you were the logical suspect, particularly when you tried to tell me that red mark around Haldane's throat was made by his collar, you thought. A doctor would know better than that. So then you and Tillman got worried."

"No, Greg, no," Woodward quavered. "You're all wrong."

"I've a hunch," Quist pursued swiftly, "you're tied into this freight-thieving business with Tillman. Anyway, you went to Haldane's door that night—I don't know on what pretext you asked entrance, and it doesn't matter—and Haldane let you in. As he turned away to light his lamp, you garroted him with a length of rawhide. Tillman now entered the room. I figure it was he fired the shot while Haldane was unconscious—"

"It wasn't me," Tillman roared. "I deny it. Doc, don't you admit a thing—"

"Quiet, scut," Ramon warned, lifting his six-shooter menacingly.

Tillman's face twisted with anger, but he fell silent and leaned back against the wall with his hands thrust in his trouser pockets.

Quist, after a quick glance at Francisca, went on, "You were both working in the dark, Doc, and I suppose you got confused. I've already told Tillman he hasn't cat's eyes. Anyway, in your hurry the gun was placed in Haldane's left hand instead of his right. Another clue. The rawhide had been dropped and somehow got kicked under the bed, where I found it later. At the time I picked it up, Doc, you promised faithfully not to tell anyone about it. From what you said that day, I guessed by that time Tillman had got around to thinking of that rawhide too. He'd wanted the key to that room, but at the moment you couldn't find it. When I left you, I went to the sheriff's office and found the section of rawhide from which the garroting length had been cut. The cut had been slashed at a sharp angle. I cut off another piece, and my piece fits the rawhide found under the bed. My cut I made straight across, so as not to mix up evidence. Later, in the sheriff's office, I discovered that the rawhide from which the pieces had been cut was missing. I knew then, Doc, you'd told Tillman of the rawhide I found beneath the bed, so he had gotten rid of evidence—he thought."

Quist let that thought sink in; then, "At first the Shattucks were under suspicion, of course, but Pitt was so insistent I find the murderer that I switched my search elsewhere. Anyway, at the time the murder was committed, the Shattucks were some miles off freighting loot from the train wreck. Later Tillman and Doc were very glib in pushing the idea that Haldane was tied in with the freight thieves. The Samuels & Tempfield six-shooter from the wreck that Tillman had brought in was left in Haldane's room to add credence to the idea and to persuade folks that Haldane had committed suicide either through fear or a guilty conscience. Tillman was so eager to make certain I noticed that gun, I grew even more suspicious of him. A couple of days ago I gave Doc the impression I knew the killer's identity, in the hope of drawing an attack on me that would bring matters to a climax—"

"I've never in my life," Tillman protested angrily, "listened to such a pack of crazy ideas—"

"It's no good, Matt," Woodward cut in hopelessly. "He's got us dead to rights, and we both know it." He forced a wry smile. "You're right, Greg. I wish I could compliment you on your work. Maybe I do anyway, rotten as I am. It was Matt killed Reed, Greg—"

An angry bellow of protest burst from Tillman's throat, but Ramon tilted his six-shooter and the big man fell silent as he slouched back against the wall again, hands thrust deeper into pockets.

Woodward continued, "I suppose you want to hear what led to all this, Greg. I'd better start away back when I first met Tillman—in a Colorado prison. He was in for cattle stealing. I'd made a mistake in my medical practice and drew a term for manslaughter. When I emerged from prison I married a good woman and came here to start life anew. For a time I prospered. Then Matt followed me here and in time became sheriff. We each had secrets to keep. Later my wife became hopelessly ill. There were several operations. Hospital bills. I became almost bankrupt. I'd borrowed twice from Reed and hated to ask again. Meanwhile, Tillman had cooked up his freight-looting plan with the Shattucks. He suggested I come in. In a weak moment I joined him, with the intention of quitting as soon as my debts were paid. But once you start that sort of thing, you're in too deeply to withdraw."

A shudder shook Woodward's body, and he kept his eyes downcast. "My job was to help Tillman dispose of stolen goods. Then one day Fate took a hand. I was at the state capital arranging with various dealers to buy our loot from wrecked trains. As luck would have it, Reed happened to enter a store where I was talking to a dealer. We started a conversation, and the dealer, thinking Reed was working with me, dropped a careless remark about cheap goods. That aroused Reed's suspicions. After he left the store I jumped the dealer for his remarks, but it was too late then. Later, in Masquerade City, Reed accused me of being mixed up with freight thieves. I admitted it. He was furious and threatened to take the whole business up with the authorities. I lied to him, told him I was turning over a new leaf, and we went on as before, without him saying anything. Though by that time he had learned someplace that Matt was an ex-convict and he was suspicious of Matt too."

Woodward mopped beads of perspiration from his forehead. "Reed thought that I'd reformed, and he was willing to forget the whole business.

313

But I was in too deep by that time. The wrecking of that T. N. & A. S. train had already been arranged. I talked things over with Matt. Well"—the others could just catch Woodward's voice now—"to save our own rotten necks, Reed had to go. That's what happened, Greg. We hoped it would be considered suicide. I—I guess skunks don't come any lower than me. I must have become insane with fear to ever do such a thing with Matt. Whatever punishment we receive is more than deserved—"

"You spineless, yellow fool," Matt Tillman snarled. "By Gawd, I'm not licked yet—" He didn't finish the words as he straightened from his slouching position against the wall and withdrew both hands from his trousers pockets. Quist tensed as he saw that each of Tillman's fists clutched a Remington .41-caliber, double-barreled derringer pistol. Small weapons they were, but vicious. "Baxter—Serrano!" Tillman bellowed. "Drop those six-shooters."

From his standing position against the wall Tillman covered everyone in the room, his short-barreled guns moving in slow arcs from side to side. Quist spoke quickly. "Drop those guns as he says. Remember, Francisca's in here." Reluctantly Chris and Ramon dropped their six-shooters. Immediately the two Shattucks scrambled to retrieve them. They were on their feet now, too, waiting for Tillman to give orders.

Francisca was deathly white but kept her nerve. Quist, in his chair, realized that Tillman would shoot at the first move, was just waiting for the slightest excuse to unleash deadly derringer fire.

Tillman sneered, "For once, Quist, you're licked. I always keep my little derringer guns on hand for emergencies. You're not the only one with a hide-out gun. And you're right to think of the girl too. We wouldn't want her to get hurt, would we? You're playing it smart, Quist. Doc can stay here and get his neck broken with a hemp noose if he likes, but the Shattucks and I have a different idea. There're horses out front. We're leaving fast—"

"And where can you go you won't get caught?" Quist asked calmly, sparring for time, intent on keeping Tillman talking. He glanced at Woodward. There was a certain look in the doctor's eyes, a sort of signal that told Quist to be on the alert. Quist nodded slightly to show that he understood, and spoke to Tillman again. "If you were smart, you wouldn't even take the Shattucks with you. Pitt has already proved that he cracks when the going gets tough—"

Pitt opened his mouth to voice an angry protest, and at that moment Woodward leaped up, shielding Francisca with his own body. For a brief instant Tillman's attention was diverted, and in that instant Quist drew and fired, moving up catlike from his chair as the shot left his .44, and throwing himself to one side. Both Shattucks were lifting their guns when Chris and Ramon, on either side, threw their weight against the brothers, causing them to crash together and sending their shots wide of their marks.

Quist caught the angry bark of the derringers and flipped a second shot toward Tillman, who was already staggering back from the impact of Quist's first bullet. Quist was on the floor now, bracing himself on one knee and hand, as his .44 roared twice more in the direction of the Shattucks.

Quite suddenly the guns fell silent. Dust was still sifting down from the ceiling rafters, shaken by the heavy concussions of exploding cartridges. Powdersmoke swirled through the room. Quist rose to his feet, glanced toward Francisca, who was still seated in her chair, one hand raised to her white face as though to stifle a scream.

Tillman lay face down, arms outstretched, hands still clutching the derringer pistols. Doc Woodward was huddled on the floor without movement. Pitt Shattuck was prone across his brother's still form, one hand clawing feebly at the floor boards. From outside the building came the sound of excited cries and running feet. Someone pounded on the closed door of the office.

Quist drew a deep breath. "And that's that," he said quietly. "Chris, get Francisca out of here, *pronto.*" He added, "Blast it, I knew I shouldn't have let you come, girl."

"It's all right, Greg." Francisca's voice shook slightly. She got to her feet. "Please see to Dr. Woodward."

"It wouldn't do any good," Quist said softly. "He took the full charge of one of those derringers. Only for him getting in front of you—well, his sacrifice squares up a little, I reckon, and gave me the chance I needed. Ramon and Chris helped too."

"*Socorro!*" Ramon exclaimed. "Nevair in my whole life have I witness' so fast of shooteeng, Greg. You were like the Gatling gun—no?"

"Never saw anything like it in my life." Chris was shaking his head in amazement. He crossed the floor, took Francisca's arm, and escorted her outside. Quist closed the door behind them, then carefully reloaded his gun and replaced it in holster. Ramon looked up from his examination of the men on the floor. "Only Pitt Shattuck is still breething, Greg. Is bad hit—but may-bee the chance. Is already unconscious. There is another doctor who live' on Apache Street—" He broke off and gave directions. "Is only the chance may-bee, but I weel go if you say—"

"I'll go for the medic," Quist said. "You stay here and keep that crowd from busting in. Clem Vincent will be along soon to take charge of things." Serrano nodded, and Quist left the

317

sheriff's office. On the street he was forced to push his way through an excited crowd that rained questions on him, all of which he ignored. Then he started at a brisk walk in the direction of Apache Street. Glancing at the cloudless sky above, he noticed three black forms silhouetted sharply against the blue—dipping, floating, soaring wing forms.

"I wonder if it is true," he speculated idly, "as old-timers claim, that buzzards possess an instinctive scent for spilled human blood that draws them to a scene of violence. . . ."

Books are produced in the United States using U.S.-based materials

Books are printed using a revolutionary new process called THINKtech™ that lowers energy usage by 70% and increases overall quality

Books are durable and flexible because of Smyth-sewing

Paper is sourced using environmentally responsible foresting methods and the paper is acid-free

Center Point Large Print
600 Brooks Road / PO Box 1
Thorndike, ME 04986-0001 USA

(207) 568-3717

US & Canada:
1 800 929-9108
www.centerpointlargeprint.com